D1246618

Pup

Pup

Christopher Slater

This is a work of fiction. Names, characters, places, and incidents are either products of the author's imagination or are used fictitiously. Any resemblance to actual events, locales, organizations, or persons living or dead, is entirely coincidental and beyond the intent of either the author or the publisher.

Studio Digital CT, LLC
P.O. Box 4331
Stamford, CT 06907

Copyright © 2015 by Christopher Slater
Cover design by Barbara Aronica-Buck

Story Plant Paperback ISBN: 978-1-61188-211-7
Fiction Studio Books E-book ISBN: 978-1-936558-64-3

Visit our website at www.TheStoryPlant.com

All rights reserved, which includes the right to reproduce this book or portions thereof in any form whatsoever except as provided by US Copyright Law. For information, address The Story Plant.

First Story Plant Printing: June 2015
Printed in the United States of America
0 9 8 7 6 5 4 3 2 1

To my family and friends who show the joy I keep inside.
You are all much braver than I.

To my family and friends who [illegible] the pa[illegible] keep m[illegible]

You are all much braver than I.

Introduction

*

This is not the story of a hero. If you were hoping to read about a hero that the biggest star in movies would play on the silver screen, then you might want to look for something else to read. There are lots of stories about heroes out there. Look around and find one of those. I'm sure there are probably some on the Best Sellers list. This is the story of a screw-up. A grade-A, monumental, epic screw-up. I wouldn't even be writing this down except that my wife wants me to record it so that our children can read it when they grow up. There's a brilliant idea! If my kids haven't figured out how much of an idiot their father is by the time they're old enough to read this, I might as well provide textual evidence to convince them! My therapist also said that it might be cathartic for me to write it all down. What a quack! He still tells me that I should be proud of myself when I look in the mirror. I look like a cartoon character. Why should I be proud of seeing that in the mirror?

All right, I suppose I should stop stalling and get this thing started. I would say that my adventures began the day I was drafted, but that would be a lie. My adventures probably began the day I was born. I often wondered if the doctor dropped me on my head after he saw me. If he did, is it possible he picked me up and dropped me again just to be certain? Whatever happened on that day, I ended up with all kinds of issues. I haven't been diagnosed with anything. Part of the reason is because I wouldn't allow myself to be tested, but there are still labels that apply to me: socially awkward, clumsy, forgetful, hyper, geek, spaz, schmo, screw-up, goofball, and clueless are at the top of the list. Those are just the labels given to me by friends and family. My grades never reflected these things. I always scored well in class. I can tell you the capital of Tajikistan off of the top of my head (it's Dushanbe, in case you wanted to know), but I couldn't tie my shoes before sixth grade, I still have to think hard to remember my left from my right, and my first attempt to boil water on the stove made it on the evening news.

Of course, everyone has their issues. I have a cousin that is scared to death of ducks. I'm not kidding. Every time she sees a duck coming toward her, she breaks out into a cold sweat and looks like she is about to have a psychotic episode. The difference between other people's issues and mine is the fact that you aren't likely to have to confront ducks on a daily basis. People are an entirely different story. I have to confront them every day. To tell the truth, I suck at it.

I could probably write a four-volume treatise on my time in school. Just imagine being in an institution for thirteen years where everyone else knows that talking to yourself in public is strange except for you, and where color-coordinating your clothes is highly suggested and you tend to ignore that suggestion. That pretty much sums up as much of my time in school as I think anyone needs to know. Oddly enough, though, I enjoyed it.

It isn't like I never had friends. I had quite a few friends. It turns out that when you spend most of your time fighting against or trying to hide your quirks, you gain a certain amount of insight into people. That insight turned me into a bit of a problem-solver. People would come to me with their problems and I would listen and help talk them through it. When you do things like that, you get a reputation as a nice guy. The funny thing is that I wasn't a nice guy. Sure, I had manners and tried to treat people decently because my mother would make my life miserable if I didn't, but that wasn't the main reason why I helped. I liked hearing these people talk about their problems because it helped me forget about mine for a little while. I never told any of them that. I'm pretty sure it would have ruined my reputation.

I admit it. I'm stalling. I could spend several pages just talking about how I managed to never touch the toilet seats in the school bathrooms (they really are gross!), but I know that I would just be coming up with ways to avoid telling the story that my wife and my quack therapist want me to tell. Here it goes. I graduated from high school and had been accepted into a college to study psychology. That's when the war broke out; I'm sure you know the history, so I'll leave the details out of it for now. I've always had a habit of reading. I read a lot. I read about a lot of stuff. At the time, I had become particularly fond of military action novels. Science fiction was my choice for television and movies, but military action seemed more "real" to me in books. It always amazed me how they could make the heroes so invincible and the villains so conniving. I think that my sense of patriotism was especially aroused by these novels. When the Second Korean War broke out I went and bought flags in every available size, got red-white-and-blue shirts and hats, and I got all kinds of posters and decorations to show my love of country. Obviously, none of this did anything to actually help the war effort, but that's just the way that I think. I figured that looking patriotic would be my contribution. I didn't really consider enlisting. I'd never shot a gun before, and I had the upper body strength of a . . . well, everything has more upper body strength than I did. So I figured I would just wear my shirts and hats and shout "U-S-A!" whenever appropriate and that would be enough.

I remember that I was wearing one of those shirts when the doorbell rang. I had been spending most of the day trying to figure out how to get along with a stranger as a roommate when I got to college. That probably scared me more than anything about going off to school. I dug into my wallet as I went to answer the door. Various groups had been doing door-to-door fundraisers to support our troops in whatever way they could. Hey, I could give a few bucks. I would do my part. I was wearing a patriotic shirt, wasn't I? When I opened the door, the deliveryman asked to see my identification. Maybe it was because he was wearing a uniform, or maybe it was because I was young and stupid, but I showed him my driver's license. He looked at it, double-checked his clip board, and then told me that I was hereby notified that I had been called to active duty through the Selective Service program. He handed me an envelope and then turned to leave. He stopped when I told him thank you. Maybe he thought I was being sarcastic. In truth, it was just an automatic response of politeness. He looked at me with an expression that I couldn't quite place. Then he told me, "Good luck, kid." He got in his vehicle and drove off without looking back.

I looked at the envelope that he had given me. I opened it up and found a great deal of information there. In truth, it was information overload. The words that stood out to me as if they had been highlighted were "active duty, United States Army." Something about those words disturbed me. Maybe it was the fact that they actually had been highlighted. I read them three times, then dropped the envelope and passed out. The least I could have done was close the door before I passed out. It took my parents two days to round up the cat and dog. My tendency to panic can be so inconsiderate at times.

It's hard to remember a whole lot that happened in the following months. I remember my mother crying a lot. That was no surprise. She wouldn't even let me walk to the neighborhood playground by myself before I was seventeen. By then, I could drive to it. I also remember watching the news a lot. I was really hoping that there would be a breaking news announcement that the Second Korean War had abruptly ended with the enemy's unconditional capitulation (I didn't actually expect it to be worded like that; I just wanted an excuse to use the word "capitulation"). I also did a lot more walking. My therapist tells me that I probably did that so that I could experience more of my familiar surroundings before leaving to a more alien environment. Quack. My mother was crying, the television kept showing depressing news stories, and the dog and cat were constantly trying to escape. I went for walks to get the hell out of there!

The day finally came for me to report for processing. I really didn't want my parents taking me. That's kind of like having your parents drop you off at school. It's embarrassing. I would know; mine did it until the last week of my senior year. Unfortunately, somebody had to drive me and they insisted. My mother kept giving me kisses when she parked the car. I finally had to speak up. "Mom! Stop kissing me!"

"I don't care if I embarrass you!" she replied. "You're my boy going off to war!"

"It's not that," I insisted. "I'm so nervous that I'm nauseous and I think I might puke all over you." Sometimes you have to hit my mom with the unaltered truth. Imagine my surprise when that just made my mom cry harder. I guess I know where I get some of my issues from.

The processing was . . . unpleasant. After getting all of my information, having me sign a lot of things that I didn't really understand, and then taking away everything that I had brought with me, the military sent me to get a physical. I'm not a big fan of physicals. I don't know of anyone who really is, but I think that I hate them more than most. People poking and prodding and asking questions that I wouldn't want to answer if they paid me. Why can't they just have a scanning device like on *Star Trek*? (Sorry! Flying my geek flag again!) To make matters worse, I had to stand in line in just my underwear with a bunch of other draftees. I guess I should point out that I have never been all that comfortable with being naked, or mostly naked, around others. I always tried to be the last to change in the gym locker room. I don't know why, probably because everyone is in better shape than me. Some people look like you could put five hundred pounds on a bar and they could bench-press it without difficulty. I look like I could be the bar. I stood in line not making any real eye contact with the others around me. I shuffled forward whenever I saw the feet of the person in front of me move. I don't know if I should have looked up or not. It might have prevented the shock of what was to come, or it might have prolonged the agony. I'll never know. I only know what did happen, and that was humiliating enough.

I shuffled forward and saw a chair in front of me. "Have a seat," a voice said. A feminine voice. A *very* feminine voice. I looked up and saw a young lady in green scrubs with a stethoscope around her neck. She was gorgeous. She was about twenty years old with red hair and a smile that could light up an entire room. I would know. She'd gone to high school with me. It was one of those rare instances that I actually recognized someone. She also recognized me. She smiled that dazzling smile. I was too nervous to smile back, but that didn't prevent other parts of me from . . . responding. While I was standing in front of her. In my underwear.

I don't think that there's any need to continue with that particular memory. We'll just say that she checked my blood pressure (it was high at the moment) and my pulse rate (which was dangerously high at the moment) and sent me to the next table. It was difficult to tell if the smile remained one of familiarity or of amusement. Of course, most people who were familiar with me were also amused by me, so six of one, half a dozen of the other. I guess that it was good news that the rest of the people involved with giving the physical were male. It prevented any repeats of that episode. I almost expected to fail the physical at the hearing test portion. I hear everything very well. The problem is that I can't seem to understand anyone. It's like everyone mumbles. Maybe everyone does mumble, and I'm the only one that didn't receive the memo. That would be about the speed of things. I was all ready to explain this with a vague hope that it might get me a medical discharge when they stuck a couple of earbuds in my ears. I heard a few odd tones come through the speakers and saw the tech look at his laptop screen. After about fifteen seconds, he removed the earbuds and put an approval on my paper. "My hearing isn't . . ."

"Your hearing is fine. Move on," he interrupted. I started to protest when he looked at me with eyes that did not broker discussion. "Your hearing is *fine*. Move on." I picked up my paper and followed instructions. At the final table was the only man in the room in an army uniform. I sat down in front of him and handed him my physical form. He took a look at it and checked off a few boxes himself. Since he was the final person in the line of tables, I figured that I had better ask him some of the questions that I had. "Sir, I have a few concerns. First, I have an unusual hearing issue. I can't always make out what people are saying. Secondly, my stomach tends to get upset when I eat unusual foods. Third, I'm not certain that I am in good enough physical condition for the military. Finally, I was just about to start college. Doesn't that exempt me from the draft?"

The corporal (I had studied up a little on military rank) had not looked up from his paperwork while I had spoken. He didn't bother looking up afterward to answer me either. "Everyone is trying to go to college now," he began in a bored voice. "Because of that, there are no more college deferments. Your tests say your ears are fine. Boot camp will get you into shape, and you can crap your pants after mess call for all I care so long as you don't foul up your weapon. Congratulations, pal. You are now a member of the United States Army." He finally looked up at me. When he saw how scrawny I was and the already-homesick look on my face, I heard him mutter under his breath, "May God help us all." And that is how my glorious career in the military began.

And the ball starts rolling . . .

*

Before I start talking about all of the things that happened to me after that fateful day I reported for duty, I feel like I should make something very clear. I may not like every veteran I've ever met, but I respect every last one of them. Anyone who has ever worn this nation's uniform deserves all of the respect we can give. They have given of themselves, voluntarily or not, so that we can all live our lives the way that we wish. They are all heroes. Of course, there are exceptions to every rule. I'm the exception to this one. My quack therapist tells me that I'm just fishing for compliments when I say something like this. He wonders why I call him a quack. I'm recognizing reality. You would think he would know the difference.

The day I reported after being drafted was a day that seemed to last forever. After completing the long and humiliating physical, I was sent into a waiting area filled with steel chairs. I was happy to get the opportunity to sit down and collect my thoughts for a moment. I walked over to a chair and sat down. I immediately squealed and jumped back up. The thirty-some-odd draftees in the waiting area immediately went quiet and stared at me. I gave a sheepish smile. "The chair's cold. Forgot I was just in my underwear. Sorry." I watched a few guys shake their heads in exasperation, and everyone went back to their conversations. True, I was not happy with this wonderful impression that I had made on the other draftees, but I'll be damned if I didn't see some of them sit down a little more slowly and carefully because of my mishap. Screwing up so that you don't have to, just another of the many services that I provide.

Once everyone had completed their physicals, we were lined up again and sent to a partitioned area that was filled with tables. These tables were all covered with military clothing. Without instructions we were shepherded through the line of tables. There was a private at each table asking us what size we wore of the various articles of clothing. I knew this was going to be bad. You see, according to clothing manufacturers, I don't exist. There is no line of clothing made for someone with my proportions. The only way that I have combated this throughout my life is by trying on various sizes until I find something that leaves the least amount of me uncovered. Pants are especially difficult. I either look like I'm trying to sag like someone from the hood or I look like I'm getting ready for a flood. The truth is, if you want to know what size I am, I'm size *me*. Something told me that they didn't carry that size uniform. The first table had undershirts on it. Without looking up, the private hollered out, "Size?"

When in a situation like this, I can be a true intellectual conversationalist. "Ummm . . ."

The private looked at me, exasperated. He grabbed a few undershirts that he must have guessed would fit me and threw them at me. I caught them and moved to the next table. I realized then that the next table had boxer shorts and was manned by a woman. Without thinking, I covered my underwear with the shirts that had been thrown at me. The female private looked at me and what I had done. "Get used to it, honey. We're all over the place now." She said it in a mechanical tone, like she had been forced to explain this a thousand times before.

"Yeah, I feel like I am right now, too, ma'am." I could feel myself blushing.

The private looked up at my red face and let out a warm chuckle. I remember hearing that chuckle and thinking that she would make a good kindergarten teacher. I don't have random thoughts; I have logical responses to stimuli. That's what I keep telling myself. She held out some boxers for me. "Here you go, pup. You be careful." I nodded in thanks and moved farther down the line.

Once we had received our clothing we were sent into another partitioned area to put on the uniforms. I almost managed to do this without incident. I had worn a lot of surplus clothing to do yard work and the like at home. I knew how most of it fit. It took me a few minutes to get my boots on and laced. That was something I wasn't used to. I had always wondered why the army doesn't use sneakers. I wore them every day when I was in school. I would have worn them to prom if my mother had let me. The boots would definitely take some getting used to. Amazingly enough, even they were not the problem. It was the Velcro fasteners. Many years before, the army had started using them on a lot of their gear, including uniforms. It makes sense. It's a useful material. Unfortunately, the hook portion of the hook-and-loop fastener also attaches to the socks issued by the army. Once we had dressed, we were led into another partitioned area where we were going to be briefed on what would be happening over the next several days.

Following instructions, I lined up as the last man in the second row. A sergeant came walking down the line, looking us over. I just looked straight ahead like I had seen in the movies, figuring he would pass me by. I should have known better than that. He stopped right next to me, looked down for a moment, and then growled, "You should attach it to your back pocket."

I couldn't continue looking straight ahead because I was completely befuddled. "What should I attach to my back pocket?" I asked meekly. He reached down and, with a tearing noise, pulled an extra green sock off the side of my pants leg and held it up to my face. If I was smart, I would have just taken the sock from him and faced forward again. Of course, if I was smart I wouldn't have to start sentences with *If I was smart*. "Why would I want to put that on my back pocket?"

"To cover up the boot print from the ass kicking I should give you!" You could look into this sergeant's eyes and see the love and respect he had for me as a newly drafted soldier. And my friends said I would never master sarcasm. The sergeant tossed the sock onto my head and then moved on. I never miss an opportunity to completely screw up a first impression.

I don't plan on spending forever describing boot camp. Hundreds of thousands of people have been through it. Some of them might have even looked more ridiculous than me. I doubt it, but anything is possible. Anything that they expected us to do after providing a manual or instructions, I did just fine. I learned how to disassemble and reassemble a carbine rifle just fine. I learned how to march and get into formation well. I was even able to write multiple reports and requisition requests with no mistakes. This made some of my training officers extremely happy.

The tasks and requirements that did not have manuals or that they didn't show us were another matter entirely. To be honest, I sucked at them. I could disassemble my carbine, but cleaning it was another matter entirely. How on earth do you use a toothbrush to clean stuff out of a spot far too small to stick the toothbrush in? Uniforms became the bane of my existence. Has anyone reading this ever had a class on how to create perfect creases? How about how to polish a scuff out of leather? I know that I didn't. Maybe it is something that most families teach at home. None of the other recruits seemed to have these problems. My mom taught me how to dance the waltz. Why couldn't that have been a skill we were tested over on the parade ground? I was in no big hurry to dance with my instructor, but I could have scored well on it if I'd had to.

I had seen a lot of movies where the drill instructors were constantly yelling and cursing and throwing the trainees around. That wasn't quite what happened to me. There was some yelling and a fair amount of cursing, but it wasn't exactly as harsh as I'd thought it would be. Don't get me wrong, I learned a lot of important lessons. For example, if a drill instructor asks if you want to go home to your mama, it is probably not in your best interest to answer "yes." I had three straight nights of guard duty for that, and they still didn't send me home to my mama. I also learned that push-ups are a form of exercise that were probably designed by Satan himself. Potatoes aren't hard to peel until you are into your second fifty-pound bag of them. I also learned that shouting "Sweet merciful crap!" the first time that a gun is fired next to you does not make many people desire to be your friend.

Obviously, I survived boot camp. I even survived infantry training afterward. What I never did understand is why they decided to make me an infantryman. I would have made a great clerk. I could write reports and requisitions. I could make people coffee. I could go and get a knit jeep cap and a teddy bear and be just like the clerk on that show my mom used to watch. Instead, someone decided that I needed to be given a gun and have others put their lives in my hands. When it was confirmed that I would be going to infantry specialty training, I remember one of my instructors muttering, "There's more proof that the brass has got shit for brains."

I don't tend to use much foul language, but I had to respond, "Fuckin' A, Sarge."

For the first time since boot camp had begun, the instructor looked up at me and smiled. "That's the smartest thing you've said in two months, Pup."

I guess that I should mention that I had picked up the nickname Pup. Someone who had been near me when we had requisitioned our uniforms so long ago had heard that woman call me that. For some reason, everyone thought it suited me. I'm not exactly sure why. Pups are cute and make everyone say "Aw!" and all of the girls want to hold them. Absolutely none of those things applied to me. I mean *absolutely none*. I didn't even reach the same level as a pug. They're so ugly that they're cute. Oh well. I guess that the nickname "Hair-brained idiot" doesn't roll off the tongue as easily. So now, I'm Pup. Nice to meet you.

I shipped out a few weeks after infantry training was completed. I got to go home and visit my family first. It was nice. My mom kept talking about how grown up her little boy had become. I don't know why she kept saying that. I did have a little more muscle. Doing a grand total of 3,500 push-ups and peeling a metric ton of potatoes will do that. Still, I felt pretty much the same as I always had. I slept in late, played video games, caught up on the latest season of *Doctor Who*, and chased after the dog and cat whenever they escaped. I've often wondered if they were trying to tell us something with how often they ran away. To be honest, I was ready to go by the time my leave was up. I was getting bored. I had gone out once to see if my uniform would get me a little attention. It didn't. There were too many others in town who had been drafted and looked much more natural in their uniforms than I did. Sure, it was good being with my friends and family, but I started seeing this tour of duty kind of like a Band-Aid. I've got lots of experience with Band-Aids. Let me rip it off quickly and get the pain over with.

I reported over an hour early to prepare to board my flight. I had only flown once before and the results were . . . unpleasant. To avoid another such event, I had taken almost every motion sickness medicine I could find. I had even purchased some of those wristbands that were supposed to prevent motion sickness without medicine. I worried that this was what I would have to do until transporter technology was invented. It turns out that multiple doses of motion sickness medicine and nearly two liters of Mountain Dew can make a person act very strangely. I guess that it's a good thing that I didn't drink. I really don't know what all I did while I was waiting to board the plane. I don't even remember actually boarding the plane. What I do know is that by the time I got aboard the plane I had lost all of my money, I was wearing the wristbands around my ears, and I can only assume that I got the black eye in a fight. Maybe it was from a doorknob. I was told that I fell down a lot. I admit that the whole affair embarrasses me. I'd been raised to act properly in public, and minutes before going off to defend our country I threw a roll of toilet paper out of the bathroom and shouted "Incoming!" Doesn't that just raise your patriotic fervor? And with that grand performance, I was off to war.

What do you call this place again?

*

I guess that it was a bit of grace that the medicines I had taken made me pass out as soon as I got on the plane. I don't remember taking off or leveling off, only nodding off. This was a blessing for me but a curse for everyone else. I snore. Actually, that's not true. People snore. Cute dogs with short snouts snore. The noise that escapes me while I sleep sounds something like a cross between a chainsaw and the mating call of a water buffalo. One of the things that forced my parents to buy a house before they were ready was the fact that my snoring had gotten us kicked out of three apartment complexes. Everyone on the plane got to enjoy the pleasure of my nasal symphony. I'm not certain how bad it was since I was asleep. I have been told an unconfirmed rumor that the pilot thought we would have to divert to another airport because he mistook my snoring for an engine fire. Thankfully a flight attendant informed him of the source of the racket. By the time I woke up, we were more than halfway to Japan and I had a pillow over my face. When I removed the pillow and looked around I was greeted with a plethora of angry looks. Who would have guessed it? My English teacher wasn't lying. I did use the word "plethora" at least once in my life.

In any case, I was a little woozy from all of the medicine and sleep. I set the pillow on the seat next to me and took the stupid wristbands off of my ears. I looked out of the window and saw nothing but clouds and water. Amazingly enough, it didn't make me ill. I rubbed my eyes and looked around the plane. It took me a minute to put together what was wrong with what I was seeing. It was a commercial airliner, not a military plane. A flight attendant who noticed that I had stopped my imitation of a dump truck walked over to check on me. With a slight slur to my words, I asked, "Did I get on the wrong plane? I don't see any green."

The flight attendant gave me one of those patient smiles that I think they drill into you at the flight attendant version of boot camp. You know, the one that allows flight attendants to put up with people like . . . well, me. "You're on the correct plane, sir. The military contracts civilian airlines to transport troops from the states. Can I get you a soft drink, sir?" I asked for a Coke, which she provided very quickly.

As my drink was being poured into a cup on my tray, I noticed that most of the people around me had turned off their lights and were sleeping. "Is it time to sleep?" I asked the attendant.

With another patient smile, she responded, "I will bring you as many drinks as you would like, as well as some snacks. We have some magazines and newspapers for you to read, or I can even send an attendant back to talk with you for a while. We will do whatever is necessary to keep *you* awake, sir. You seem like a nice young man, so please do not take it personally when I read the instructions that the captain left for me." She pulled a piece of paper out of her pocket, unfolded it, and read it aloud to me. "'If that human lawn mower tries to go to sleep again, you are to stuff him into his duffel bag and place the duffle bag into the cargo compartment so that I can open the cargo hatch and send him plummeting into the Pacific.' I would rather not see that happen to you, sir." And with that warning, the attendant poured me another soda, gave me three bags of pretzels, two newspapers, a crossword book, and her own personal iPod to listen to. The rest of the flight was surprisingly uneventful. At least now I understand why my parents insisted I bring portable video games on long family drives. Bad video game music is bound to be better than snoring that sounds like a hacksaw cutting through a stick of dynamite in a fireworks factory.

We landed in Tokyo. It was absolutely huge. The view from the air was incredible. I had never seen so many people crowded into one place. Sure, I had been to several cities. I'd been to Atlanta. I almost got assaulted there when I commented that I thought someone's pants were falling down. I'd been to Cincinnati. I wore the Braves hat I had gotten on my Atlanta trip and I barely made it out alive. I had been to San Francisco, where I rented a bike to ride around town. My legs required therapy for a month afterward. But I had never seen a city the size and scope of Tokyo. I felt lost just looking at it. It suddenly hit me that I wasn't home anymore. Part of me started to shake a little, and I had an almost uncontrollable urge to call home.

The landing was blissfully smooth. The flight attendant told us all to keep our seats so that a military liaison officer could give us our instructions. I sat there for a little while longer enjoying some of the sounds of home on the iPod while the other soldiers around me yawned and stretched out their in-flight cramps. It took about ten minutes before the military liaison officer made his way onto the airplane. He was a young lieutenant who looked like he had been stationed in Japan a while and knew where all of the good restaurants were. I heard several of the soldiers mutter things like "FOBbit" and "desk jockey." One soldier behind me muttered, "You know he's never seen action on the Hiss." I didn't even know what that meant. What I did know was that he was a superior officer and that I hadn't "seen action on the Hiss" either, so I just kept my mouth shut.

The lieutenant picked up the public address system, blew into the microphone a few times to make certain that it was on, and then began speaking to us. "Ladies and gentlemen of the United States military, welcome to Tokyo. I am Lieutenant Reed. I am the officer in charge of transportation of American personnel through Tokyo. I coordinate with the Tokyo airport to make certain that you all get where you are supposed to go. Enjoy your time here in Tokyo. It is the last bit of peacetime you will see before getting to the war zone." Well, that was a freaking ray of sunshine. "You will be traveling to Korea on military transports from this point onward. The flights will be escorted by fighter aircraft due to the possibility of enemy attack. This is why you will not be continuing on civilian airliners." This guy really needed to learn how to sugarcoat stuff. "Your transports are scheduled to depart from this airport in four hours. You are not to leave the airport terminal. Information on where the flights will be boarding will be announced over the intercom in the terminal in English." He stopped to take a drink of water. I looked closely and noticed that he was sweating. I think this might have been the most exercise he'd had all day. "The shops in the terminal take American dollars, so buy whatever you like, as long as it fits in your duffel bag and is not fruits, vegetables, or alcohol. Your American cash will be traded for military scrip before boarding the plane. Please remember that you are representatives of the United States of America and conduct yourselves accordingly. Good luck, and I will see you in four hours."

After Lieutenant Reed left the airplane everyone began gathering their gear to get off of the plane as quickly as they could. I was in no rush. To be honest, I was a little afraid. I had never been out of the country before, and I wasn't certain of what I might see. Besides that, my seat and the seat beside me were a mess. I had made certain that I stayed awake by reading and eating and drinking and even making little paper airplanes. Once everyone else had deplaned I began to clean up my seats. The flight attendant who had lent me the iPod walked through the cabin, cleaning up after the departed soldiers. She looked up and saw me cleaning up after myself. "You don't have to do that, sir. I'll take care of it."

I responded without really thinking about it. "My mother would kick my butt if she knew I didn't clean up after myself." I might as well have said that she picked my clothes out for me, too. She did that for way too long. Wow, I can say some stupid stuff.

Much to my surprise, the attendant didn't think it was stupid at all. "Well, thank you very much. It's nice to see that some people are still raised with manners."

"Speaking of which," I reached down into the seat and picked up the iPod and earbuds that she had lent me. "Thank you very much. It was kind of you to let me borrow this.

With a warm smile, she accepted the iPod back. Her smile warped into something a little different and then she handed the music player back to me. "That's OK. You keep it." I thanked her profusely, thinking maybe it was just her way of helping out a young soldier. I looked at the earbuds and then remembered that I had run out of Q-tips recently. Awkward!

I left the aircraft and entered the concourse for the airport. At first, it looked pretty similar to the other airport I had seen in my youth. The people were different, for the most part. There were a lot more soldiers and a lot more business-types walking around here. I didn't seem to see as many families on a relaxing vacation. I put my waxy earbuds back in and started listening to music as I began walking down the concourse. One difference between this airport and the other I had been in was that this thing was huge! I continued walking along, seeing the occasional aircraft taxi or take off out of a window. Imagine my surprise when I looked out a window and saw a train zoom past! I was in awe. I pressed my nose to the glass like some sort of child so that I could get a better view. I heard some giggling and saw two pretty Japanese ladies looking at me. There were a couple of soldiers from my flight standing there trying to talk to them. I continued my walk. As I walked past I heard one of the soldiers telling the ladies, "He's not with us. I don't even know where he got his uniform." I didn't take it personally. Hey, I embarrass myself.

I continued walking until the concourse opened up into the main shopping area. It was incredible! Here I was, in the middle of an airport in the largest city in the world, and there was a six-story-tall shopping mall! While hundreds or thousands of people walked past me, I just stood there and stared. I expected a small newsstand and maybe a little fast-food eating area. I didn't expect to find just about everything I could ask for and a lot more that I wouldn't know how to ask for. I finally made myself begin walking so that I could look around. There seemed to be a little of everything there. I found stores that carried nothing but high-end watches and stores that carried cheap souvenirs. There were stores that carried glassware and stores that carried music. I was like a kid in a candy store (they had those, too!). The problem was that I didn't have a lot of money, and the shopkeepers started to get annoyed at my constant browsing.

My stomach started growling after about an hour of looking in slack-jawed awe at the wonderment around me. I decided to check out one more shop before I ate. I looked up and found a rather large one that looked like it carried a bit of everything. I read the sign and saw that it was the duty-free shop. I still had my music playing, so I didn't realize that I was shouting when I announced, "That says doody!" Yes, I said it! I'm not proud of it! I told you that I had some social awkwardness. Of course, that goes beyond social awkwardness. That falls straight into the this-is-too-stupid-to-even-put-into-a-slapstick-comedy category.

Naturally, everyone within a hundred feet looked up to see what I'd said. The good news is that most of them didn't speak English and had no clue how moronic I just made myself appear. The bad news is that there were some soldiers nearby. Some shook their heads in disgust. Others closed their eyes and said a small prayer hoping that I wouldn't wind up in their unit. A few responded with rude hand gestures. One suggested that I perform an anatomically impossible act. Another suggested that I perform that same anatomically impossible act with a relative. Hey, some of these guys were creative!

I decided it would be smart for me to skip the shop and get some food. There was a massive variety of food available as well. Some of it looked exotically delicious. Some of it looked like it would fight back when I tried to eat it. I decided to play it safe. A meatball sub became the last peacetime meal that I would eat for a year. Man, that was a good sub! I kept my earbuds in and dragged my duffel bag to a chair where I enjoyed my sandwich, closed my eyes, and sang along with the music. I really didn't care who stared at me as they walked by. See, Quack? I have some self-confidence.

Why are some engineers sadists?

*

It never occurred to me that focusing so much on my music could cause any problems. It's music. When has music ever been an issue? If I have any history buffs reading this, don't try to correct me. Surely you have better things to do with your time. The problem with focusing so much on my music was that I couldn't hear the public address system in the airport. I didn't hear the first call for my flight. I didn't hear the second call for my flight. I didn't hear the final call for my flight. What I did notice was a number of soldiers running past me trying to catch the flight. At first I thought that they might be running because of some kind of emergency. That instantly made me concerned. Then I realized that they were running to catch a flight. That instantly made me terrified! I grabbed my duffel bag and started to run after the other soldiers. I had no idea what gate I was supposed to get to, but I figured following someone in the same situation as me couldn't hurt.

It turned out that I was a pretty fast runner. In fact, my body ran faster than my brain did. I turned into a tall, skinny bulldozer in a uniform. I plowed over luggage, chairs, shoeshine kits, and one annoying, yapping dog. Don't worry. It was OK. It yapped at me afterward. Even all of those little accidents were nothing compared to what was on the way. I continued barreling through the terminal and found myself baring down on some poor Japanese lady. She was dressed in a very nice business outfit that looked wonderful on her. She was only about twenty years old or so. I was running right at her, but because my body was faster than my brain, I never considered trying to dodge around her. I do remember thinking about how pretty she was. Stupid hormones. She turned toward me just in time for the collision.

I'm not certain exactly how everything happened. I know that I almost tripped over her luggage. I also know that we were fortunate not to have our heads bonk together. What amazed me about the collision was that she didn't fall down. In an unusual move of self-preservation, the young lady wrapped her arms around my neck and her legs around my waist in order to keep from falling down. I had not even slowed down, and I had a young lady along for the ride with me. I looked over at her and her shocked expression. For reasons that even I cannot explain, I smiled at her. Her face went from shocked to disgusted. Stupid hormones. I started telling her that I would let her down as soon as I reached my gate, but I stopped when she started yelling at me in Japanese. Obviously, communication was going to be an issue, so I stopped bothering with trying to talk and just kept running.

Thankfully, the gate wasn't very far away. I started to run through the door, but my arm was grabbed by an MP at the gate. I came to an abrupt halt and almost lost my balance, but the MP was remarkably strong and held me up. Once I had recovered he looked at me and then at the young lady who had accidentally attached herself to me. With mixed amusement and utter amazement, he said, "I don't care how much you love her, you can't take her with you." I looked at him, confused at first, then I connected the dots about what he was referring to. The young lady lowered herself off of me. At this point, she seemed uncertain of what to make of the whole situation. She looked at the MP, then at me. Still unsure what to do, she bowed at us a little, then walked off muttering something in Japanese that I couldn't understand.

I turned to the MP, who was snickering. "What was she saying?"

The MP smirked. "It was the Japanese equivalent of Whiskey Tango Foxtrot." He picked my duffel bag off the ground and handed it to me. "You better get on your way to the Hiss. Good luck, Private." I gave the MP a salute, accepted my duffel bag, and walked through the gate onto the tarmac.

As I walked onto the tarmac, I was led over to a table. There I was required to exchange my American money for military scrip. It looked like fancy Monopoly money. I swear, I was going to protest and accuse the corporal there of stealing my cash, but then I heard someone with obvious authority to their voice begin speaking over by the airplanes. I stuffed my toy money into my pockets, hefted my duffel bag, and ran over to where the other soldiers had assembled. At the front of the group was an Air Force officer in a flight suit. He looked about three decades past the mandatory retirement age. His legs creaked when he walked. He wore glasses that looked so thick that NASA could use them to track near-Earth asteroids. It was like receiving a briefing from Mr. Magoo. "My name is Lieutenant Colonel Thomas Kiernan. I've been in the Air National Guard for twenty-five years now. I will be piloting aircraft two." He pointed to one of the C-17 cargo planes on the tarmac. He was one of the freaking pilots. The man looked like he should be selling Metamucil on a television commercial that only comes on during morning game shows, but instead he was a pilot of one of the planes. I started to worry less about fighting in a war zone and more about getting killed in a plane because the pilot couldn't see the airport terminal. "We will divide you among the aircraft for the flight to Daegu, South Korea. The three C-17 aircraft will be escorted by four Japanese fighters for the first half of the flight, and then by four American fighters when we reach the Sea of Japan. Enemy aircraft have attempted to attack cargo transports before, so be prepared. Stow all of your gear so that it will not move in the course of evasive maneuvers." I started to feel my stomach knotting up. "Should evasive action be necessary, remain in your jump seats and listen for any orders. Pick up your gear and the loadmasters will assign you to your aircraft."

We all picked up our duffel bags and began filing toward the waiting planes. Three non-commissioned officers, the aircrafts' loadmasters, were checking name tags and assigning each soldier to one of the three aircraft. As I moved closer to the front of the line I found myself muttering, "Not number two. Whatever else happens, don't put me in aircraft two." I got to the front of the line (technically it was the end of the line since I was the last one) and looked up expectantly. Imagine my unadulterated amazement when they assigned me to aircraft two. I'm sure the Fates were giggling at that one. With the look of a whipped puppy, I approached the rear of the aircraft and made my way aboard.

I had seen pictures of this particular aircraft set up for carrying troops before. They were designed to use seats that were certainly not as comfortable as airline seats, but that were padded and decent for long journeys. Unfortunately, as a means of saving weight and money, this plane had been equipped with the old-fashioned web jump seats. The loadmaster instructed me on how to stow my duffel bag, and then led me to my seat. I sat down and immediately considered jumping out of the plane. Maybe that's where the name came from. The seat was evil. I don't even understand how it could be referred to as a seat. It was three metal bars with nylon webbing stretched between them to take the shape of a seat. The loadmaster screamed at me to buckle my harness, which I did, and then I returned to contemplating the sheer masochistic qualities of those seats. It was in a perfect "L" shape, so I had to sit straight up. However, when I sat straight up I had a metal bar going under my knees, another right on my tailbone, and the third right at my head. I felt like I had a migraine, hemorrhoids, and arthritis in my knees all at once. What sadistic engineer put these things together? Did he have any bones, or was his entire body made of cartilage? It was absolutely mind-boggling.

It must have really boggled my mind because by the time I stopped contemplating why anyone would design something so uncomfortable and what I would do to them if I met them in a dark alley, we were well over the Sea of Japan. At least the loadmaster claimed that we were. It's not like we could see out of the airplane anyways. I finally began noticing some other things about the flight. First was the smell. There were over a hundred troops on our plane, and most of us had been traveling for nearly twenty hours. It turns out that when you are lugging a heavy duffel bag around, sitting on a hot tarmac, or sitting in an airliner seat for that long, you tend to sweat. The stench was almost unbearable. The next thing I noticed was the noise. It almost overwhelmed the stench. I had thought that things were a little noisy on the airliner because I was sitting near the engines. The cargo compartment we were flying in sounded like they had stuck us in the engines and cranked it up. I dug out my newly acquired iPod and tried to listen to some music, but I couldn't seem to turn it up loud enough to drown out the noise of the compartment. I'd thought that the flight to Japan had been long. This flight was going to be excruciating. I started wishing for a bunch of motion sickness medicine and a Mountain Dew again.

Just as I was contemplating asking the loadmaster how much longer the flight would be, I heard him yell out, "Hold on to something!" He'd barely gotten the words out when my butt dropped out from underneath me. I had ridden a few roller coasters in my life. I always liked the twists and turns and even the loops, but I had always hated the dips. Now I remembered why. The plane and my body seemed to be diving faster than my food was. Like a complete idiot, I allowed my mind to remember what my last meal had been. The thought of having the meatball sub make an encore appearance made me feel even worse. I could tell I was turning green, and I began feeling myself break out into a cold sweat. The very large and intimidating soldier next to me must have seen the way I looked, because his deep voice bellowed out over all of the racket. "If you puke on me, boy, I will rip your nose off and eat it!" The urge to vomit ceased almost immediately. I believe that this occurred for two reasons. The first reason was that the man threatening me scared the living hell out of me. That man could have snapped me like a twig, compressed my body back together, and then turned me into a living accordion like they used to do in old cartoons. He probably could have done all of that without breaking a sweat. The other reason that I forgot to be sick was because of the manner of his threat. I mean, really? Rip my nose off and eat it? I've been threatened in a lot of ways, but nasal cannibalism was a new one. Rip my nose off and eat it. And *I'm* the one seeing a quack therapist these days?

The dive finally started to level out, but then the plane began to make sharp, banking turns. I had no idea an airplane that big could come close to moving that much. During one of the turns, I discovered that there were, in fact, a few small windows in the cargo hold that had been blocked by the heads of some of the soldiers sitting there. I looked through the window and saw nothing but ocean. I don't mean I saw ocean until the horizon. I mean that I saw *nothing but ocean!* We were so low that I could make out the whitecaps of the waves. I had almost decided that it was time to freak out when I felt something slip out of my pocket. The sudden movements and shaking must have loosened something. I reached down to check my pocket and realized what I'd lost. This couldn't possibly end well. I had no sooner gotten the thought out when I heard someone yell, "Ow! What the hell?"

I looked over and saw a soldier holding his ear with some blood dripping from between his fingers. As the plane started to level out, the loadmaster rushed over to check on the wounded man. Something had scratched a pretty good cut across his ear. He would be fine, but the wound bled a lot. He and the loadmaster searched around for the culprit that had caused the cut. I knew what it was. I tried to shrink down lower in the sadistic seat that they had me strapped into. It only took a moment, and then the loadmaster held up a set of keys. "Who the hell brought their house and car keys with them on deployment?" he shouted loud enough for all of us to hear.

I guess I should explain that I am a creature of habit. I always had car keys in one hip pocket and a wallet in my back pocket. I'd been doing that since my parents had gotten me a set of house keys in middle school. I was accustomed to having them there. If I didn't have my keys and wallet in my pockets, I spent the entire day feeling like something was missing. It never mattered what I was doing or what I was wearing, I always had those with me. Being . . . well, the way that I am, it never occurred to me that I wouldn't be needing to unlock my house or drive my car for the next year. That realization hit me fast enough to keep me from claiming the keys as mine, though. I'd just have to get a spare set when I got back home, because both the loadmaster and the cut soldier looked mad enough to kill.

The landing at Daegu was much smoother than the flight. As the cargo doors began to open and the soldiers began to unbuckle, the loadmaster shouted out to all of us, "Welcome to the Hiss, soldiers. Enjoy your stay. If you should have the pleasure of flying with us again, keep your keys at home, dumbass." I didn't look directly at the loadmaster on my way out.

After I walked down the cargo ramp, I looked over and saw Lt. Col. Kiernan exiting the plane. I ran over to him and saluted. "Colonel Kiernan. I wanted to thank you for getting us away from those enemy fighters."

The pilot quickly returned the salute and replied with a twinkle in his eye, "What enemy fighters?" He and his copilot were laughing as they walked off. I'd been bested by a hundred-year-old living cartoon character. All right, Humility. You've won this round!

I guess I just need to learn the language . . .

*

After landing in Daegu we were quickly ushered into a bunch of green busses. Getting on the bus was kind of disturbing. It was like a flashback to being in school. When I got on the bus all of the seats were taken. There was literally nowhere left to sit, and the other busses had already pulled away. I was left with no choice but to stand in the aisle with my duffel bag at my feet and with me holding on to the rack above everyone's head that was holding their duffle bags. Everyone was fairly quiet as we pulled out of the airfield and began traveling to our destination, Camp Lincoln.

Camp Lincoln was only about five miles outside of Daegu, but Daegu itself was a large city with three million people. Even though we had a police escort, our convoy ended up moving slowly through traffic. Most of the soldiers were looking out of the metal bar windows, but I couldn't see through them while I was standing. As much as I wanted to gawk at the new sights like a tourist, I found myself faced with two other problems. The first problem was that I realized that I had to go to the bathroom. The second problem was that my legs were getting tired from standing up. I tried shifting my weight from one leg to another so that both of my legs wouldn't be so tired, but I realized that when I shifted my weight, it shifted my hips, and the person to one side or the other received an uncomfortably close view of my butt. It also made me want to cross my legs since I had to use the bathroom, and that was a decidedly unmanly pose. I eventually forced myself to stand straight and face ahead in a stalwart, manly pose. It just about killed me.

One thing that I was truly grateful for was the fact that despite there being a war on, the roads through Daegu were well paved and smooth. If the bus had been bouncing around a lot over potholes or gravel, I probably would have been the victim of a terrible biological accident. As it was, by the time we took the exit off of the expressway, my eyes were literally watering with discomfort. Being on the plane while it was diving and banking (Kiernan had better be glad I never saw him again!) was nothing compared to this. I began to believe that if someone had offered me a Porta-Potty in exchange for replacing every piece of furniture I own with web jump seats for the rest of my life, I would have taken the deal. It was excruciating.

Just when I thought that life as I knew it was about to end thanks to bodily functions, a miracle happened. This is not something that anyone else would have viewed as a miracle. In fact, most saw it as a disaster. However, I like to think that I take a much wider view of events than most people do. That is how I saw this miracle. Kids, if you're reading this, try to remember that. You can find miracles in the strangest places. In this case, it was the miracle of an oncoming Hyundai.

The bus had just taken the exit off of the expressway and merged onto a smaller highway. There must have been a sharp rock or piece of glass somewhere up ahead. Whatever it was, it shredded the tire of a Hyundai traveling in the other direction. The driver struggled to regain control, but he flew across oncoming traffic directly in front of our bus.

The bus driver swerved to prevent a collision. He was good. He managed to avoid the car cleanly, but stress and fatigue on the rear axle caused it to snap. The bus was careening along the shoulder with the driver trying to bring it to a stop. Everyone was holding on for dear life, but no one more than me. I was the only idiot standing up. As the bus took a particularly vicious swerve, my duffle bag began to fly off to my right. I let go of the overhead rack I was holding on to with my right hand and reached out to grab my duffle bag before it could hurt someone. I was keeping my balance by holding on for dear life to the overhead rack on my left. Unfortunately, the weight of the duffle bags it was carrying and the stress of the maneuvers on top of the pressure I was placing on it was too much for it to take. The support I was holding on to ripped itself out of the metal body of the bus. I flew to the right but was caught out of reflex by the soldier sitting there. The soldiers sitting on the left were not so lucky. The rack tilted downward and all of their duffle bags began falling on top of them. There was a lot of angry shouting, cussing, and even some language that I couldn't quite identify. Thankfully, the bags were loaded mostly with uniforms and the like, so they were more of a nuisance than a hazard. Even so, by the time the bus came to a complete stop, almost everyone on board looked ready to chew nails. Lucky for me, they all thought that the bus was just getting old and that the rack fell on its own. If any of those soldiers are reading this now, I would like to ask that you not try to find me. I have a family to take care of now, you know.

Some may be wondering how on earth this could possibly be considered a miracle. Well, the miracle is the fact that the bus came to a stop just in front of a restaurant. That restaurant had food, drink, and, thank goodness, bathrooms! While waiting for a replacement bus to arrive, we were allowed to avail ourselves of the hospitality of the owners. They actually fed us at no cost. I left money for them anyways. They had shown so much concern when they saw me running at full sprint toward their bathrooms.

It took another two hours before we finally reached Camp Lincoln in a replacement bus. We were all looking forward to ending our long journey from the United States to the war in Korea. When I think about it, that was probably the most illogical feeling that we could have ever had. We were relieved to end the safest part of our journey so that we could begin the most dangerous part. I've heard the term "young and stupid" many times in my life. I may just now be getting to the point where I understand it. I even breathed a sigh of relief when they ordered us off of the bus. It made perfect sense to me at the time. Of course, most comic books made perfect sense to me at the time, too. Wow, I am getting old.

When we arrived at Camp Lincoln we were told to find a bunk and to be ready for inspection at 0600. Why does the military have to do everything early in the morning? Do they have something against sleeping in? I wonder if we would have a more peaceful world if we all just snored a little while longer. There's some philosophy for a PhD candidate to write about. Regardless, it was getting late. It was already dark before we had arrived, which made getting around colorful, but it also meant that none of us were chosen for sentry duty that night. The barracks we entered were made from plywood and had obviously been thrown up in a hurry, but they were air-conditioned, much to my surprise, so I couldn't complain. There was only one bed still open, and it was right next to the entrance to the latrine. No wonder it was still available. The smell and the fact that people would be walking past you all night long is why no one else had chosen that bunk. This never happens to anyone else that's "fashionably late."

I tossed my duffle bag next to my bunk and laid down. Why is it that we can control a little remote control car on another planet but we can't design a decent bed for soldiers to sleep in? Yes, it is certainly better than the ground. I know that intellectually and from experience. Still, those things cannot be healthy for someone's back. I was tired, but not so tired that I was going to fall asleep right away. I started to make up the bunk and noticed the soldier next to me doing the same. It was odd. He looked almost exactly like me, but he seemed older and more in shape. He couldn't have been much older than me, but there was something in the way that he moved and the look in his eyes that contained a lifetime of wisdom that I lacked (and that I'm still looking for). I didn't realize I was staring until he looked over his shoulder and said, "Why don't you take a picture? It'll be easier to study."

I blinked and immediately looked away, ashamed at my ill manners. However, when I looked back, he was smiling at me. I realized that the tone of voice he had said it in was not reproachful but more conversational. He wasn't angry at me. He was breaking the ice. He held out his hand to me. "My name's Ian."

I shook his hand. "They call me Pup."

He nodded his head a little. "I can see that. You must have been on that late bus. Welcome to Camp Lincoln. Don't get too comfortable. You won't be here long." The whole process of what was going to happen to me and what they expected me to do was never really clear to me. I had stopped asking people about it because I got tired of being told not to ask stupid questions. I'm not entirely sure if I have any other kind of questions. Ian gave me a little half-grin. "Go ahead and ask me stuff. I know what it's like when no one explains anything to you."

There are days when I wonder if he ever regretted giving me permission to ask questions. I had a million of them. That isn't even much of an exaggeration. He explained to me what to have prepared for inspection, when I would be issued gear, and when mess call usually was. He gave me a list on how to pack a rucksack and even helped me find ways to get my boots on and off more quickly. That man probably saved me from more embarrassment than any other individual in my life. I finally remembered a question that I had been wanting to ask all day. "This is going to sound stupid." He snickered. I figured he was used to that by now. "But there are two terms I've heard recently that I don't understand. First, what is Whiskey Tango Foxtrot?"

Even as patient as Ian had been, he looked at me like I was clueless. Well, that's because I was. "You've never heard the term WTF?"

I had to think about that for a minute. I had never bothered trying to convert the military alphabet terms to actual letters. It took a minute, but it finally hit me what he meant. "Oh! I guess that poor Japanese lady at the airport really didn't like me." I didn't bother trying to explain that one to him. He was wise enough not to ask. "OK, I can understand that. One thing that I have heard a lot more is Hiss. What on earth is the Hiss?"

"You're standing on it, Pup." He laid back on his cot and propped his head up on his arm. "The term started back near the beginning of the Second Korean War. Soldiers started calling this place the Hiss."

I also laid down on my cot and faced him. "Why?"

"You ever look at a map of Korea?" I nodded. "It looks like a 'thumbs down.' Boo, hiss."

I nodded again. "I take it the South Koreans don't care for the name?"

"Not really. The South Koreans are impressive. I've seen their soldiers fight harder than anyone could ever expect, while the civilians are tough and resourceful. I wouldn't want to get on their bad side."

I was still shaking my head. "I can't believe someone could be so callous like that. How can you disrespect the people that you're fighting alongside?"

Ian sat back up. He obviously wanted to drive his point home. "Pup, when you get out in the field, you're going to think that a lot of the people you meet are assholes. Some of them will be. The rest are just trying to survive. When you get out there, you're going to try and hold on to a lot of the lessons you were taught in kindergarten, and you'll manage to hold on to a few, but most you're going to let go of because you don't have time for them." He looked away for a second. I guess he was remembering some of what he had seen and heard. "I've heard the South Koreans say some nasty stuff about the American soldiers. Don't forget, this is a United Nations effort. There's a lot of different nationalities out there, and you are going to hear them say things about each other that would result in a brawl on the streets back home." He shrugged. "It doesn't matter so much right now. When you're out there, you really find out what is most important to you. Being polite is all well and good when you are on leave. In fact, you'll get yourself in trouble if you aren't. But in the field, you worry about getting home. That's all anyone worries about." He closed his eyes in remembrance and laughed. "I had a South Korean soldier on a joint patrol with me that called Americans every name in the book and a few I think he made up. Part of my mind told me to hate the guy. Still, most of my mind told me to watch his back. He didn't just insult Americans, he insulted me directly a few times. Not twenty minutes into our patrol, we got ambushed. He almost got himself killed saving me. He still calls me all sorts of names, and I still buy him a beer every time I see him. I don't forgive some of what people say out there, but I can get past it."

I watched Ian lay back down and look up at the ceiling. He had given me a lot to think about. I was eighteen years old. I knew all about people trash-talking one another. But I had always felt that there was a line that you didn't cross. Ian was on his way home. He had served his year in the Hiss. He knew what he was talking about. He knew that such a line didn't exist or even matter out there in the field. The important thing was that you survived and made sure the soldiers around you survived. Everything else was secondary. For a kid who had managed to avoid fights at school, much less true combat, it was a lesson that I had not learned yet.

After a few minutes, Ian rolled back onto his side and looked at me. "One other thing, Pup. There's something else that will be a lot different out in the field. They don't have time and space to set up separate facilities. Everything is coed. You'd better start getting over that now." He looked at me to make sure that I had heard him, then he rolled back over and fell right off to sleep.

I laid there thinking about all that he had told me that night. He had taught me a whole lot. I also started to realize that before he had arrived, he'd probably been a lot like me. Maybe that's why he was willing to be so patient with me. So he was what I would be like when I ended my tour? Thinking about the way that he had treated me, it seemed like a pretty decent way to end up.

I'm sure by now some people are wondering when the next stupid thing is going to happen to me. Well, nothing else happened that night. Even a blithering idiot has a calm night once in a while. Plus, this was a war, not a sitcom. I could end that evening talking about some of the more creative ways that soldiers in the latrine expressed their flatulence, but to be honest, it's more true to point out that I went to sleep wiser than I had woken up that morning. (See, honey? You always think I can't take anything seriously.)

But they could have been four-legged people . . .

*

We were all awakened at 0400. That's four o'clock in the morning for you uninitiated out there. Four o'clock. It is physically painful to even mention that time of day. No civilian that I have ever spoken to gets up at four o'clock unless they have to. It's a whole different story in the army. Not only do they wake you up that early, but they do it with a trumpet call, like you should be celebrating the lack of sleep. I know, there's tradition behind it. I don't care. Let tradition lose sleep.

I dragged myself out of my bunk and made my way to the latrine. After taking care of the biological necessities that had put themselves on hold in order for me to sleep, I proceeded to the sink to shave. I hated shaving. I was eighteen years old and didn't grow much facial hair at the time, so shaving just reminded me that I wasn't as "manly" as some of the others. I preferred to use an electric razor because regular razors made my skin break out, but I learned very quickly in boot camp that the military has a certain prejudice against rotary blades. I sprayed some shaving cream in my hand and proceeded to spread it on my face when I felt something odd. I looked in the mirror and noticed something on my nose. I squinted to get a better view and realized that it was one of those strips that some people wear to keep them from snoring. I started replaying the events of the previous night in my head and never remembered putting one on. "You snore," said a voice at the sink beside me. I looked over and saw Ian beginning the same ritual of shaving that I was about to begin. "I put that on you last night so that you wouldn't get mugged in your bunk by sleep-deprived soldiers. I put the rest of the box in your duffel. It won't last long, so make sure to hit the PX before you get shipped out."

I nodded and proceeded to shave. "Thanks a lot. I owe you. The flight attendant on the way over would have sacrificed body parts for me to have had those on the plane." A sudden thought occurred to me. It caused me to nick my chin. Stupid razors! "Why do you have these things?"

"I have a bit of a snoring issue, too." He stopped for a moment as he shaved over his Adam's apple. I patiently waited. I didn't want him getting nicked, too. I looked ridiculous enough for the both of us. "When I first got here, someone duct-taped my mouth shut in my sleep. It wouldn't have been a big deal, but it was the heavy duty duct tape. I was kept from the front line for an extra week because the tape took some skin off with it."

I smiled and went back to shaving. "What do you do if you run out of the strips while you're on patrol?"

"You won't need them while you're on patrol."

"But what if I . . ."

Ian stopped and looked over at me. "You won't need them. Trust me, Pup." I nodded. I had to trust him. He had a clue. He pointed to my sink. "Make sure you are using cold water to rinse your razor. It will help some with the irritation."

I nodded and changed the water flow. It didn't even occur to me at the time to be appreciative of the fact that we had hot water at Camp Lincoln. Oh, the lessons that we learn. "Thanks a lot, Ian. I swear, it's like you know how screwed up I am and how to prevent it from getting me into trouble."

He toweled his face dry and patted me on the back. "Come on, Pup. You aren't screwed up. You're special. I'm sure your mommy told you so." We both laughed. She had. Several times. "Seriously, I've been through the same stuff you have. You grow up quick here. I had to find out a lot of stuff the hard way. I see no reason that you should have to learn the same way." I turned to him and shook his hand warmly. It had only taken a day for him to become my best friend. He returned the gesture, and I could tell he understood. After a second, he broke out into a wide smile again. "Don't go getting a man-crush, there, pal. I'm heading home tomorrow."

I let go and finished shaving. I only nicked myself twice more (stupid razors!), which was a new record for me. I donned my uniform and walked with Ian to the mess hall. The food wasn't too bad. It was cooked, warm, and at least resembled what it was supposed to be. The colors were fairly close. I sat with Ian and traded stories about home. I didn't ask him too much about his time in the field. I figured that if he wanted to tell me anything that he would.

The time came for us to fall in for inspection. Ian told me to just live with it. He explained to me that inspection wasn't something I'd be having to deal with much at the front, but some of the rear bases required it. The lieutenant looked us all over with a minimum of fuss. It's a good thing. I realized later that my name tape was on upside down. I saw a smirk on Ian's face. I never could prove that he did it. Man, with friends like that . . .

The next thing they did was start assigning us to details. I wasn't all that thrilled about that. I don't mind doing work, but come on! I'm just supposed to be at this base long enough for you to figure out where you want to send me to risk my life! Why do I care if your buildings are painted or trash disposed of? Still, that's how things worked. They picked people pretty much at random, without regard to whether they had the ability to do the job or not. That's how I saw it. In truth, most people were probably more than capable of doing these jobs without real instruction. Then there was me. I needed instructions to figure out how to use a refrigerator magnet. In the end, Ian and I wound up on separate work details. He was supposed to help raise the walls for a new set of barracks. I was ordered to help set out new razor wire along the base perimeter.

Let me see if I can explain this. Razor wire is sharp. Hence the name, razor wire. Its purpose is to create a barrier that an enemy trying to enter the base would have to cross over. It won't kill them, but it is an obstacle that can slow them down. Because it's sharp. It's a wire. With razors. Razor wire. I can't prevent myself from getting cut when shaving. With a safety razor. This was a wire. With razors. That weren't safe.

I'm not going to get into all of the details of what happened that day. I know that my quack therapist says that talking things out is good for the healing process, but this wasn't emotionally painful. It was physically painful. Very physically painful. Besides, I can't go into all of the details because I don't remember them all. What I do know is that getting tangled up in razor wire ranks right up there with skinny-dipping in Siberia on my list of things I never want to do. It's true that the razor wire will probably not kill you. What it will do is cause you to have to receive so many bandages from the medic that a special requisition has to be sent to the quartermaster for resupply. I still wonder why vampires in books didn't make use of razor wire. It turns out to be a very effective bloodletting tool.

I managed to survive without the need for a transfusion and met up with Ian in the mess hall for supper. I discovered quickly that use of the salt shaker when one is covered with cuts is an excruciating means of flavoring one's food. I finally decided it was safer to eat it plain. Ian couldn't help but laugh at me. "Wow!" he exclaimed. "Talk about death from a thousand cuts!"

I winced a little as I raised my food to my mouth. Man! I felt like I had cuts everywhere! How did I get cuts between my toes? I was wearing boots! "I think they only counted nine hundred and ninety-nine," I countered. "There is life left in me yet." We had another good time talking and laughing over a bland meal of . . . something. I learned it was better not to try and identify the food. You might not like what you figured out.

Our fun was interrupted by some grumbling of soldiers elsewhere in the mess hall. I saw a sergeant walking around and pointing at people. Whoever he pointed at usually responded with a frown or a muttered curse that the sergeant pretended not to hear. In the corner of my vision I could see Ian starting to shrink into his uniform, like he was trying to make himself invisible. I wasn't sure why until the sergeant walked up and pointed at me. "You! Sentry," he growled.

"No, Sergeant. They call me Pup. I don't know anybody named Sentry." I spend a lot of time these days looking back on things that I have said and done. Most of the time I realize that my responses to questions and situations are about two steps below moronic. This would be one of those times.

The sergeant slapped the back of my head. Technically, I suppose that's an assault. However, compared to what I'm sure he wanted to do to me, the head-slap was perfectly acceptable. "Smart ass," he growled as he moved on. I had to wonder if that was his natural tone of voice. When he told his children, "Good night. Sweet dreams," did it sound like a threat?

My train of thought was derailed by Ian snickering again. "I'm sorry, Pup, but that was funny. In all honesty, I probably would have responded the same way last year."

I rubbed the back of my head. "Now comes the part where I ask what it was that I just responded stupidly to."

"The sergeant was assigning people to sentry detail. You have to stand guard in one of the bunkers tonight." He watched my face fall like someone had just proclaimed that my dog was deceased. "Don't worry. It's not that bad. You'll be in the bunker with one other soldier, and you'll split the shift. I'll help you draw the equipment from the armory when we get done eating."

A few minutes later, Ian was talking me through the requirements for sentry duty. (I know. I said "doody.") It turned out that even I could figure it out. I and whoever was stuck in a bunker with me would split up the watch. I would sleep while the other soldier had watch, then they would wake me up and I would take watch. I would have to check in regularly on radio and scan with my NVGs (Night Vision Goggles) occasionally. Mostly, I would be watching out for flares. The perimeter of the base was lined with trip wires that had flares attached to them. If someone crossed, a flare would be fired and we would make their night a whole lot more difficult. I doubted even I could screw it up. I should have more faith in myself as a screw-up than that!

Since it was summertime and the sun set late and rose early, night watch was just from 2200 to 0400. At about 2130, I arrived at the armory and was issued a carbine to keep with me that night. I reported to the watch officer who assigned me to a bunker on the north corner of the base. I found the bunker easily. Thankfully, someone had labeled the bunkers well enough that I could read it in the minuscule light.

I crawled into it and then stopped in my tracks. There was a belt-fed machine gun mounted on a stand at the front of the bunker. There was already a radio set up in the front corner, within easy reach for whoever was on watch. There were two MRE packets open with their contents laid out near the machine gun. There was also another soldier there, and *she* looked at me impatiently.

I guess that I have to explain a few things. First of all, I was an eighteen-year-old guy. I was a not-very-popular eighteen-year-old guy. I was a smart guy that thought about a lot of things. However, like most eighteen-year-old guys, I thought about women a lot. I was pretty sure that I had dreamt about this particular scenario before. The woman in the bunker was not gorgeous. She was not going to make a career in modeling. She was too well filled out for that. She had obviously gotten a lot of exercise, and it wasn't in an attempt to lose weight. She could probably punch a hole in the side of the bunker to shoot out of if I got in her way. Her eyes were of a distinctly feminine shape, but the look in them was hard and cold. A little wisp of red hair escaped from underneath her cap. She looked like she belonged in a uniform, and that made life . . . difficult for me. I had a thing for women in uniform. I had a thing for women not in uniform. OK! I admit it! I was eighteen! I had a thing for all women! Any delusions I had of romance were quickly destroyed when she spoke. "Are you gonna get in here, Private, or are you gonna stand there like a friggin' moron?"

I quickly squirmed the rest of the way into the bunker. "I'm sorry, Corporal . . ." I checked her name tape. "McKall."

She glared at me for another moment before offering me her hand. "Folks call me Rabbit." I shook her hand but looked at her curiously. She finally felt compelled to explain. "My first name is Jessica. I have red hair. Apparently there is some old movie that I need to see to understand. Whatever the movie is, some of the guys started calling me Rabbit."

"OK. Well everybody calls me Pup."

"Great," she mumbled. "Get a couple more animal nicknames and we could start a friggin' zoo." I laughed at her joke a little too hard. Stupid hormones! She glared at me again, and I got quiet quickly. "Whatever. I'll take first watch. Are you a cherry?" I looked at her in shock. I couldn't believe that she would ask me such a personal question when we had just met! It really threw me for a loop because I think that the woman in my dream asked the same question. I'm so glad I've learned to think with my brain since then. Rabbit rolled her eyes at me. "I meant is this your first tour, perv?" I nodded, too afraid to speak. "Fine. We're post Delta Thirteen on the radio. We'll do a check-in each hour. If a flare goes off in our area of responsibility, you'll wake me so I can report it on the radio, and you'll look for the problem with the NVGs. If it's a sapper, you'll take them out. Simple enough?" I nodded once more. "Good. You can sleep over there." She gestured to a corner of the bunker.

I proceeded over to the corner that Rabbit had indicated and got ready to sleep. Ian had made certain that I brought a nose strip with me so that I wouldn't give my position away to enemy listening posts all the way at the North Pole. I put one on my nose and glanced over to say good night to Rabbit. She was already looking through her NVGs and reporting on the radio that we were secure. I decided that it would be smart not to disturb her. I was pretty sure she hated me already. I wrapped myself in a poncho liner and got ready to sleep. It took about four seconds. Poncho liners are so cozy.

I'm not sure if I had any dreams during that brief rest. I hope not. I have a feeling that I might talk in my sleep, or at the very least make noises in my sleep. There is a high potential for humiliation there. I tend to dream that I am a captain of a starship. That could be tough to explain. Whether I did or not, Rabbit never said a thing about it. She just woke me up when her shift was over. She checked in on the radio and informed them that we were switching watches. I listened closely to what she said on the radio so that I could duplicate it. She passed the NVGs to me and shuffled to the corner of the bunker and placed her carbine within arm's reach. She asked to borrow my poncho liner, which I readily agreed to. She gave me a curious look and then settled down to sleep. I started to put the NVGs on so that I could look around outside, but I was interrupted by a drowsy sounding Rabbit. "Pup?" I turned around to see what she wanted. "If I wake up and find you staring at me like some kind of weirdo while I sleep, you won't be able to walk for a week."

I rather awkwardly replied with a "Yes, ma'am," and she settled back in. I was completely confused by her threat. Why would she think that I would be watching her while she slept? I had a responsibility to monitor the perimeter, and I took it seriously. Who would shirk that responsibility to watch someone sleep? I turned to ask her about that, but she was already asleep. I was about to turn back to monitor the perimeter when my curiosity got the better of me. Why would anyone watch someone else sleep? I started to watch her to see what might be so unusual about a sleeping person. I had never watched someone sleep before. I had never had a reason to. Now I watched Rabbit sleep, and I was mesmerized. It wasn't some odd sexual thing. That was one of the things that amazed me the most.

My therapist and I have spoken at length about that. I don't know why he's so obsessed with it. I'm starting to think that he has some issues. Quack.

I noticed how her lips were parted just slightly. Barely enough to let air enter or escape. You could see her taking deep breaths as her chest rose and fell under the poncho liner. OK, yes I noticed it was her chest. Stupid hormones. Her eyes were moving back and forth under her eyelids, almost as though she were reading a book in her sleep. One of her legs twitched slightly. I began to wonder what she might be dreaming of. I wondered how much of the world she was aware of right now and how much she was oblivious to. Was she seeing things with her eyes or her mind? I really have a tendency to overthink things.

I was so focused on my thoughts and analyzing my observations that I never noticed that the twitching and eye movement had stopped. I almost screamed out loud when I heard her voice speaking to me. "I mean it, Pup. I will hurt you."

"Uh, yes, ma'am. Sorry ma'am," I stuttered. I quickly turned around and made a concerted effort to not look back at her. Amazing. I was just doing something quasi-scientific and I still got busted. I had no luck whatsoever.

I learned a few important things during my first hour or so of sentry duty. The first thing I learned was that when it gets dark outside of the city, it gets *dark!* With no streetlights or headlights to bring about any ambient light, it can get remarkably dark outside. When I say dark, I mean that anything more than ten feet away from me was invisible. It was amazing. It wasn't total darkness. I had experienced that on a tour of Mammoth Cave once. I still have nightmares. The quack is trying to talk me through those. However, it was still dark enough that my mind had trouble grasping it. I had never gone camping in the woods or anything. My mother hadn't let me join the Scouts. She'd been scared of me learning how to start a fire. I also discovered that the darkness made the stars much more visible. I knew there were a lot of stars in the sky, but I had never realized how many I couldn't see while living in the suburbs. It was like someone had plopped me down in the middle of a planetarium and turned the projector up to "ultra." I learned that NVGs gave you a headache if you wore them for very long. I also learned that once you got past the darkness and the view of the stars, sentry duty was incredibly boring. I mean mind-numbingly, coma-inducing, singing-to-yourself, creating-finger-puppets-out-of-clay-and-putting-on-a-play boring!

I have a habit that I started when I was a child that I still have to this day. It's something that occurs when I'm bored, confused, or angry. I talk to myself. No, I don't think there is another person talking back to me or anything like that. I just do it as a way of voicing my thoughts. Sometimes hearing things out loud changes your perspective on them. I had gotten so incredibly bored by the end of the second hour that I had to have some kind of sensory input before I lost my mind. The radio was digital, so it didn't have any kind of static that might have broken the monotony. Rabbit didn't snore. I didn't want to sing for fear that I would be accused of violating the Geneva Convention, dealing with torture of the enemy. I started talking to myself. I mostly replayed the events of the last few days. I spoke through the different conversations that Ian and I'd had. I even replayed conversations I'd had with others, but the way that I wanted them to go instead of the way that they went. By the time I was done with my faux conversations, the Japanese lady in the airport had to be pried away from me by the MP while she begged to join me on my deployment. Ah, reality, thou art a harsh mistress.

I was so deep into my thoughts that I almost didn't notice the flare shoot into the sky. It was the movement that caught my attention more than the light, but regardless of what drew my eyes out of my dream world, it caused my adrenaline to surge. In the flare light I saw one thing move rapidly along the perimeter, then I noticed something crawling low. *Sappers!* I thought. I knew what I was supposed to do, but I was afraid that if I took the time to do things right that the sapper might accomplish his mission. *It's all up to me*, I thought. I had seen way too many movies. I grabbed the machine gun and fired off a burst. Wow! What a rush! I had been trained on how to load and operate a belt-fed machine gun, but I had never really gotten to fire one with live ammunition. It was a blast! Something about the rapid recoil and the ear-splitting, ripping-a-hole-in-the-sky sound was more than the pleasure center of my brain could handle. I remember smiling widely after that first burst. Unfortunately, the burst was high. Really high. If there were any owls out there that night, I was a big danger to them.

The burst of automatic fire woke Rabbit up immediately and apparently did the same to everyone on the perimeter. Rabbit was asking me what was going on. The HQ radio operator was demanding a report. Why couldn't they all shut up? I was busy trying to aim and be a hero. The flare light was starting to dwindle, and I wanted to get my target before it went out. I fired again, much lower this time. Dirt was thrown into the air only about twenty feet from my bunker, but I didn't let off of the trigger. I walked the fire all the way to what looked like a man that was surprisingly fast on all fours. The bullets finally started landing near the intruder. They turned and started to retreat. Man! They were fast on their hands and knees! I could see Rabbit donning the NVGs next to me. Good. She could help spot for me. I followed the retreating figure. Just as I heard Rabbit shout "Cease fire!" I hit the target. I heard a noise I hadn't expected. A yelp. Not a man shouting in pain, but the yelp you hear from a dog that just discovered the odd object it was sniffing was a snapping turtle (don't ask how I know that). I immediately took my finger off of the trigger about the same time that Rabbit grabbed my arm to get my attention. Things suddenly got very quiet.

I turned toward Rabbit. The grin was gone from my face. I realized that I hadn't taken a breath for the last thirty seconds or so and started gasping for air. Rabbit removed my hand from the gun and then took off her NVGs. She looked like she was going to ask me a question, but she realized I couldn't speak then. She instead went to the radio to report our situation. "HQ, Delta Thirteen. Our position's clear. A wild dog breached the perimeter, and the kid got antsy. Over."

I didn't catch the response from the operator. I was busy replaying the whole event in my head. How come I didn't notice that it was a dog? Why didn't I put on my NVGs? What was my hurry again? I was used to screwing up. It was kind of my thing. But this time I screwed up and I hurt something. That really bothered me.

Rabbit stayed up with me for the rest of the shift. I could tell that she wanted to chew me up one side and down the other. I wouldn't have blamed her onc bit for doing it either. Still, she held back. I guess she knew that I was busy punishing myself. If my kids are reading this, I hope you don't inherit my conscience. It's torture. My conscience never leaves me alone, and it sounds just like my mother! Then again, if it keeps you out of trouble . . .

The sun came up eventually, and we were given the all-clear signal. I decided to go and see what I had done that night. So did Rabbit and the occupants of almost every bunker on the north side of the base. I walked toward the perpetrator of that morning's "invasion," following the bullet holes in the ground that I had created. I'd damned near dug a trench. I wanted to remember that next time somebody wanted me to dig one with some little shovel. That machine gun was easier. As I started getting closer to the target I saw bits of brown fur spread out over a wide area. It was finer than dog hair, and I wasn't sure where it had come from. I was thinking about that until I nearly tripped over the victim of my adrenaline-surged rampage.

Calling this dog a mangy mutt would be an insult to mangy mutts everywhere. This dog had likely never seen the inside of a home and had definitely never seen the inside of a bath tub. I'm sure that it had fleas and ticks, it had some kind of skin condition, and it was ugly. I mean ugly. I look like a cartoon character that is meant to frighten small children and I still had the right to call this thing ugly. Much to my surprise, it was also alive. The bullet had struck its right front leg. It lay there panting and unconscious but alive. I knelt down and placed my hand on its side. It growled a little but otherwise remained asleep. Someone from one of the other bunkers asked in a bad Australian accent, "Why were you so mad at it? Did a dingo eat your baby?"

I ignored them and found myself asking, to no one in particular, "Who can help it?"

The soldier with the bad Australian impression replied, "Help it? That wild dog is beyond help. We'd be doing it a favor, putting it out of its misery."

His partner seemed a little more sympathetic. "There's a K-9 unit stationed near here. I know they have a vet. I'll get it moved there." I watched him carefully lift the dog and carry it off. It never occurred to me or him that the dog could have woken up and torn his face off in a fearful rage. I'm not sure that he really cared. I discovered long after the war that the soldier got to take the wild dog home after the vet fixed him up. The dog only had three legs but wound up being a wonderful family pet. Rumor has it that the dog passes out if you show it a picture of me. I always joked that I frighten children and small animals. I didn't realize that it was true.

Rabbit came walking up with some of that brown fur in her hands. "It looks like the dog was chasing a rabbit. No stupid jokes, please. You must have hit it because there's fur everywhere. You really should have . . ." She stopped after she looked up at me. She had noticed that tears were welling up in my eyes. "You pussy." Some insults seem to carry extra weight when they come from a woman. That was certainly one of them. "It was a wild dog. You should have followed procedure, and I'm sure you'll catch hell for that, but it was just a wild dog. Are you going to cry over the first enemy soldier you shoot?"

I had never considered that question. I know that she didn't mean to ask it as some deep philosophical debate, but my mind really started churning because of it. Sure, I had gone through all of my training, and some of the targets we shot at were designed to look like enemy soldiers, but how would I feel when I hurt true flesh and blood. I didn't have a good answer to that. "I might," I mumbled.

Rabbit looked right at me, and for a second the cold, hard quality of her eyes softened a bit. Then she tossed the fur in her hand on the ground, turned around, and stomped off. I'm not completely certain, but I thought I heard her whisper, "I did, too."

Word travels fast around a small base. I went through the chow line for breakfast with people patting me on the back and thanking me for preventing an assault by those deadly wild dogs. A couple even howled as I walked by. It was almost like being back in high school. I sat by myself. Ian had left earlier that morning, and I already missed him. I ate quickly and then went back to the barracks to catch a quick nap. When I got to my bunk, some of the other soldiers had left me a gift. They had taken one of the tabs that can be added above a division patch and written on it. Now instead of saying "K-9," the patch read "K-9 Killer." My first thought was to throw it in the toilet or set it on fire in front of the barracks. Then I remembered what one of my teachers had taught me. I took the tab and placed it on my left arm of my uniform. My teacher once said, "If you're going to screw up, own it!" I looked at the tab and smiled. It labeled me the guy that screwed up big. I could live with that. It really was just like being in high school again.

Definitely not like camp . . .

*

My embarrassment at Camp Lincoln didn't last very long. The day after the infamous "mutt incident," I was informed that I would be shipping out to an infantry unit as a replacement. I have to admit I was a little disappointed to hear that. I was kind of hoping that I would wind up in some other type of unit. Something that wouldn't force me to walk everywhere I went. The sergeant informing me of my assignment smiled at that. "From what I hear, you can run a full on sprint with a duffle bag in one hand and a scared-to-death Japanese woman in the other. I'd say your legs work just fine." It always did amaze me how no one can remember when you do something good, but when you do something stupid, even people you have never known always seem to find out about it. "Get to the quartermaster and draw your gear before you ship out tomorrow."

I reported to the quartermaster's depot. I walked in and a supply clerk greeted me with, "What's up, killer?" See what I mean about how stupid news travels? "What can we do for you?" I informed him of where I was shipping out to. He took a few minutes and gathered up all of the gear he was supposed to issue to me. The idea of having to haul all of that stuff around made my back hurt just thinking about it. He yelled something to someone in the back and then started going over all of my gear and filling it in on a form. Once he was done, he had me sign the form and virtually dumped all of the gear into my arms. I was about to walk off, but he stopped me. A moment later, the one he had yelled to in the back came running up and handed him a couple of pieces of Velcro-backed cloth. He handed them to me. They each said "Pup." "The LT you'll be serving under likes to have his soldiers wear name tags with their nicknames. He thinks it builds unit cohesion. It's a violation of uniform code, but nobody cares about that out in the field. Good luck to you."

I hauled all of my stuff back to the barracks and spent the day organizing it into something that could almost be portable without using a two-ton truck to haul it. I wrote a few notes to myself in the hopes that they would remind me of important advice that Ian had given me. I think the one that I remembered the most was, "Right now and in the future, you say you're fighting for your country. When you're in the field, you're really fighting for the soldier next to you." I felt a brief wave of pity for whoever the soldier next to me was going to be. I slept surprisingly well that night. I was scared out of my wits, but something in me also knew that this was likely to be the most comfortable rest I would have for a while, so I drifted off quickly. I was fortunate that I remembered to put on one of the nasal strips before I did. To be more accurate, everyone in the barracks was lucky that I remembered.

The next morning I found myself in a Humvee heading north. There were four of us in the vehicle. One was the driver. He apparently made this run often and never bothered looking at a map or GPS. That impressed me. My father used to joke that if he sent me out the front door and turned me around twice that I wouldn't be able to find my way home again. Of course he was exaggerating, but I'm also glad he never tested his theory. I was riding shotgun. Behind me was Rabbit. She had already changed her name tape. She didn't seem very thrilled to see me, and she didn't bother saying hello. The man sitting next to her was the one that concerned me the most. He was built as solid as a bulldozer and looked like he could defeat one in a tug-of-war match. There was no evidence on his face that he had ever smiled. To make matters worse, I had met him before. He was the soldier who had told me that if I vomited on him in the airplane that he would rip my nose off and eat it. I looked at his name tape. Hannibal. Of course. How could this not be fun?

A lot of the drive was on highway roads. The farther north that we traveled, though, the less comfortable the highways became. Not only did it seem to be suffering from a lack of maintenance, but I started seeing pits and holes in it that could only have been caused by artillery or bombs. Then I started to notice hulks of burned-out vehicles off of the side of the road. Some were military, but even more were civilian. The sights put a sudden lump of ice into my stomach. You could almost hear the voice on a GPS announcing: "You are now leaving civilization. You are now entering war zone. Turn right for minefield, left for artillery bombardment, or continue forward for unspecified imminent death." I couldn't decide if it was a good thing that we were continuing forward or not.

We eventually turned off of the highway, but at that point it was kind of hard to tell. The highway was in such bad condition that the ride on the highway and the ride on the barely marked unpaved road were pretty similar. I think that I am the only one who noticed the discomfort in the vehicle. It was hot. The noise was almost unbearable. I'm pretty sure that my rear end felt every single pebble that we drove over, and we drove over a *lot* of pebbles. When I looked around, though, the other occupants of the Humvee were completely unfazed. The driver just focused on his driving. I guess I can appreciate that. I might have been a little unnerved if the driver decided that texting on a cell phone through a war zone would be an enjoyable pastime. Rabbit and Hannibal apparently knew each other, and they proceeded to talk about their previous deployment and all of the things that they seemed to be looking forward to about being back out in the field. I really wanted to take part in the conversation so that I could pick up a few things from them, but the look I received from Hannibal when I turned around to speak left no room for translation. I was not welcome in the discussion. I just turned back around and stared out the windshield.

On rare occasions, timing actually works in my favor. I was so bored after a while on the drive that I was about to start singing to myself. The problem with that is I am never just singing to myself. Everyone around me gets to hear it, too. That never goes over well. I have caused bats to run into cave walls with my singing before. I barely avoided committing a major crime of sound pollution by noticing the approach of a series of tents. We had finally arrived at our new home. A hand-painted sign on the side of what sadly passed for a road read "Welcome to Camp Wildcat." In scribbled writing below that was a second message. "North Koreans and Duke fans may not enter."

I looked questioningly at the driver. He was smiling. For the first time in the entire interminable (there's another of those words I thought I'd never use) drive, he spoke up. "The officer who planned the locations of these forward bases two years ago was a huge college basketball fan. He named all of the forward bases after his favorite college teams. It's grown into its own rivalry between bases ever since."

"Aw, crap," I mumbled. "I hate basketball."

The driver continued to smile. "Good. That means you probably aren't a Duke fan. So unless you are a well-disguised North Korean, you should be safe here."

"The local dogs, however, are history," I heard Rabbit say to Hannibal in the back. He grunted. That was probably as close as he could come to a laugh. I didn't respond. I knew that the comment wasn't meant for my ears. What I didn't know was whether Rabbit was just being funny or if she really thought less of me for what had happened. Probably the latter, I decided. I always tend to err on the side that makes me look worse. I think it prevents me from being let down.

The camp was made almost entirely of tents. There were trenches dug around it and machine gun nests at various intervals. A few radio antennas were visible and the sound of a power generator in the distance was a constant drone. I also noticed a few solar panels set up in one area. I guess it helped cut down on how much diesel was used. A few guys were playing basketball while others were manning sentry posts. There were several Humvees off to one side and a helicopter sat on a helipad. I started having flashbacks of old episodes of *M*A*S*H*.

The driver brought us to a stop and announced that we had arrived. I gathered up my gear, and we all got out of the Humvee. This is where I tended to run into problems. I had no idea where to go from here. Usually, I just followed someone who looked like they knew what they were doing and duplicated their actions. The problem was, no one was doing anything. Rabbit and Hannibal were standing behind me. It would have been incredibly awkward for me to pick up my gear and then walk around behind them. Don't get me wrong; I don't often shy away from awkward. Still, that would be tantamount to writing "moron" on my forehead. I've had someone do that to me before. It makes for a very long day.

Thankfully, the driver came to my rescue again. He shouted toward the guys playing basketball. "Professor! Your replacements are here!"

One of the basketball players called time-out and started heading toward us. He was probably in his mid-twenties and was in incredible shape. Movie stars would have had posters of this guy on their walls. He was just over six feet tall. He was muscular, but not in a grotesque, bodybuilder fashion. His sandy hair was cut short, and it worked for him. He had a bright smile and looked friendly. You could also see a sharp mind at work behind his eyes. He was the total package. It pissed me off. I wasn't even the box, and here was this guy being the total package. Couldn't he have backed off just a little? I mean, how were guys like me supposed to ever have a chance when Mr. Perfect there was hogging all the attention and the ladies . . .

Sorry. Inferiority issues. I'm working on that. In any case, this officer had apparently been playing for the "skins" team because he walked up to us shirtless (I'm jealous! I admit it!) as Hannibal and Rabbit lined up on either side of me. The officer hadn't quite reached us before he started greeting the others. "Rabbit! Hannibal! Glad that they accepted my request to have you brought back for another tour. This must be our other grunt."

I did exactly what I thought I should. I stood at attention and saluted the approaching officer. I thought I would start things off by doing something right. You can imagine my surprise when Hannibal roughly grabbed my wrist and forced it down. "You idiot! You wanna get him killed?"

I obviously looked as confused as I felt. The officer put a placating hand on Hannibal's shoulder. "Easy, big guy. He's a cherry. It will take him a little while to learn." He gestured to Rabbit and Hannibal. "You two know where everything is. Go ahead and get yourselves settled. We have a couple of days before anything major is planned." The other two soldiers nodded and walked off. The driver made some comment about food and headed off to the mess tent, leaving me alone, still standing at attention, with the officer. He looked me up and down for a moment, glanced at my name tape, and then said, "At ease, Pup." I relaxed a little but not much. "Close enough, I guess. Everyone calls me Professor. I'm the lieutenant in charge of your platoon, and Hannibal didn't want me to become a target for a sniper. They can easily identify someone as an officer if they see other soldiers salute them." I have to admit I had never thought of that. In basic I would have wound up getting up close and personal with more potatoes if I didn't salute an officer. I guess it was all kind of like some of the tests they made me take in school. Some of it didn't translate into the real world for me. The Professor gestured to the bumper of the Humvee ,and we both sat down on it. "I was working on my doctoral thesis in American history when the war broke out. That's where I got my nickname. You look like someone who is probably pretty intellectual yourself."

"I can be about some things," I admitted, wondering where this was going.

"Good. Tell me what you know about the Second Korean War."

I almost breathed an audible sigh of relief. Finally, something that I knew about. I'd been following everything with rapt attention as it happened on the news, Internet, and documentaries. I was like a junkie for this stuff. I thought I might be able to impress him. "Well, sir, Mount Baekdu in North Korea erupted violently. It was the second loudest sound in recorded history, just behind the eruption of Krakatoa. Because of the prevailing winds and the violence of the eruption, several cities all the way to the coast were damaged or covered in ash. There has been no official estimate on the casualties. The North Korean government did not have the resources to recover from the disaster. They were about to begin accepting aid from western nations in exchange for ending its nuclear program when the generals in their military staged a coup. They told the population of North Korea that the volcanic eruption had actually been a nuclear attack by the United States. They turned this into an excuse to begin a new war. They used chemical weapons to attack our forces along the demilitarized zone and launched their only long range ballistic missile at Seattle. The missile was knocked off course by our defensive batteries, but the warhead still exploded roughly sixty miles off the coast of Washington. It has disrupted shipping and caused a lot of environmental damage there."

I felt like I was on a roll. The Professor was watching me in rapt attention. I was certain that I was getting on his good side. "Congress passed a declaration of war, and the United Nations also authorized military action in the security council. Multiple nations joined us in the fight, and the war should have ended fairly quickly. Even though the North Koreans were better equipped than anyone expected, they were heavily outnumbered. Unfortunately, every nation that had a problem with the United States joined in the fight. We were no longer facing just the North Korean Army, but a massive collection of disparate groups that were determined to defeat us. These groups ranged from jihadi terrorists to Venezuelans still loyal to the late Chavez. There have also been rumors of assistance from hard-line military commanders from China and Russia, but that has never been confirmed. That brings us to where we are today."

The Professor nodded and smiled. "That would have been an excellent answer in one of the classes I was an assistant in." That made me feel great. I was starting to get over this guy's perfection. "You know, a lot of soldiers don't like intellectuals in the field. They think that intellectuals don't have common sense and can't be men of action. Some intellectuals do still make the transition well, though. I like to think that I have. You, Pup, obviously haven't yet." So much for feeling good. "I want to demonstrate the difference. When I ask what caused the Second Korean War, an intellectual would give the answer that you gave. A soldier's answer would have sounded something like this: 'The North Koreans and their pals killed a bunch of Americans, so we came over here to fuck their shit up.' Both answers are correct. But out here, the second one gets the job done." The Professor stood up, and I followed his example, trying not to look disappointed. "You'll learn the soldier's way over time, Pup. Don't overthink everything; just follow the examples of the veterans. For various tactical reasons, we organize ourselves into half-size squads. Your squad will point you in the right direction. You've already met Rabbit and Hannibal. Hannibal is in charge of your squad. The rest you can meet in the enlisted tent." He pointed to one of the large tents in the center of the base. "It's that one there. You need to grab a bunk and stow your gear. You can have one of them show you the ropes. Dismissed." I almost saluted but managed to stop my hand halfway up. It turned into an odd and very un-military wave. The Professor smirked and I started to walk off. I stopped when he shouted after me. "Pup! Forget about the incidents with the Japanese lady and the dog. You're squadmates' lives depend on you. You can't let past screw ups hold you back." Great. That didn't put any extra pressure on me at all. And how the hell did he know about those things? Was I on some freaking reality TV show and no one told me? I was most of the way to the tent when I realized that he said Hannibal was in charge of my squad. Wonderful. I wondered if there was a special form that the military sent home if you had your nose bitten off by your superior.

Yes, I'm ignorant. It makes me a blissful person . . .

*

I made my way into a large tent near the center of the camp. I was worried that I would be stuck in pup tents for my entire tour, but this thing was massive. I mean park-your-car-next-to-the-bus-and-your-pet-tyrannosaurus huge. As I walked in and began walking toward one end, the first person to look up at me was Hannibal. Tyrannosaurus, check. He and Rabbit were talking with what must have been the rest of my squad. The first thing that I noticed about them was that all of their uniforms and gear had that lived-in look. Even Rabbit and Hannibal, and they'd just arrived. Everything of mine was brand-new and virtually shining. It really made me stand out. It reminded me of watching my dog in the yard. He used to always lay on his back and writhe on the ground. I always thought that he was just scratching his back. Now I wondered if he was just making himself fit in with the other neighborhood dogs. I had a brief urge to step out of the tent and roll around on the dirt for a few minutes, but something told me that would make the wrong impression with my new squad.

Hannibal and Rabbit shook hands with nearly a dozen people, greeting them and exchanging both pleasantries and unpleasantries, depending on the level of sarcasm called for. I didn't know what else to do, so I just stood there and grinned like an idiot. What else could I do? It wasn't like this was a party in someone's house where I could go over to the potted plant and carry on a conversation with it (yes, I did that once. It cut off all future invitations to parties for my entire high school career). People kept glancing over at me, wondering what I was doing, but they would always get drawn back into the conversation of the group. My legs were starting to get tired by the time that about half of the squad wandered back outside to join the basketball game. With fewer people shouting for attention, my presence became harder to ignore. One of the soldiers sitting on his bunk looked at me, still standing there with that damn fool grin, raised an eyebrow, and asked to no one in particular, "What is he, some kind of wax dummy?"

"You're half right," Hannibal grumbled as he turned and walked farther into the tent.

Rabbit, who was the only other person in the tent who knew who I was, felt obligated to make the introductions. "Guys, this is our FNG. Call him Pup." Everyone gave a half wave before glancing over at Rabbit again. "Yes, he's the dog shooter." She pointed a finger at an empty bunk. "Stow your gear there, sit down, and please stop grinning like that. You look like that clown everyone has nightmares about."

I followed her instructions and then looked back at everyone else. They stared back at me for an uncomfortably long time. I found myself grinning again and forced myself to stop. I can't help it! It's a defense mechanism! Finally, the guy closest to me leaned forward from his bunk and held out his hand. "How ya doin' there, Pup? They call me Jethro," he drawled. I'd never really heard a drawl before, but there was no way to mistake this accent. He was short with sun-bleached hair. His build showed that he had spent plenty of time working hard in a field somewhere. This soldier's country accent was so thick that he could have had a successful reality program just sitting on camera and reading Shakespeare. The thought made me laugh. He didn't care for it much. "You got some kind of problem with me, city slicker? You're the FNG here, so you better watch your attitude or I'll be stuck on you like hair in a biscuit!" I'm not entirely certain what that meant, but it did convince me that I never wanted to eat a meal at his house.

Rabbit made no attempt to hide her amusement, but she did try to rescue me, sort of. "Give him a bit of a break, Jethro. He's already pissed off Hannibal, shot a stray dog, and nearly got the Professor killed saluting him. He's had a full week."

Jethro seemed to mull that over for a moment. "I reckon I can give a little slack. My momma wouldn't let me back in the house if she knew I didn't do the Christian thing and give you another chance. Just tired of people puttin' flies in my soup 'cause I'm the only one 'round here that knows how to talk." Yep, that clinches it. I'm never eating at his place. "Just watch yourself, FNG. I might forget what my momma taught me next time." He laid back in his bunk and started whistling "A Country Boy Can Survive." He was a living, breathing stereotype.

I turned to Rabbit and asked, "FNG?"

Still amused by the conversation, she replied, "Fucking New Guy. The term has been around since Vietnam, so treat it with respect."

I rolled that around in my head for a moment. "Is that an official designation?" I should probably point out that I do have rather long legs. Besides allowing me to run more quickly, this also gives me the ability to kick myself in the butt. I am doing that as I am writing this out of shame for my sheer stupidity.

Amazingly, everyone thought it was a joke. Everyone nearby started laughing. I could have sworn that even Hannibal let out a chuckle. Either that, or his stomach growled. I unconsciously checked my nose to guarantee its continued existence. "This guy's a trip!" the soldier in the bunk next to Jethro exclaimed. He reached out his hand. "Whassup Pup? They call me Nickel." Nickel was an African-American of average height and with a look to him like he'd done an awful lot, and none of it was what he wanted in life.

"Why do they call you Nickel?" I asked after shaking his hand.

Jethro didn't even sit up to answer. "Because he likes that rap crap. Thinks he's gonna be the next 50 Cent, but he only has a tenth of the talent. So he's Nickel."

At this point I expected a fight to break out between the two, but Nickel had a smile on his face as he responded. "Only reason you don't appreciate my talent is 'cause you think all music has to have a harmonica and a fiddle."

Jethro looked over at him. "Only the music that's good. Let's test out your future as a rapper. Give me a rhyme for the word 'last.'" Several seconds passed. A cricket started chirping. Hannibal stomped on it.

After an agonizing fifteen seconds had elapsed, Nickel finally exclaimed, "So I'm not so great at rhyming under pressure! That doesn't mean you have to stomp on my dreams!"

"Actually, hoss, I think it does," Jethro replied with a grin.

"Screw you, redneck!"

"Not even if a skunk threatened to take a bath with me." I swear that guy had to be coming up with those sayings on purpose. I've seen cartoon characters that sounded more realistic than him.

I turned to the last person in the group that hadn't introduced herself yet. I didn't try to speak because I couldn't.

She was gorgeous. And in uniform. She was tall and athletic. She was of Hispanic heritage with long, dark hair and eyes that you could get lost in if you didn't keep a compass handy. And I was staring. That wouldn't have been so bad if I had just been staring at her face, but I ended up staring at all of her. (Yes, Mom, I am aware of how rude that is. I didn't mean to.) It turns out that you can't do that without moving your eyes and head. When you do that, the person that you are looking at knows that you are checking them out. When that person is an unbelievably attractive woman who also happens to be trained in hand-to-hand combat, you are taking your life into your own hands. Without warning, this amazing-looking woman reached across and slapped the living snot out of me. (That's another of Jethro's phrases. I wonder if he has ever seen dead snot.) I fell back on my bunk and sat there shaking my head, trying to stop the ringing. That was no love tap. "Keep your eyes in your head or I'll pop 'em back in there with a bayonet for you!" she exclaimed before stalking off to another part of the tent that was partially blocked off by a canvas divider.

Rabbit looked almost giddy in her amusement. "That's Boom. She's got an explosive temper. She has greeted every male FNG that way since she's been here. Of course, they've all done the exact same thing you did when they first saw her."

Rabbit, still smiling and giggling to herself, got up to follow Boom. "Rabbit," I called out. She stopped and turned to look at me. "Does my discomfort really amuse you that much?" I don't know what made me ask that question, but for some reason I felt like I really needed to know.

Rabbit took a moment to pretend that she was thinking about it, nodded once, and replied "Yep," before turning and disappearing behind the canvas divider.

"Hell, I just met you, and I find your discomfort amusing," chimed in Nickel.

"You aren't nearly uncomfortable enough to amuse me yet," Hannibal grumbled.

From his relaxed position, Jethro offered the closest thing to consolation. "Ain't it fun being the FNG?" I checked to make sure that everything was organized the way that Ian had told me to organize it and then laid back in the bunk. I'm sure that I should have been upset about how things had gone, but I still couldn't help but smile. It had still worked out better than my first day of high school. No swirlies so far.

No . . . really . . . I'm perfectly comfortable with this . . .

*

I'm not entirely certain where he is right now, but if I could see Ian, I would shake his hand. If my squad could meet him, they would hug him, kiss him, and offer him drinks for life. The brief time he spent giving me lessons saved the entire platoon a great many headaches and me several beatings and possibly a bitten-off nose. I put the snore strips on after preparing for sleep and did not snore in any appreciable way the entire night. I know this because I was still in my bunk and not in the middle of a minefield when I woke up. Thanks, Ian. We all owe you a big one!

I have never been a morning person, and I never will be. I don't care what kind of coffee you give me or sayings you throw at me (I'm never going to be healthy, wealthy, or wise), I do not want to rise, and I will not shine come hell or high water. Many attempts have been made to change my attitude, and none of them ever worked. I was certain that the hatred of mornings would get me into all kinds of trouble in the army. It turned out that another thing Ian told me was true. Once you were deployed, the sun would wake you up every day. He wasn't kidding. I woke up with the sun and knew that I would not go back to sleep. That was great for the army, but it sure sucked for me. I did rise, but I still did not shine. I absolutely refused to let the sun win!

I grumbled and rolled out of my bunk and noticed the same movement throughout the tent. I noticed that the canvas divider was closed completely so that freaky little pervs (not me!) couldn't stare at the female squad members while they slept. There were only two of them in our tent, but I think the canvas was up for the men's protection. I think that anyone trying to peek in on Rabbit or Boom would face a beating that most mixed martial arts fighters would cringe at. We all formed up outside and did some morning calisthenics. I'm not a huge fan of exercise myself, but ever since boot camp I was at least able to do them without passing out.

Once we were done with calisthenics I started heading toward the showers. I'm not a big fan of being all sticky and sweaty. My quack therapist calls it an insecurity. I call it manners. Do I really want others to smell me if I can avoid it? I don't think so! In any case, I started walking toward the showers and noticed a couple of other soldiers heading that way as well. I know I've already mentioned that I'm not a big fan of being naked around others. I knew I would have to get over that because privacy was a luxury in the Army, so I kept walking toward the showers. I'm glad that something in my head told me to take a second look, because when I did I realized that the soldiers preparing to take showers were a clerk, a grunt, and a medic. They were also all women. Without even trying to pretend that I was doing anything else, I immediately performed a textbook about-face and walked to the mess tent.

I walked through the line in a bit of a daze. I was trying to work out some logistics in my head. There was only one shower tent. There were two genders. I hadn't noticed any posted orders about shower usage. How was this supposed to work? How were we supposed to know when it was safe to shower? Why were my eggs so runny? Were they even supposed to be eggs? Sorry. Not all of my questions remain relevant to the situation.

After getting a tray full of something that had the potential to grow into food someday, I looked around the tent. I had the distinct feeling of being back in school and trying to figure out where to sit in the cafeteria. The problem was that I had positively no friends here. I decided that if I couldn't find anyone friendly, I would at least find someone familiar. I saw several members of my squad at one table and decided that was where I would sit.

I sat down next to Jethro and across from Nickel. No one really acknowledged my presence, which worked out pretty well as far as I was concerned. No attention meant no chance of screwing up. I smiled just a little and prepared to dig in when every member of the squad that was present reached over and snatched something off of my tray. Anything that was halfway decent disappeared in a flash. By the time they were done the only things I had remaining were a glass of water, runny eggs, and something that helped answer the question of how sausage was made. I looked up in mild surprise. "Price of being the FNG," Boom managed to say between bites of my toast.

I thought about speaking up and standing up for myself. Really, I did. I wasn't scared. I didn't have an urge to cry or anything. Really! I was just remembering something sad from my childhood. In the end I just accepted the reality and started eating (or slurping) the eggs. I waited until it seemed like everyone had enjoyed my food before I decided to seek some advice. "Um . . . is there a shower schedule for girls and boys here or something?"

Boom looked at me in disgust. "Girls?"

"I . . . I . . . I . . . meant . . . I meant ladies," I stammered. I was flustered. I had made two mistakes. I had used the term "boys and girls" like we were in third grade, and I had looked directly at Boom. She was beautiful when she was angry. Stupid hormones!

Rabbit didn't even look up as she snickered. "Damn, Pup! Can't even ask a question right!"

"The menfolk tend to let the women go first. It is polite, after all. But there ain't no published schedule. Sometimes you wind up in there at the same time. The dividers are tall enough so it ain't no big thing. You get used to it. Hell, my pappy had a duck fit when he heard about it," Jethro explained.

"What exactly is a duck fit?" I found myself asking.

Jethro started to answer when Nickel jumped in. "No! No! No! I cannot sit through another story from Crap Hole Creek or wherever the hell it is you said you came from."

"It's Snake Lick Creek, city slicker, and I was just answering Pup's question."

Nickel turned to me. "Do you really want to know what a duck fit is? Understand that if you say that you do then I'm gonna shave your eyebrows off in your sleep with a dull, rusty combat knife." I had to wonder if Hannibal got together with everyone and came up with new and unique threats just for me. I shook my head. "See, hick? Boy didn't really want to know." Nickel took another bite of my fruit before continuing. "Better be happy while you're here, Pup. At least you get a little bit of privacy. When we go on patrol, you gonna be steppin' all over each other day and night. And no showers, neither. If we go out enough days, you don't give a damn what you or anyone else looks like. The only thing you care about is what you and everyone else smell like."

I have to admit that the thought of being able to smell each other that vividly made me lose what little appetite I still had for breakfast. I excused myself and got up from the table. As I was walking away, I thought I heard Boom and Rabbit speaking to each other in a conspiratorial whisper. I couldn't tell what they were saying. That was most likely the point of them whispering. And people say that I have no common sense.

I turned in my tray and headed back to my bunk. I figured that enough time had passed and that most everyone was eating their breakfast, so it seemed like the best time to hit the showers. I opened the door slowly and took a look around. I didn't hear any water running and didn't notice any movement, so I decided to go on in. I confirmed that there was no one else in there and prepared to take my shower. That was when I learned that I am not the only one that makes odd assumptions. You see, the thing about a big canvas tent is that if you are around them enough, you start to think of them the same way that you think of buildings. You assume that they will keep the rain off of you, which they do; that they will help keep you warm, which they at least make a mild attempt at; and that they will give you privacy, which they do not. Sound travels through tent walls like they aren't even there. Since I had just arrived at camp, I knew that fact and had not had enough time to forget it. Some others were not so fortunate. I realized that when I heard a familiar voice say, "That FNG is too damned shy. He can't go into the field that way." It was Nickel.

"He'll get himself as lost as last year's Easter egg trying to get some privacy in the field if he ain't careful," Jethro added.

There was a little bit of mumbling between them all before I heard Rabbit proclaim, "He's in the showers now. Boom and I will get him over that shyness quick. We go out in the next day or two. I'll be damned if I'm gonna risk him getting lost 'cause he can't get over himself." I heard their footsteps walking off as she added, "After all, what if we stumble across another dog? Who's going to protect us?"

It didn't take me long to decide what to do. I might not be the most confrontational person out there, but I will try to find ways to protect myself, even if they are a little . . . passive. After I made my preparations, I stepped into the shower. I have to admit that I was a little surprised at having hot water. I took a couple of seconds to enjoy it before getting out the soap. I found myself deep in thought as I washed. I was a little embarrassed by Rabbit's parting shot, but mostly I felt appreciation for the actions of my squad. Yes, I am well aware of the fact that they didn't think highly of me. I'm clueless, but I'm not self-deluded. The thing is, they were making an effort to try and make me a more useful part of the team. I'm sure that they didn't see it that way, but it was going to be the end result of their actions. That was certainly something that I could stand behind. I wouldn't walk headlong into it, but I could certainly get behind it.

It took just a little bit longer than I thought for my squad to put their plan into motion, but since I knew something was going to happen, it was easy for me to spot it when it did. The bottom of the tent was lifted up a few inches and an arm reached in and began searching around. I stifled a laugh as the arm fumbled for several seconds before locating my towel and clothes, grabbing them, and pulling them back underneath the tent. I nodded and continued my shower. Just a few seconds later, the door opened and Boom and Rabbit walked in. They pretended not to notice I was there and proceeded to the showers on the opposite side of the tent. They positioned themselves so that I would not be able to leave the tent without being in their full view. The trap had been set.

I expected the two of them to just stay there and wait for me to exit the shower, but then they did something I truly didn't expect. They prepared to take showers themselves. As soon as I realized that they were removing their uniforms, I turned around and pretended to be washing the back of my hair. Don't get me wrong; I was a young man who found both of these women attractive, but I was also raised with manners. These manners told me that if I were to try and watch these women that my mother would find out about it and beat me with a telephone pole until she felt better. So in the battle of hormones vs. manners, manners scored the first goal.

I heard the other showers begin and then tried to think through the next step. My decision of what to do was made for me when a blast of cold water hit my skin. Before realizing what I had done, I let out a yelp and turned off the water. Finally acknowledging my existence, Rabbit called across the tent, "Each shower only has three minutes of hot water, Pup. Better learn to shower faster."

Now the trap had been sprung. My shower was over, and there was no way for me to leave the tent without being seen by the two women in there. This was how they intended to get me over my self-consciousness that they worried could hinder me in the field. To make matters worse, with my clothes and towel gone I was going to have to go halfway across the compound to get to my bunk and a uniform. It had been a well thought-out plan. If only they had remembered about sound traveling through tent walls.

I stepped out of my shower soaking wet and made my way to the exit. I heard both Boom and Rabbit turn off their showers. I walked into their field of view, and they started to call out, "Hey, Pup! How's it . . ." They both stopped as soon as they saw me. I stood there, dripping water on the floor, in my soaking wet boxer shorts. I was still a little more exposed than I was comfortable with, but I just kept telling myself that it was like a pair of swimming trunks. A good ten seconds passed as the two women looked at me and realized that they had been outmaneuvered. A look of slight admiration passed over Rabbit's features before she leaned against the shower partition and said, "Well played, Pup. Well played." Boom even gave me a brief round of applause.

I inclined my head in acknowledgement and exited the tent. Outside, other members of my squad waited, prepared to force me out of my shy nature. They all reacted with silence as I walked out of the tent with at least a modicum of clothing. I walked up to Jethro, who was standing there with a slightly stunned look on his face and his arms full, holding my towel and uniform. I took them from him and began drying my hair. "Thanks a lot," I said as I began to walk off. "I'd hate to drip on my bunk." I smiled all of the way back to my tent as they argued about how I had pulled one over on them. I wore boxers in the shower for the remainder of my deployment. Just in case.

And now it's time to see the elephant . . .

*

I really wouldn't have minded more time to get used to life at Camp Wildcat. I think that, given the opportunity, I might have been able to get used to it. Unfortunately, I wasn't there with the Boy Scouts. I was there with the US Army, and they don't sing songs or teach you how to make a campfire, and they don't tend to send you somewhere unless you have a job to do there. Our job was to fight. The day after The Great Shower Victory, Hannibal called the squad together for a briefing. I listened with a certain amount of apprehension as he spread a map out and began explaining our mission. "OK, children, as most of you know we are approaching harvest time in Korea. If the enemy holds true to past patterns, they will become very active during the harvest."

"Why?" I blurted out without thinking.

Hannibal looked at me with slight annoyance for the interruption, but I was surprised that there was no trace of annoyance in his voice when he asked, "Why do you think, Pup?"

I thought that he was asking a rhetorical question. I usually don't catch the hints when people do that, so I was kind of proud of myself when I decided to stay quiet. I should have known better. I realized that he actually wanted me to answer when he made an impatient gesture for me to hurry up. I tried to snap my brain into gear. "Well . . . uh . . . the farmers have to be in their fields."

"No shit," he replied. "What does that have to do with an enemy offensive?"

I was scared to answer, but I had already opened the door. I had to walk through it. "Well, if there are civilians in the field, then we can't simply carpet-bomb an area or use drone strikes without killing a lot of civilians. So the enemy can move through the farming areas with the knowledge that one of our best assets is partially neutralized."

Hannibal shook his head. "Pup, you make me wonder if smart people really exist." I hung my head a little, disappointed. "You took three or four sentences to explain what could have been said in one. The farmers get in the way. Basically, the FNG is right." I perked up at that. I had gotten it right! I had a huge smile on my face when I looked at Hannibal. He was still stone-faced and looked hungry. I immediately stopped smiling and unconsciously put my hand over my nose. "We aren't going to wait for an offensive. We are going to sweep through these areas and rout enemy forces before the harvest." He pointed to a spot on the map. "Birds will drop us off here. We will be the northernmost squad. The tip of the arrow. The rest of our platoon will be angled on our left flank and a platoon from Camp Aggie will be on our right flank. We sweep northward and push back any enemy forces we encounter. Any questions?" I had a million. Most of them had to do with food, sleep, and survival. Something told me it was smart not to ask them. For once, I listened to that little voice in my head.

Hannibal folded up the map and then looked at each of us. He seemed to be evaluating our readiness for deployment. He had a mild look of disappointment when he looked at me. Honestly, I was used to it. My therapist seems to give me the same look whenever we end a session. Quack. "Good. Draw supplies for three days of marching. If we are out there any longer the birds will resupply us. This is going to be straight grunt work. No vehicles, just using our feet, our eyes, our ears, and if necessary, our trigger fingers. The Professor and his aide will be with us on this patrol. I expect everyone's best, and for you all to keep an eye on the FNG. We may see the elephant, and I don't want him freezing up on us. We take off in two hours. Dismissed!" I started to walk off when I felt a steel grip on my shoulder. It was Hannibal. "Pup, the first time that you salute the LT on this mission, I will kick you in the kidneys." At least he didn't threaten to eat them. I nodded and walked off. I started to wonder if I was more likely to get hurt in combat or in my own squad.

I received my next surprise while we were preparing our gear. Jethro walked up and grabbed my carbine from me. "I'll turn this in for you, hoss. You get to carry this beast." I watched in dismay as my nice, lightweight carbine was carried off. It was replaced with a big, hulking squad automatic weapon and all of the accompanying ammunition.

Let me see if I can paint the picture for those of you who do not know about the military weapons we were carrying. A carbine is, in essence, a short rifle. It is nice and lightweight and convenient. It weighs about seven pounds when loaded. A squad automatic is supposed to provide covering fire for the whole squad. It is larger, heavier, and carries a lot more ammunition. Fully loaded, it's about twenty-two pounds. Plus it goes through ammunition a lot faster, so you have to carry a lot more with you. My weapons load just tripled. I turned to Nickel to protest, but he explained before I could even ask. "One of the perks of being the FNG, Pup. It helps build character and muscle." He suddenly turned serious. "It also means that we are all depending on you to keep the bad guys off our asses. Don't screw it up." So basically, no pressure.

I reconfigured my equipment for the squad auto and packed my rucksack for a three-day patrol. It always surprises me how much can be involved in keeping you alive and moving for just three days. By the time I was done packing up, I was certain that the pack weighed as much as I did. I had it sitting on a table with the shoulder straps facing me so I could put it on more easily. I decided to test it out and make sure that everything was nice and comfortable. I put the shoulder straps on, fastened the support straps, and then slid the rucksack off of the table. The next thing that I felt was a severe pain in my backside. I shook stars from my sight and took stock of my situation. I was sitting on the ground with my legs straight out in front of me. I deduced that I had fallen straight down as soon as the full weight of my ruck had been placed on my shoulders.

Hannibal and Rabbit showed up on either side of me. Without a word they both reached down and grabbed my harness with both hands. In what I considered a feat of strength worthy of Hercules, they pulled me straight up into a standing position. I stared at them in slack-jawed awe for a few moments before I finally placed my feet firmly on the ground. Hannibal looked over at Rabbit, nodded, and they both released my harness. I remained vertical for about three more seconds. After that I had fallen backward onto my rucksack and began to squirm like a turtle turned onto its shell. I heard several others laughing at my predicament. I can't blame them. I have no doubt that I looked stupid. I also have no doubt that if they had chosen to leave me there like that, I would have still been in the same position three days later when they returned.

Hannibal and Rabbit, who didn't look so amused, reached down and hauled me back up again. Once I was vertical again, Hannibal looked over at Rabbit and grumbled, "Fix him!" before he let go of my harness. I stumbled a little under the added weight, but Rabbit still had ahold of me and managed to keep me from falling once again.

I tried to get control of my balance, but the added weight and my lack of coordination caused me to fail miserably. "How am I supposed to walk like this?" I asked. I didn't whine. Really, I didn't. I don't care what anybody says!

"Are all smart guys as stupid as you?" Rabbit was still holding me up, and I could tell she was getting sick of it.

"No," I answered honestly.

"Hunch forward," she instructed. I hunched my back forward. The weight of the rucksack continued to press down on me, but my center of gravity had shifted enough so that I wasn't falling backward. "The weight will improve as the days go by and you dispose of some of your stuff."

I stood there for a few moments just making certain that I was going to be able to stand on my own. A few experimental steps showed that it was possible. "This isn't very comfortable." Honestly, I never whine!

Rabbit gathered up her own gear as she replied. "What has ever happened to you that makes you think the army gives a damn about your comfort?" I thought about that and was forced to agree. Everything that we had and used was functional. It all performed its task properly. However, none of it was designed for physical or aesthetic (another word I've been dying to use!) comfort. I looked around and noticed most of the other soldiers around me were also hunched over under the weight of their rucksacks, although not nearly as much as I was. Maybe they'd just packed less. Yeah. That must've been it. "Grab your weapon and get to the bird," Rabbit ordered. "We've got a long three days ahead of us."

I walked around a few tents with all my gear and weapons to try and get used to it. I came to the simple conclusion that it sucked. There was no comfortable way to walk with everything that I had. Don't get me wrong. I could do it. I just didn't like it. I began to equate wearing my gear with eating my vegetables. It might be necessary, but that didn't mean I would smile while doing it. Worse, I couldn't feed my gear to my dog. I should have never drawn that parallel. I didn't eat vegetables for another two years. I think that my mother actually threw one of those duck fits that Jethro kept talking about.

One good thing about the whole situation was that even I knew when it was time to leave. Multiple helicopters began circling Camp Wildcat like birds of prey. They were impossible to miss because they were as loud as my older sister's music. I took that as a cue to move to the landing pads on one side of the base. Once there, I found all of the members of my squad and lined up with the ones I knew. Hannibal was walking down the line and checking to make certain that everyone had their gear squared away and was ready for the patrol. When he got to me I noticed that he seemed to be a little less rough when moving some straps or checking to make sure things were secure. Apparently he didn't feel like picking me up again if he were to knock me over. He took a look at my arm and noticed the "K-9 Killer" patch. I couldn't tell if he was amused or annoyed. With a face like his, it was hard to tell the difference. "At least if we get attacked by Lassie we know you can protect us," he muttered before moving farther down the line.

I spent a few minutes double-checking my own weapon and any gear I could reach until I heard Hannibal shout that we were next. With some apprehension, I turned with everyone else in my squad to watch the helicopter land with its side doors already open. I promptly remembered all of my kindergarten lessons and followed the person in front of me as we boarded the bird. Jump seats. Yay. As if my back weren't already in pain, now I was going to endure torment worthy of the Spanish Inquisition. I didn't have time to dwell on it as the person behind me pushed me forward. I went to the next open seat and strapped in, still wearing my rucksack. I looked around and noticed that I was the only one that was strapped in. I never figured out if that was because I was the only one skinny enough to fit in the harness with my rucksack or if I was the only one convinced that I was going to fall out of the helicopter. We managed to board the helicopter pretty quickly before we took off with a lurch.

Several thoughts competed for my attention as I took off for my first patrol. I thought about what I should expect when I faced combat for the first time. I ran through the immediate action drills for my weapon. I wondered if a supply drop would include fresh toilet paper. I noticed that the side doors were left open (yikes!). I remembered with great fear that I had not packed any snore strips. I realized that Boom looked incredible even when wearing a helmet (stupid hormones!). And I also remembered that I hated flying and that it usually made me sick. Add to that fear the previously mentioned fact that the side doors were wide open, and all of my previous thoughts lost the competition for my attention as I tried to control a wave of vertigo and trembling.

I floundered for something to take my mind off of the entire flying situation. I looked out the doorway at the beautiful landscape passing by. This worked for about six seconds before my brain latched on to the fact that I could see so much of the beautiful landscape because I was flying over it in a helicopter with wide open doors! I tried focusing on the door gunners and imagining their job and the power of firing those huge miniguns. That worked until one of them thought I was staring at him too much and told me to mind my own damned business. Finally, I looked at where I was sitting. Rabbit was on my right, and Boom was right in front of me. That gave me an opportunity to ask a question I had been wondering for the past day. "How did you know?" I shouted over the sound of the wind and rotors.

Rabbit and Boom looked at me, then at each other, then back at me, then back to each other again. Do I seriously confuse people that much? Don't answer that. I don't want to know. Boom finally shouted back, "How did we know what?"

"How did you know that I wouldn't look when you went to the showers?"

Boom looked at me like I was an idiot. Trust me. I know that look well. "We didn't. We expected that you would look."

I tried to digest that for a minute, but my brain couldn't wrap around it. Thankfully, Rabbit came to my brain's rescue. "That was the whole point, Pup. We are going to be living together in the field, and you have got to get over your stupid hormones and embarrassment!"

Boom spoke up again. "When we're in the field, survival is all that is important. I promise that you won't give a damn what is underneath this uniform when you're facing down an enemy ambush. I can guarantee that I won't care what you look like when we are in the middle of combat." There must have been a subtle change in my expression because Boom's face took on a dark tone. "I don't care what you look like outside of combat either! I swear! What is it with men?" That brought our conversation to a rather abrupt end.

"Are you starting to understand what I mean about you thinking things through too much?" I almost jumped out of my seat. The only thing that kept me from startling myself straight out of the wide open door (seriously, why don't they close those damned things?) was the fact that I was harnessed to the seat. I hadn't even realized that the Professor was sitting next to me. He smiled and waited for my pulse to return to something less than that of a hummingbird's before continuing. "There was a simple lesson in what happened, but rather than learn it you decided to analyze it."

"But that's what helped me succeed in school and get into college."

Still smiling, the Professor pointed at my uniform, then at my weapon, and then out the door. I looked at everywhere he pointed except for out the door. I had seen enough of that. "Does this look like a classroom to you? Don't misunderstand me. I've got no problems with intellectuals. I like to consider myself one. But there is a time and a place for it, and this is neither. War is complex. Fighting is simple. It comes down to survival. You can talk about the war when you get home. Here, you have to fight." His smile was gone, and he was looking at me like a teacher to a student. I understood his nickname more with each conversation. "Now get your fangs out. It's time to go hunting."

I forced myself to look out the door and realized that we were starting to descend. I heard someone shout out that we had fifteen seconds. I made certain that my weapon was ready and closed my eyes for a quick breath. I felt the bird settle into a hover and heard the order to deploy. I opened my eyes and got out of my seat . . . or tried to. I hadn't unfastened my harness yet. I stretched against the harness and yelped when it didn't give. It hurt in places that it's not fun to hurt in. I actually managed to shift that to the back of my mind and unfasten my harness. I knew I had just held several soldiers up for an extra second or two, and I could only hope that it didn't cause a problem. I made it to the door and hopped down, surprised that I didn't break my leg under the weight of my rucksack. I followed the rest of the squad as they ran to a tree line about fifty yards away. Once there, we spread out and made sure that the small copse of trees we were harboring in was clear of any enemy soldiers or booby traps.

Everything happened so fast that I didn't have time to think about anything. I heard the helicopter gain altitude, fly a few miles, and then descend again to make a false insertion. I looked around to make certain that I had some clue who was near me. Jethro was the closest to me. He gave me a thumbs up and then whispered across to me, "You OK, Pup?"

I nodded. "Yeah. Why?"

He let out a little laugh. "You were running pretty funny to the tree line. You reminded me of a three-legged dog I once had." I thought about what he said and wondered why I might have been running oddly. That was when I remembered what had happened with the harness and where it had hurt. I also realized that while I had been running in a crouch, I hadn't been hunched over under the weight of the rucksack. I then had an almost irresistible urge to hurt Jethro. The pain from the harness came back full force, and the weight of the rucksack and gear became unbelievably noticeable. That was when I truly understood the meaning of the notion that ignorance is bliss. Jethro must have known what he had done because he laughed again and whispered, "Don't mention it!" Asshole.

The Professor checked in with HQ and then gave the order to move out. Nickel took point and set the pace out of the copse, and the rest of us fanned out according to our training. I tried to position myself exactly as I had been taught and concentrated with every fiber of my being on what was around me, the location of the rest of the squad, the smells, sounds, and sights of the environment, the position of the sun, and anything else that could possibly give me the slightest advantage if we should happen to make contact with enemy forces. I stayed at that level of alertness for about twelve minutes. It was exhausting! Finally, I decided to look at what the rest of my squad was doing. It looked like they were alert but at a much lower level than I was. They looked to be prepared for the long haul whereas I had approached the patrol like I was playing a video game. Of course, I had never played a three-day-long video game marathon, so I decided to adjust and tone things down to the same level as my cohorts.

The truth was that there was very little cover where we were. Most of the land we were walking through was pasture or short crops surrounded by remarkably steep-sided mountains that seemed to pop up out of nowhere. The bad part of this was that we were in the wide open. That was dangerous from a tactical point of view but unavoidable. The good part was that we were seeing some amazingly beautiful countryside. Sure I was looking out for enemy movement, but you couldn't do that without looking around, and you couldn't do that without noticing the landscape. It was a nice way to pass the time for a while. I could picture several of the areas that we were marching through on postcards.

It didn't take long for the landscape to stop holding my attention. I would say that occurred about five or six miles into our patrol. That was about the time that I remembered that I had feet. Put more accurately, my feet reminded me that they were there and that they were very unhappy at the punishment I was putting them through. I began to believe that I could feel every pebble that I stepped on at first, then proceeded to feeling every blade of grass. I tried to take my mind off of it by watching the landscape again, but rather than finding it picturesque anymore, I saw everything as a potential obstacle that we might have to march through.

When I realized that approach wasn't working, I tried working out chemical equations in my head. This was something that I used to do whenever my parents were lecturing. It used to bring me great comfort, or at least great distraction. How many times must I remind you that I am a nerd? Intellectual challenges relax me! Unfortunately, they also take a great deal of concentration. I was reminded of this fact when I almost smacked into an outbuilding belonging to a farm we were marching through. You've heard the saying that someone can't hit the broad side of a barn? Well apparently I can, with my nose. Finally I tried to just ignore my feet, but they seemed to keep shouting at me for attention to make certain that I noticed their discomfort. I finally snarled "Shut up!" at them. It didn't work and earned me a very concerned look from Jethro. I finally just put up with the pain and accepted it as part of the march.

The rest of the day went without incident. We stopped a few times along the way, whenever we found a defensible position, to drink water and once to eat an MRE. The MRE, or Meal Ready to Eat, wasn't bad, although it took me most of the time we were given for lunch just to get the packaging open. I ended up eating my pound cake dessert as we marched. As the sun began to descend, we began looking for a good place to set up for the night. We found a slightly wooded area that backed up to an old dirt road through the countryside. The Professor called for the squad to halt and informed the platoon over the radio to begin setting up their evening defensive perimeter. I was hoping that would mean we could settle down and rest. Nope. That wasn't in the cards. While Hannibal and Rabbit were sent up the road to find a good spot for an evening listening post, I was put to work with an entrenching tool and dug a series of foxholes that we could use if we were attacked during the night. An entrenching tool is basically a little shovel that you can fold up and carry around with you. They are convenient for carrying, but they certainly do suck for digging. By the time I was done, my hands were shouting at my feet to shut up because they hurt more. Once I was done with that detail, I had to dig out my own scrape to sleep in. Finally, I had an opportunity to sit down and eat my MRE.

I expected to be chosen for a shift at the listening post. After all, I was the FNG and I figured that detail would fall to me. Amazingly enough, I was told that I wouldn't be pulling a shift that night. I was about to express my appreciation to Hannibal, but he cut me off before I could. "I'm not doing this as a favor to you, Pup. I'm doing it for my squad. Last time you were on guard duty you fired over a hundred rounds to shoot a stray dog. If I send you to the LP and you detonate our claymores because a rat ran by, you would give away our position to every enemy soldier within a ten-mile radius. Now get your hands and feet cleaned up. All that blood is gonna bring in the bugs." You could almost feel the concern oozing out of him.

I looked down and realized that I was bleeding where blisters had formed and burst on my hands. I was certain that the same had happened on my feet. I stumbled over to the medic, who cleaned and disinfected my hands and feet. That man should be sainted. I didn't even want to go anywhere near my own feet after that long march. He didn't seem to notice. Once that was done, I managed to drag myself back over to the scrape I had dug for myself. It had gotten dark by this point, and it was getting tough to see. The Professor and Hannibal were going over a map using a red-tinted light and preparing the next day's march, but that was just about the only light to be found at the sight. It was obviously time to get some sleep.

I had a multitude of problems flowing through my mind when I started to crawl into my scrape. The first thing that I realized was that I wasn't sleeping in a tent. That kind of creeped me out. I had never really slept out in the open before. I just had my poncho and poncho liner to wrap up in. I've never been much of an outdoorsman. I had camped once or twice, but one of those times was in a camper, and the other was in a really nice tent. Now it was just me and the open air. Maybe my mother just swaddled me too tightly when I was a baby. I needed that extra support. I also wondered if the listening post would be enough to warn us if enemy troops decided to go wandering at night. I also never felt very comfortable sleeping in boots and uniform, but even I was smart enough not to bring a set of pajamas on a patrol. I remembered that I had not brought any snore strips with me. If I started snoring, seismic monitors were likely to pick it up all the way in China.

With all of these worries, I wasn't certain that I would ever get any sleep. I wrapped myself in my poncho and liner and pulled my weapon into the scrape with me. I made certain that the safety was on. The last thing I needed to do was wake up the entire platoon by firing off a dozen rounds in my sleep. I laid my head on my rolled up jacket and prepared for a restless night of worries. My exhausted body was asleep before I finished adjusting my makeshift pillow.

I woke up with a sunrise in front of me and an angel looking down on me. I smiled at the dreamy vision of beauty that my imagination had conjured up to accompany the sunrise. My blurry consciousness had just barely started to realize that the angel I was imagining was wearing a uniform when she started yelling at me. "Wipe that dumbass grin off of your face and wake up, Pup! Time to grab some chow and get ready to move." I nodded blearily to Boom as she turned and stormed off to wake up some other lucky soul. It still amazes me how much I managed to tick that woman off. What a talent I had.

I grabbed my rucksack and pulled out some food for breakfast. My mother had sent me a care package that included beef jerky. For some reason it tasted like the perfect breakfast food. After chowing down, I stood up to start gathering my gear and just barely managed to suppress a scream. I was sore. I don't mean that I was a little uncomfortable. I mean that my body was staging a revolt against my mind that made a nuclear exchange look like a spitball fight. There was not one single part of my body that didn't fight against every move that I made, and thanks to the incident with the harness, I do mean *not one part of my body*! I saw some people stretching and walking like they were trying to work out cramps. I decided to stretch to see if it could help work out some of this soreness. Guess what? If you stretch with this many sore muscles, it just makes it hurt worse! Like the pain in my feet the day before, I figured that I would just have to push through this. I went about getting my gear together, though it probably took me twice as long as it should have.

It was about time to begin our march, and I was trying to figure out how I was going to get my rucksack on. There wasn't a table for me to work with like there had been at Camp Wildcat. I looked around and saw everyone pairing up and helping each other get up off of the ground with their rucksacks on. I knew this wouldn't work for me because it required pairing up with someone. I think people still thought that I had cooties of some sort after the whole dog shooting incident. I sat down and put my rucksack on and then started trying to get up on my own. It didn't help that I was in so much unbelievable pain that blinking my eyes even hurt. After a few minutes of struggling, I saw someone's hand reach out for me. It was Nickel. I took his hand and he pulled me up. He took a look at the bandages that the medic had placed on my hands the night before. "Don't worry about it, Pup. You won't get nothin' but callouses after a while." He smiled and smacked me good-naturedly on the arm before moving up to take point. I don't think that he ever realized how much I appreciated that help and that simple comment. It really helped me get on with my morning. I also don't think that he realized that I almost burst into tears from the pain of his slap on the arm. Man, I was sore!

Once we started moving, I managed to fall into the routine of the previous day. I admit that the routine was quite a bit tougher because my body felt like it had just danced the tango with a taffy puller, but at least it was becoming familiar. As we marched, I noticed the terrain beginning to change. The mountains that seemed to pop up out of nowhere were beginning to coalesce into a range. The terrain was beginning to put us into valleys, which made the squad understandably nervous. I could sense the tension beginning to creep into everyone's movements. While we had not been chatty during the patrol, an absolute silence followed the squad into the valleys. That silence was shattered by what sounded like distant thunder and a loud whisper from the Professor for Hannibal to join him.

The rest of the squad kept their eyes out for enemy activity while the Professor and Hannibal discussed things in an excited fashion and gestured continuously at a map. After about two minutes of this, Hannibal called for his squad to gather around while the Professor moved away and began making several calls over the radio net with his aide logging down the information. Hannibal looked up to make certain that we were all paying attention before pointing to a spot on the map. "OK, guys, we are here. A platoon from Camp Tiger is on our left flank and SoKos are on our right."

"South Koreans," Jethro whispered into my ear. I must have looked confused . . . at least more so than usual.

"The platoon from Camp Tiger made contact with enemy soldiers about five minutes ago," Hannibal continued. "They estimate they are looking at a company-sized force." I heard a few low whistles at that. "They are calling in air support and a Bone will be carpet bombing ahead of them in ten minutes. Warthogs will then be on station to help with close support. Our job is to hit the enemy's left flank and mop up from the bombing while the SoKos sweep around and cut off retreat. Rapid reaction forces are also on the way to try and even things out. If you bothered looking at the map, you saw what is involved for us. You know how I operate, so let's do it." Hannibal nodded sharply and then walked back to the Professor to coordinate with him.

I turned back to Jethro. "I caught a word or two of that but got a little lost toward the end."

"Simple," replied Jethro. "One of our platoons kicked a hornet's nest full of enemy soldiers. Our planes are going to bomb the snot out of them while we prepare to hit what's left of them from the side while the South Koreans move to cut off their escape."

"OK . . . so what did he mean about how he operates?"

"He's talking about his nickname."

"We have to eat people?"

Jethro had been taking a drink from his hydration pack when I said that and had some of it squirt out his nose. "Boy, you are dumber than a sack of hammers! He's called that because he once saved another squad by marching his men over a mountain to surprise the enemy. You know, like that general that sent elephants over the Alps?"

I was about to ask him how he could judge the intelligence of a sack of hammers when what he was saying sank in. "You mean we are going to have to march over that mountain?" Jethro nodded. "Could you please beat me with that sack of hammers you mentioned?"

There was no time for more complaining or really even noticing my pain because Hannibal called for us to move out. Everyone double-checked their weapons and gear, and I figured that I would do the same. As we moved out I noticed that we were in a more correct formation than we had been using, and most of the soldiers were expressing the same level of concentration as I had displayed at the beginning of the patrol. This made me truly nervous. This didn't strike me as paranoia from them. It told me that they knew we were going to see action, and I didn't think that I was ready for that.

We started up a fairly steep mountain. I began to gain great appreciation for the boots I had been issued. Their grip was exceptional as we made our way up the steeper gradient. I should have felt like my feet were ready to separate from my body, but I was too concerned with keeping an eye out for an advanced enemy patrol. Part of my mind expected to see an enemy scout around every shrub or rock. Another part of my mind hoped that the platoon from Camp Tiger had mistaken a herd of water buffalo for enemy soldiers and that we were on our way to a barbecue.

We were a little over halfway up the mountain when the sound of a large jet aircraft reached our ears. Like spectators at some macabre tennis match (yes! Another cool word!), we all looked to the south and followed the flight path of a B-1 bomber as it moved with incredible speed across the sky. It opened its bomb bay doors and then released what looked like every bomb ever created to fall on unseen targets on the other side of the mountain. I realized quickly that it wasn't every bomb ever created when a second bomber dropped a similar payload. The bombs dropped out of our line of sight and hit on the other side of the mountain. Earlier, I had heard a sound that seemed like distant thunder. Now I heard what the thunder must have sounded like from inside the cloud. The noise was horrendous. Some childish part of my brain curled up into a fetal position in the corner of a room and cried for Mommy at the sound of the explosions. A more primal part of my brain snarled in satisfaction.

I heard several members of the squad let out a quiet cheer. "Those Bones just decimated their reserves," Rabbit said in a virtual growl.

"Why not their front lines?" I found myself asking.

She never stopped looking toward the rising smoke on the other side of the mountain. "Because our guys are too close for that. The Warthogs will help them, and we'll start to roll up the enemy forces." She said all this with a certainty and even a little glee in her voice.

With the destructive air show over for the moment, we continued up the mountain. I realized that we were all moving at a faster pace than before. Apparently we wanted to get there before the effects of the bombing run wore off. The heightened pace paid off. We reached the top of the mountain a short time later. That was when I saw my first real view of war.

My quack therapist loves this part. He seems to think that the view of the bombed-out landscape was some kind of psychological turning point for me, triggering both a survival instinct as well as a sympathetic connection to my fellow man. Why couldn't I have gotten a job like his? I could string a whole bunch of words together that make me sound like I have a clue and charge people eighty bucks an hour for it. Someone remind me to cancel my next appointment.

Quack therapist aside, it was a life-changing sight. On the other side of the mountain was a wide, beautiful valley. There were crops being grown that were ready for harvest, and off in the distance I even saw a small village that looked like it was straight out of a theme park, but almost directly ahead of us was the sight of the bombing. There was little to no green to be seen. Everything was a charred black. There were deep craters in the ground as if a meteor shower had hit only that one spot on the earth. Several vehicles, some civilian but most obviously military, were charred or still burning. It seemed like nothing over three feet tall was still standing. I had to clamp down on the part of my brain that pointed out that most people were over three feet tall. The sight was, in a word, terrifying. And we started marching down the mountain toward it.

We didn't march long. As we began our descent, I saw something in the distance that didn't seem right. I couldn't stop to try and take a more analytic look, but I filed it away in my mind. We continued our descent, and my attention was drawn to the same spot about thirty seconds later. This time I did stop. My brain was trying to process what was wrong with that picture. Was it my imagination? Was I seeing things? That was when I saw it again. That was when things got bad.

Now I will be the first to admit that I am not a man of the world. I can't talk about a whole bunch of exotic stuff with firsthand knowledge. While I had read a lot about Korea and knew its history and geography, I also knew that there was a lot of stuff there that I had never experienced and would find nowhere else in the world. However, despite the inherent exotic nature of the locale, even I knew that a bush shouldn't move from one spot to another.

"Pup! Keep moving!" Jethro called to me in a loud whisper.

Without thinking about it, I pointed toward the moving bush and shouted, not whispered, *shouted,* "Contact front!"

About that time the world exploded all around me. Everyone in my squad raised their weapons and opened fire on the enemy formation concealed ahead of us. The enemy formation returned the favor. I learned a very important difference between video games and real combat right then. In video games, you usually know you are being shot at when tracers fly past or you hear someone shouting a stock phrase in a foreign language at you. In combat, you know you are being shot at when you feel the bullet whiz past you. Yes, I said *feel*, not hear. Unlike some of my favorite shows and movies, you know that those bullets can't be set for stun, either. Some people who play video games try to stay alive by jumping a lot. Believe me when I say that when the real fighting starts, you try to make yourself as short as a munchkin and are permanently rooted to the ground. Don't bother jumping. You'll just die dumb.

I'm not going to go into a lot of detail about the engagement. I'm not trying to tell some big war story. I will say that I'm not sure if I had a true thought during the entire fight. The only thing that I had were reactions that I didn't even know were part of my mental repertoire. I guess training did teach me more than peeling potatoes and doing push-ups. I simply responded to everything that I saw and heard. When I heard a member of my squad announce that they were going to move or advance, I directed covering fire to help them out. I made certain that my squad didn't get far ahead of me. Whenever I heard the Professor give orders to another squad, I mentally noted where he said they were so that I could be sure not to send fire their way. I took cover when I was told to take cover, advanced when I was told to advance, and I wet my pants. That last part wasn't the result of any orders or training. I'm pretty sure that it happened after I felt that first bullet pass by.

I also don't see any good reason to describe what I saw during the fight. I think that we can all agree that it was disgusting and horrible. I don't actually think I saw much of it during the fight. At that time, my head was on a swivel, and I was too busy trying to survive to worry about whether what I was seeing was real or special effects. After the fight was when I probably saw the first grisly results of combat. Yes, it haunts me. How could it not? Note to self: don't cancel next therapy appointment . . . but he's still a quack.

I don't know how long our part of the fight lasted, but by the time we were done the sun was going down, I had missed lunch, and we were at the bottom of the mountain and into the blast radius of the bombing run. I guess that I knew it was over when I saw a group of fifteen North Koreans approaching us with their arms raised and a white flag in their hands. It occurred to me that the surrendering soldiers outnumbered the squad that they were surrendering to. Of course, we had held the high ground and they'd had about a million tons of explosives dropped on their heads. I reckoned that I would've been ready to surrender at that point as well.

While Jethro, Nickel, and Hannibal secured the prisoners, the Professor walked up to me, still talking on his radio. Once he was finished, he clapped a hand down onto my shoulder and said, "Well, Pup, all of our platoon is in this valley, the platoon from Camp Tiger inflicted heavy damage on the enemy, and the SoKos are pursuing the retreating North Koreans. Congratulations. You just saw the elephant. You made it through your first battle."

When I answered, my voice was croaking. I don't think I had spoken without shouting for the past several hours. "Do you mean that it's over?"

The Professor nodded. "That's right, son. You've survived your first taste of combat." I nodded, thought about what he just said, and then promptly puked what I can only assume was the beef jerky I'd had for breakfast onto the ground.

OK . . . breathe . . . no, seriously, you have to breathe . . .

*

If there is one thing that I have found out about adrenaline it is that it should never be turned into a drug. It may cause you to achieve things that you never thought possible, but coming down off of it is evil. After losing my breakfast, I got a severe case of the shakes and had trouble catching my breath. I actually remember gasping out that I couldn't breathe. With something like amused patience, the Professor told me, "What do you think that noise you're making is?" Damn that guy was good. That bit of logic pierced right through my bubble of panic and I immediately stopped gasping for air. I was still shaking though, and my knees were weak for reasons well beyond the weight of the rucksack, especially since I and the rest of the squad had dumped our rucksacks before the fighting began. *Oh crap*, I thought. *I'm gonna have to go halfway back up the mountain to collect my gear.* I let out a groan of annoyance and fatigue and slumped against the hood of a burnt-out Hyundai. The Professor gestured to me and said, "Rabbit, watch him."

Rabbit walked over to me with an air of frustration. Once she realized that she didn't have to watch me because I'd screwed something up, most of that annoyance evaporated. She leaned against the hood beside me and waited silently as the shaking slowly receded. When she spoke up again, it was in the most normal tone I had ever heard her use. There was no command in her voice, no sarcasm, no attempt to separate her behavior from mine. It was the friendliest thing that she had ever done for me. "It usually happens like this the first time. It won't hit as hard next time. Some people try to hide the crash. Some think that it's worth the crash to experience the rush. I just figure it's a necessary part of survival. Nothing to feel bad about."

Rabbit was looking off into the distance at nothing in particular. I turned to her and said, "I threw up my breakfast." What I still don't understand is how I could have ever been confused about why I couldn't get a girlfriend in high school. I would think that comments like that would have made it plain even to me.

Much to my surprise, Rabbit smiled and even let out a little laugh. She reached into one of the cargo pockets on her uniform, pulled out a granola bar, and handed it over to me. I don't know if I even thanked her before tearing open the wrapper and attacking the granola bar like some kind of predator. Of course, if I were some kind of predator, a granola bar would probably be all that I could catch, so I guess it all evens out. Once I had eaten the granola bar, Rabbit stood up and asked, "You good?"

I also stood up and found my legs able to support my weight without doing their imitation of an earthquake on a caffeine rush. "No," I replied. "But if you waited until I'm good, you'd be here until the sun blinks out." We smiled and started to step away from the Hyundai when a bullet ricocheted off of the frame. We both hit the ground and began looking for the source.

When the next shot was fired, Rabbit saw the muzzle flash. "Sniper! My ten o'clock. Mountainside. Eight hundred yards!" Wow. It was amazing to me how some people could size up information like that so quickly. I had to manually count how many cans were left in a carton of sodas. "We need Jethro up here," she said to me. "He's our marksman. Be ready to give him cover." I looked down and realized I was still carrying the squad automatic weapon. Amazing how some things slip your mind even when they weigh as much as a toddler.

Setting up the bipod, I got myself into a firing position. The problem was that I still hadn't seen a muzzle flash and had no idea where the sniper was. I tried aiming toward roughly where Rabbit had described, but it was remarkable how much ground that covered. "You ready?" she asked. No, I wasn't ready. I was firing blind. Before I could say that to her, she shouted, "Covering fire!"

Multiple things happened at once. Jethro began running toward a better firing position. The sniper tried to take a shot at Jethro. I saw the muzzle flash and adjusted my aim as I was pulling the trigger. I also gained a new appreciation for Rabbit's lungs. Man, that woman could shout loudly! I don't think I heard the first three rounds fired because my ears were ringing from her voice.

I continued to hold the trigger until I was certain that my rounds were impacting near the sniper. Then I fired a short, controlled burst. I heard Jethro let out a growl, and then I heard a scream come down from the mountainside. I ceased fire, and the screaming continued for a few moments before ending in a kind of strangled gasp. I watched Rabbit run over to Jethro and then call for a medic. Nickel and the medic got to him at about the same time, and Rabbit stepped aside to let them work. I kept my weapon aimed at the mountainside and began moving up toward where most of the squad was.

Hannibal checked with the medic. Jethro had just been grazed. He would need a few stitches but no permanent damage was done. Hannibal then came over to me and Rabbit. "Rabbit, you and me are going to go pull that sniper out. Pup, you come along to cover us."

I was a little shaky again when Rabbit walked up next to me. "Don't puke up my granola bar," she said quietly. "You aren't getting another." Then she began spacing out from Hannibal for the trek up the mountainside to discover the fate of our assailant. We were a little over halfway to where I had seen the muzzle flash when it occurred to me that I had been the only one shooting when the sniper supposedly got hit. I hadn't been aiming to shoot him, exactly. I just wanted to keep his head down while Jethro got into a better position. I might have been fighting the entire day, but I had not had time to think about whether I had shot anyone or not. This time, I not only had time to think about it, I was going to have to see it. Only the fear that I would go hungry kept the granola bar from coming back up again.

All three of us noticed the sniper rifle on the ground a little bit in front of a rather large rock that the sniper must have been using for cover. Even though the sniper no longer had his rifle, we all kept our weapons raised as we worked our way around the rock. Rabbit and Hannibal made it around the rock first while I covered them a few feet away. They both looked at the ground, looked at each other, gave a nod, and lowered their weapons. Following their lead, I did the same. Hannibal activated his radio and spoke into the microphone. "Wildcat Actual, this is Wildcat 1-2. We have one enemy KIA this position. No other signs of activity." He exchanged a few more words before signing off and turning to me. "Good work, Pup. Birds are on their way to take us back to Camp Wildcat. Seems that our success and that of other platoons has helped cut the mission short. Go rejoin the squad and help get all of the rucksacks gathered and ready for exfil."

I nodded and looked over at Rabbit. She had a sad look in her eyes. I guessed that she was remembering my answer to her question the morning after I had shot the dog. I turned away and made my way back down the mountainside. I don't know if they heard any of my sniffling or not. To be honest, I don't give a damn if they did. If either of them are reading this, don't take that personally. I'm not trying to make a point about you, but about me. You see . . .

Sorry. I tend to get a little carried away trying to make sure I don't upset too many people. Anyway, I got back to the squad's location and found that the rucksacks had already been recovered and found mine waiting for me. I didn't check in with the Professor but instead opened my ruck and pulled out some of the MRE crackers and peanut butter. I sat there next to my rucksack, clearing the tears from my face, and eating what seemed like the tastiest peanut butter and crackers I had ever had. "They always taste better when you realize you're alive." I damned near jumped out of my skin. I had never even noticed the Professor walking up to me. What was with him being all sneaky like that? He stepped over to my rucksack, reached in, and pulled out the chocolate bar from the open MRE. He sat down in front of me. My eyes must have shown some kind of protest because he tapped his rank insignia and said, "The bar gave me permission." He took a bite and pointed to the location of the now dead sniper. "That's what war is. Right or wrong, ready for it or not, war is death. You either kill or wind up dead. You feel bad about what you had to do, and that's good. Shows that you're still human. But you're going to have to put that self-recrimination aside or it will eat you alive."

I finished off my bite of cracker and drank some water before I responded with a somewhat quiet voice. "I'm not a soldier. Up until today the only thing I've done is hurt a defenseless dog for no reason."

"Not exactly. There's something I haven't told you. When we get back to camp, you are going to receive two things. The first is your Combat Infantry Badge. The second is a letter of commendation for your actions in preventing a major sapper attack on a US Army camp." I'm not going to claim to have the best memory in the world. My memory is surprisingly selective. I can give you unusually obscure details about a commercial that I might have seen a decade ago, but I often forget the names of people I just met. Despite that, I'm pretty sure I'd recall fending off an attack, and I told the lieutenant as much. "You didn't hurt that dog on accident. The sappers had released stray dogs toward the fence line in order to set off the perimeter defenses but make it look like a bunch of accidents. While the sentries dealt with the strays and let their guard down, the sappers would have snuck in. Your actions scared the dogs away and convinced the sappers that their plan wouldn't succeed. We captured one two days later and managed to get him to confess to all of this."

I ran that evening through my head again. I thought that I had seen something slower moving along the perimeter at the time. Of course, if he had told me that Captain Kirk had personally trained the dogs I probably would have remembered seeing a transporter beam somewhere along the way. Memories are easily influenced like that. "Why didn't you tell me before?"

The Professor finished off the chocolate bar and stood. "I wanted to see if what I thought about you was true. You did well out here today. You didn't overthink everything, and you responded based on your training."

"I didn't have time to think!" OK . . . maybe I whine a little.

"And you usually won't," he responded, still patient. "The point is that you have good instincts. Let your instincts and training take over, and you should do just fine. Just like you did today. Just like you did that night on sentry duty. Give yourself some credit, Pup. Nobody is a perfect screw-up." He began to walk off but then stopped long enough to add, "Although you seem determined to try and achieve that in your own mind." He walked away, leaving me to think through what all had happened. Of course, he had just told me to stop overthinking things, so I stopped thinking and started acting on instinct. My instincts told me that I wanted something sweet, so I dug through what was left of my food. I felt my first flash of anger at the Professor. That jerk had eaten my last chocolate bar.

It's basic chemistry . . .

*

Jethro was lifted out along with the medic before the rest of us so that he could get himself stitched up back at camp. Within the hour, another flock of blessed but unbelievably loud metallic birds arrived for the remainder of us. Most of the rest of the members of the platoon were talking about the battle, which they said was a remarkable victory against a larger enemy force, textbook execution, etcetera, etcetera. I have to admit that I didn't care much. I just wanted to get back to camp and find an opportunity to think, eat food that I didn't have to fight with, and put my feet in either warm water, cold water, or a vat of sulfuric acid for all I cared as long as it did something about the pain my body was starting to remember. One thing that had been foretold, and was a true blessing, was the fact that my rucksack was much lighter than the way it had begun. I boarded the helicopter, strapped in, squirmed some because I was still uncomfortable with the injury caused by the harness from my last helicopter ride, but I didn't even care that the doors remained open this time. The wind felt pretty good.

Most of the squad still seemed to be pretty hyper from the adrenaline, while I was pretty well drained from it. It was getting dark, and even though we had only spent one night on patrol and were being pulled back out early, I felt like I had been away forever. I actually started drifting off to sleep when someone smacked my knee. It was Boom. "Hey, Pup! Congratulations! You lost your cherry! How do you feel?"

I was pretty groggy, so I didn't think through my answer before I gave it. At least, that's what I keep telling myself. Truthfully, I probably would have responded the same way. "It's remarkable. We spend the night in the field, we march over a mountain, we fight in a battle, and you still manage to come out of it looking amazing."

Now, for some women, that would have been the biggest compliment. I have known women that would go through days of spa treatments to look like Boom did after a few stressful days in the field. I honestly believed that I was being polite and complimentary. It became obvious that Boom felt differently. "You little shit! You keep your eyes off of my body, and I swear that if I find you taking pictures of me or anything like that, I will rip off any parts of you that respond to them!" I'm pretty sure that she would have stormed off if we weren't a few thousand feet off the ground and going one hundred and fifty miles per hour.

Boom wasn't looking at me anymore, and something told me that it wasn't safe for me to look at her. Instead I looked out the door. Thinking back on it now, I reckon that is proof of how much I was intimidated by her. I found more comfort in looking out an open doorway that made me think I might plummet to my death than looking at her. While I watched the darkened countryside pass by, I started thinking about home. It was something that I hadn't really thought about much since I had gotten to the Hiss. That alone surprised me. I had to leave a summer camp once because I had gotten so homesick. I'm sure that happened to a lot of people when they were young, but my summer camp was just three miles from home and my mother visited daily. Maybe that was why I left. Maybe her visits embarrassed me. Kids, if you are reading this, please let me know if I do something embarrassing enough that it makes you want to leave somewhere. On second thought, don't tell me. We probably will never go anywhere as a family again.

I felt a little bit better about what had happened with the dog after what the Professor told me, but I still felt sad because I missed my dog. I wondered if he had tried to run away since I'd left. My parents hadn't mentioned it in any of their letters. It made me wonder if he hadn't run away because I wasn't there to accidentally leave the door open, or if my absence removed his reason for running away. I could still hear my mother's voice shouting at me. "Close that door! Were you born in a barn?" In a middle school-age fit of sarcasm I once asked her if she kept saying that because she couldn't remember. I wasn't allowed outside for the remainder of my seventh grade year. I did ask her with honest curiosity a few years later if it was a bad thing to leave a barn door open as well. That ended the summer of my ninth grade year.

Most of the flight back to the camp was a blur. I found myself chuckling at the memory of my dad causing a small explosion the first time he used a gas grill. I shook my head in wonder at the memory of the first time that the dog and cat met each other. Since they both were convinced they were hairy humans, they appeared to decide that they were siblings. That's when their rivalry began. For a moment I thought I could almost smell my mother's cooking . . . as I burnt it in the microwave trying to reheat it. When the bird landed, I was a confused mess of joyful, thankful, sad, and homesick. Even with that, I made sure to exit the bird on the opposite side from Boom.

Once we exited the helicopter, everyone went about their own personal rituals that they had honed over time for a return from a successful mission. Nickel ran straight to the medic tent to check on Jethro. The Professor went to his tent to start writing his after-action report. Hannibal went straight to the mess hall. It looked like most of the platoon were running to the tents that served as enlisted and NCO drinking clubs. For me, I secured my gear and decided that I needed a shower. We may have only been in the field for a couple of days, but I felt grimy and dirty and would be happy to revel in running water, be it hot or cold.

I entered the shower tent, checked for other bathers, saw there were none, and stripped down to my boxers. I stepped into the shower and started the water. The screech that I let out reverberated through the surrounding hills and set flocks of birds scattering for safety. I had forgotten about the busted blisters all over my hands and feet. When the water touched them, my scream was involuntary. I choked it off as soon as I could, but the pain still blurred my vision for a few moments. Eventually, the pain became manageable. I realized that no one had come to find the source of the scream. Either everyone was too tired or too drunk to care. Either that or they recognized my voice and figured I had just done something stupid . . . which was true enough.

I was a minute or two into my shower and starting to feel human again when I heard someone else enter the tent. I looked up and saw Rabbit making her way to the other side of the tent. She got to the shower stall that she wanted and began to remove her uniform. I promptly turned away and cleared my throat to make certain that she knew I was there. "Hello, Pup," she said without the slightest hint of surprise. "You can stop trying to cover up. The shower divider keeps you pretty well hidden." I looked down and realized that I was trying to cover myself with my arms, which was a remarkably stupid looking thing for a man to do. I rather sheepishly stopped trying to cover myself and proceeded to use my soap.

Once I heard Rabbit start up her own water and I was certain that she was behind her own shower divider, I turned back around. We both showered in silence for a few moments before I heard her say, barely loud enough for me to hear, "I heard about the dog. Sorry for jumping your case."

"No reason to apologize," I replied, a little more loudly to let her know that I didn't consider it a big deal. "I don't care what the Professor says about it, I didn't do it because I have good instincts or anything like that. I did it because I am excitable and easily confused sometimes and am really good at screwing things up."

"I can definitely agree with the part about screwing things up." Oh, so now she decides to speak up! "Still, you saved a lot of lives even if you didn't mean to. You performed well in the valley today, too. Nothing imaginative or innovative. Everything was straight out of the training manual. Still, that's a useful thing, too. Boom told me you were able to keep several guys away from her until she could reach a better position. Exactly what support fire is for."

At the mention of the name, I figured that I would take a risk. "Why does she hate me so much?"

Rabbit seemed to think about that before replying. "You know how you can care about someone so much that you start to hate them?" I certainly did. I had hoped that was the situation. I had dreamed that was the situation. I mean that literally. I had dreamt several nights before that Boom yelled and cursed at me before grabbing me and kissing me with great passion. I woke up and was making out with my pillow. I'm so glad that everyone else in the tent had slept through that one. "Well, that's not the case with you and Boom." Thanks, Rabbit. Way to burst my hormone-filled egotistical bubble. "I'm sure you've noticed that she got her nickname because of her explosive temper. She got her temper because of her past."

I sat there, awaiting further explanation. None was forthcoming. My skin was starting to prune. "Let's operate under the assumption that I know nothing about her past and proceed from there."

"You see, Pup, most people would have prodded me by saying 'and . . .' You have got to stop being so . . . so . . ."

"Loquacious," I offered. Wow. I think I am going to ask for a review of my transcripts and see if I can get my English grades raised after this.

"Wordy," she corrected. Why was everyone trying to teach me this lesson? A conspiracy theorist would be very paranoid by this point. "Boom has always been hot. Before she was in the army, she had two serious relationships. Both of them were guys that told her everything that a woman wants to hear. They complimented her, they were polite to her, and they bought her nice things."

"So you are saying that I'm not being nice enough to her?" I'm not sure what else I could have done, but I was willing to try anything. I really don't like people being upset with me.

"I'm saying that you are an impolite little punk for interrupting my story." I may not like people being upset with me, but I have an uncanny ability to make people feel that way. "The problem is that both of these guys just wanted eye candy. She overheard her first boyfriend talking with his buddies about how much he hated hearing her talk about things she liked and how if she wasn't so hot he'd dump her at the side of the road. The second boyfriend, who swore he'd never treat her that way, never showed up on their wedding day." Rabbit turned off her water and began to step out of the shower. I promptly turned away. "Boom was at the recruiter's office the next day. Now, any guy that compliments her reminds her of her ex-boyfriends, and it sets her off." It occurred to me that Rabbit's voice was moving. When I looked up, I saw her standing at my shower stall wrapped in a towel. I once again tried to cover up, even with my boxer shorts on. She pretended not to notice. "It isn't that you aren't being polite to Boom. The problem is that you are trying to be polite, which makes her think that you want to use her like they did. I know you don't." It made me feel for a moment like Rabbit understood me. "Because I know you can't possibly believe that you have a chance with her." Like I said, for a moment. "So maybe you just need to back off for a bit. Also, you might want to turn off the water. It's obviously cold."

As Rabbit left the tent, I realized that she was correct. The shower water had gone cold halfway through our conversation and I was shivering violently. I turned the water off and stepped out to get my towel, which was gone along with the rest of my uniform. I heard Rabbit laughing as she walked back to the tent. Damn. What happened to the good old days of "kick me" signs? They were easier to deal with and didn't feel like hypothermia.

We had a couple of days of stand-down while higher authorities contemplated what to do next. I discovered on the first night that while I had not needed the snore strips while on patrol (I couldn't believe that Ian had been right about that), I still required them in camp. I tested sleeping without it one night. I woke up to the other members of the tent rifling through a toolbox and trying to decide what tool would be best for making me shut up. I'm glad I was able to find my snore strips because they had decided unanimously on the tin snips. I cringe to think of what they'd planned to do with them. I also managed to get through a shower for the first time without someone stealing my towel and clothes. I shouldn't have been so happy about it. In my joy, I celebrated loudly in front of some of the members of my squad. My towel and uniform promptly disappeared the next day. On a high note, I was able to eat in the mess tent at least three times without spilling a substantial amount of food on myself. It was a decent few days.

About five days after my first taste of combat, we were sent on another three-day patrol. I was forced to carry the squad automatic weapon again (I mean, seriously, how long does this FNG crap go on?), and we were out there for the entire three days. We saw absolutely no action during the patrol, unless you count the pack of stray dogs that ran away when they saw me. My feet were even more injured than from the previous patrol, but I managed to stifle my scream when I stepped into the shower this time.

I had barely spoken a word to Boom since the first patrol. It was the morning after we returned from the second patrol that the situation changed. After calisthenics, I wound up walking to the mess tent for breakfast at about the same time as Boom. When we reached the wood-framed door, I reached out and opened it for her. She looked at me with fire in her eyes and said, "I don't need your help, Puppy!"

I stared right back at her but with a lot less fire. "Boom, I am not one of your exes. You are gorgeous, and I have noticed that, but I don't care. The only thing that I am trying to be is polite. I don't expect anything in return from you. I don't want to do anything to hurt you. If the only thing I ever get out of my efforts from you is a smile, then it is well worth it. I'm truly sorry that people have treated you like that. I truly am, and I am here if you ever want to talk about it, but you have got to stop biting my head off just because I keep acting the way that my mommy raised me." Yes, I actually said "mommy." Not "mother," "mom," or even "female parental unit." Mommy. Insert face-palm here.

Boom continued to look at me with that same fire. It occurred to me that these could be the last few moments of my life. One of the reasons Boom looked so good was because she was very fit. That meant that she could probably pop my head off and play volleyball with it without much effort. One of her eyes started to squint a little bit as though she was planning something. That seemed to guarantee the end of my existence. When I saw her hand start reaching for me, I prepared for the end. She lightly, playfully slapped me on the cheek. "Damn, Pup. Survive one battle and you suddenly grow a pair." Then she smiled.

I'm not a typical "man's man." A man's man would have been thinking at this point how he could capitalize on this moment to go further with this beauty. I had three thoughts that occupied my mind, and going further wasn't involved in any of them. The first thought was that this had been the closest I had come to wetting my pants since the battle. The second thought I had was that I needed to say a few extra prayers tonight to give thanks for still being alive. The third thought was that I had made someone smile a genuine smile. It made the entire journey to the Hiss worthwhile. I'm a softy. It makes me easy to please.

I continued to hold the door to the mess tent open, and Boom finally walked through it. That was when we both realized that everyone in the tent had stopped eating their breakfast and were watching our exchange. The population of the tent consisted mostly of men, and they were all nodding at me with the unspoken male message that they were proud of me because they thought I would be able to use this moment to go to the next level. I felt my eyes get wide and my head shake slightly from side to side. Boom was a lot less subtle. She looked at the tent, saw their reactions, and growled at them. I kid you not, she growled like some kind of feline hunter. Everyone in the tent startled away from her, including me. Satisfied that she had properly cowed the men, Boom proceeded to walk to the line. After she passed, some of the men still turned to me and nodded. I guess that we men really are that thick.

A few hours later we had mail call. Although we had access to the Internet, it was often interrupted for various reasons. We could receive e-mail and the like, but because of the unreliability of our electronic services, old-fashioned letter writing had come back into fashion. Mail call was once again the favorite time of day for soldiers throughout the Hiss, just like in the olden days. I had received quite a few letters from my parents, and even a care package with more beef jerky (if you tell my mother that you like something, you will receive an overabundance of it for years afterward), so I looked forward to mail call as well. When they called my name this time, I took possession of a letter that had unfamiliar handwriting on the envelope. Curious, I carried the letter back to my bunk.

Once I had made myself comfortable, I took a good look at the return address. I didn't recognize the address, but the name was memorable. It was from Korika. Even with my bad memory for names, I remembered that one. Korika was a friend from high school. A sweet girl at heart, she had the uncanny ability to find bad relationships and get into them. Being so many people's "big brother," I was always there to help her whenever she realized how bad the relationships really were. I was always a good shoulder to cry on, and I was usually happy to do it. I hadn't heard much from her since high school, so I was pretty surprised to receive a letter from her.

I opened the letter and began reading. Apparently, there had been a brief story in the local newspaper about how I had received my Combat Infantry Badge. They even mentioned my letter of commendation, although they didn't mention me accidentally injuring a dog. It's probably a good thing. PETA would have had me for dinner, accident or not.

She talked about how she had read the story and become scared for my safety over here. She went on to describe how much she appreciated that I had been there for her in the difficult days of her high school years. Thinking about it made her realize that she had never really thanked me for doing so much for her. She wanted me to know that she did appreciate it, and she'd decided that she wanted to show her appreciation.

Kids, if you're reading this, please skip to the next chapter. Trust me, it is better for all involved. Honey, you might want to skip to the next chapter as well. Otherwise, you may not let me attend the next high school reunion.

I reached into the envelope and pulled out her token of appreciation. It was a picture. Of her. It was one of *those* pictures. Of her. My eyes just about popped out of my head. I looked around and realized that the tent was full of people who were reading their mail or the mail of others to get a feel for home. I *really* didn't want any members of the squad to get that kind of a feeling for my home! I stuffed the picture back into the envelope before anyone could see it.

Yes, we all know that I'm a guy, but that didn't mean that I was really comfortable with the situation. It wasn't that Korika was unattractive. She was actually very pretty. But she was also someone that I might see again when I returned home. I didn't think that I could even begin to imagine how that conversation might go. I have no doubt that there are sitcoms and movies that show how to deal with these situations, but my mother would never let me watch any of them. It was a sheltered childhood.

I decided that I needed to dispose of the picture in a way that would prevent anyone else, including myself, from seeing it again. My brain quickly conceived of a plan to remove the picture from existence permanently. I looked in the envelope once more . . . you know . . . to make sure the picture was still in there (stupid hormones), checked my pockets, and then hightailed it out of the tent.

I was at a sprint by the time I was three steps out the door. People looked at me with concern at first. They thought that maybe I was running to a post to repel attackers or something. When my destination became apparent to them, the jokes about mess hall food proceeded. I made it to the latrine in record time and closed the door behind me, thankful that it was empty.

The latrine was really just an outhouse, so there was no way I could flush the picture. I had other plans to deal with it instead. I reached into my pocket and pulled out the instrument of the picture's destruction: a pack of matches. I removed the picture from the envelope, looked at it again... you know... to make certain it was the right picture (seriously, those hormones get annoying), and then struck the match and lit the picture on fire. I then dropped the picture into the latrine and prepared to walk away.

With my level of education and intelligence, I can tell you precisely what happens in the process of decomposing human waste. I can tell you exactly what happens when the byproducts of that process come into contact with the chemical combustion known as fire. I can even write out the chemical equation involved in the process. However, that is all theory. I'm really good at theory. What I'm not always good at is application. This was a case where "intelligence" and "knowledge" were not exactly the same thing. Because they weren't the same thing, I never thought of what might occur when a flaming picture is dropped into a hole filled with human waste. You never have to be taught that lesson more than once.

The explosion sounded comparable to the ones that I'd heard during the bombing run in the valley. The entire latrine blew up in a fireball that would have done any Hollywood filmmaker proud. I received the privilege of experiencing the miracle of flight without wings. I would have settled for the experience of landing without a painful *thud*. I flew a good twenty or thirty yards away from the latrine with the back of my uniform on fire, looking like a human comet. An incredibly stinky human comet. I turned the hard landing into a roll. It did absolutely nothing to cushion the landing, but it did at least put out the fire on my uniform. I lay there for a moment with the breath knocked out of me trying to figure out what the odd noises coming from all around me were. Once I was able to breathe again I opened my eyes and looked to my left and right. That was when I realized that the odd noises I was hearing were the contents of the latrine returning back to Earth after their own flight.

Korika, I hope you understand that this is why I turned away from you without speaking when I saw you years later. Sorry. Some associations just never go away in your mind.

I heard several people yelling at me to see if I was all right. I gave a weak thumbs-up, and they all stayed where they were. It took me some time, but I finally surmised that they were waiting for the literal shit storm (sorry, Mom) to end before they came to get me. Eventually, what had went down and then up, came back down again. Several people started to move toward me, then they abruptly retreated. They returned a couple of minutes later wearing gas masks and protective gloves before approaching me. They picked me up and carried me to the medic tent. The medic took one look at me (and one whiff of me) and ordered them to set me outside of the tent. He donned his own gas mask and protective gloves before coming outside to check on me. He began tending to my wounds while others did their best to wash me off.

It turned out that I had some mild burns on my back and buttocks from the explosion. After washing me off as best as they could, the masked soldiers carried me into the tent where I was ordered to stay and rest on my stomach overnight. I was ordered, not asked, to strip down, which I did with a great deal of my now-legendary shyness. I then lay on my stomach on a cot, and, after some creams were applied to the burns, a light cotton sheet was placed over me.

I lay there the rest of the day, scared to death of what was going to be done to me. For goodness sakes, I blew up the latrine! I don't know if there is an actual charge in the Uniform Code of Military Justice for destruction of a bathroom facility, but I'm sure that something in there applies. It is one of the moments of my life that makes me fantasize about having a time machine so I could take it back . . . partly because of the danger in what I did but largely because burns on your buttocks really hurt! I was given a reprieve, though, when the medic came in and told me that military intelligence thought that the incident might have been an example of enemy sabotage. Seriously? How could they have come to that conclusion? Did they interrogate a prisoner that said they were planning to bring this war to an abrupt end by blowing up our crappers? Could I please see the transcript of that interview?

After my initial disbelief, I realized that this was my salvation. If the brass thought that the exploding latrine was a result of enemy action, then I wouldn't have to face charges for it. This was my ticket out of trouble. Of course, my conscience kept telling me (in my mother's voice) that I should tell the truth. I couldn't tell my conscience to shut up. In my mind, that would have been like telling my mother to shut up, and I like to think that I have a little more respect than that. So instead, I did the next best thing: I delayed. I told my conscience that I would tell the truth . . . someday. That seemed to settle my conscience, and I remained silent. See,

Conscience, I didn't lie. And now that the statute of limitations has run out, I don't have to worry about visiting the stockade either. Everyone's happy . . . except those poor guys that had to build a new latrine.

I fell asleep that night with a certain level of peacefulness and a snore strip provided by the medic. When I woke up the next morning, I found two gifts and a note sitting next to the cot. I picked up the note and read it. *One gift is for you, the other gift is for us.* I looked at the items on the ground. One was a donut pillow, the other was a can of body spray. The note was signed by Boom. Boom, if it matters to you now, it made me smile.

How do you say Whiskey Tango Foxtrot in Japanese?

*

The Great Latrine Sabotage kept the camp talking for several days, and it surprised me to discover that they weren't making fun of me in the process . . . exclusively. There were some jokes about my burned rear end. That's no surprise. I made a few of them. Someone also set off a firecracker outside the first time I made use of the new latrine. I admit to falling off of the seat, but I managed not to fall out of the door. Of course, it didn't exactly shock me when I found the burnt remnants of the old toilet seat mounted above my bunk with a Purple Heart painted on it. I actually found the Purple Heart a nice touch. However, most of the discussion was about preventing another possible sabotage. That largely resulted in beefing up the perimeter security with new razor wire, digging new trenches, and increasing the number of night sentries. Sorry guys. I hope you understand.

I found myself volunteering for sentry duty on a fairly regular basis. I had begun to appreciate the quiet time and the opportunity it gave me to think. It also gave me a chance to make use of the night vision gear a lot. After my run-in with the stray dogs when I first arrived, I had come to appreciate the use of the night vision gear a lot. If I'd had this type of equipment when I was a kid, I could've ruled the world. There wouldn't have been a single person on the planet that could have beaten me at hide-and-seek. I could have snuck out of my house and back in again without ever being caught . . . um . . . not that I ever did that kind of thing, Mom . . . really. I began reading the tech manuals on all of the different night vision gear that we had available. It was excessively boring reading, but it gave me something to focus on. My only other option would have been to write letters home, and I hadn't done that since I'd been launched into orbit from an outhouse. I just couldn't figure out how to explain that one to the folks, so I didn't try. On the next patrol, I was picked to man the listening post for the second shift. When I arrived, the first shift informed me that the night vision goggles had malfunctioned and were useless. Everyone was impressed when I returned the next morning with fully functional goggles and a small essay on the nocturnal bird life in that region of Korea (nobody read it, but they were certainly surprised).

Because of my newfound expertise in the field of night vision technology, the Professor asked me to join him and a few NCOs for a briefing in the mess tent on some new technology that we were going to be field testing. He told me that a civilian representative for the Japanese company supplying the gear would be there to answer questions and demonstrate the gear, and he wanted my opinions and questions. Yes, I will admit that I was very happy. It was kind of like being the teacher's pet again. Everybody likes to knock teacher's pets, but those are usually people who have never been one. It's really great. It makes a person feel special, and I am special. My mommy told me so.

A slight wardrobe malfunction caused me to be late to the briefing. If anyone from the army is reading this, I hope you realize that button flies might be more serviceable than zippers, but when one of those buttons pops off, and they *will* pop off, it creates a bit more of a breeze than some of us are comfortable with. So after sewing on a new button to close the barn door (OK, after paying someone else to sew on a button; I can't sew), I rushed to the mess tent, where the briefing was taking place. I should know better than to rush. Nothing good ever happens when I rush. This was no exception.

I flung open the door and ran to where I thought a good spot would be to listen and see. Unfortunately, the tables had been rearranged for the purposes of the briefing. Rather than running toward a seat, I plowed into one of the tables. This created a chain reaction of collapses that sent night vision goggles flying, NCOs and officers tumbling, and a table of donuts brought by the tech rep crashing to the floor. I guess I should mention that I never remained a teacher's pet for long. I began apologizing profusely and attempted to rescue the donuts. Some were beyond help, and I put them out of their misery with my digestive system. I didn't try to help any of the soldiers up, because I feared what they would do if I reached my hand out to help them. I had just replaced the last table when the tech rep looked up at me and screamed.

There was something about the scream that was familiar. The Japanese oath that she spat out sounded remarkably familiar as well. I looked up at her and tried to place where we had met. She was wearing an olive drab uniform with no insignia except for her company's logo and a name tape that read "Ogawa." She had on an olive drab baseball cap that forced her to pull her long hair back in a ponytail, but she still managed to make the entire thing look good. She couldn't have been older than her early twenties. Her face held youthful beauty, but her eyes displayed great intelligence . . . and hostility. I'm certain that the former had gotten her the job she currently held, and the latter was reserved for clumsy, ignorant American soldiers that interrupted her during her aforementioned job.

It wasn't until I happened to catch a whiff of her very subtle perfume that I finally placed the scream and the curse. Without the slightest thought about what I was saying, I pointed to her and said, "You're that woman that I picked up at the airport!" A few snickers spread among the attendees. "No, I mean that she wrapped herself around me . . ." More laughter. "I meant that . . . well an MP had to separate us . . ." The laughter was pretty endemic now. Really, do some of us ever grow up? Then again, I'm the one that still laughs whenever anyone uses the word "duty."

"Could you please just be quiet and go away?" I looked again at the tech rep and realized that her English was quite good when she wasn't being involuntarily carried through an airport by a frantic soldier. She was blushing, but she was also trembling with anger. In a very brief time I had managed to embarrass her, wreck her presentation, and possibly also her reputation. I screw more things up by 8:00 a.m. than most people do all day. "I would like to keep my job, and I don't know if I can do that if I take one of our products, walk up to you, and shove it where the sun doesn't shine."

"But if they are any good, we'd still be able to see through them there." I have no idea what made me say that. Maybe I was trying to be sarcastic. Maybe I was nervous. Maybe this was some awkward method of flirting for me.

Whatever it was, it worked. Shaking a little less, she nodded and said, "In full, living color." I found myself raising my eyebrows in surprise and took a seat. Ms. Ogawa raised her voice loud enough to be heard by everyone in the tent. "As Private," she glanced at my name tape, "Pup, here, just heard, the best feature of this product is that it is the first night vision system to provide this important ability in full color, not the green-and-black or white-and-black monochrome that you have become accustomed to." She picked up one of the sets of goggles from off of the floor where it had fallen. "The private also has helped to demonstrate that these devices are fully prepared for use in the field and can survive rough handling without losing functionality. Grab the closest set off of the floor, and we can finally demonstrate."

Looking around, I found a set near my feet and picked them up. Ms. Ogawa demonstrated how the goggles could be worn and how they turned on. She then had the mess tent darkened. It never occurred to me how dark that tent could get with everything sealed up. I discovered that the hard way when I smacked my knee on the table in front of me. I could have sworn that I heard a satisfied chuckle come from the young tech rep. I turned on the goggles, and the world opened up to me once again. While there wasn't quite as much detail as I would have seen with the naked eye in daylight, all of the colors were exactly the same. I could clearly make out all of the names and ranks of the soldiers around me, I could tell which donuts were chocolate or maple glazed (I tested them, just to be sure), and I could see that olive drab did a wonderful job of showcasing Ms. Ogawa's skin tone and highlighting her intelligent eyes (stupid hormones!).

Lights were brought back up, and we were all sufficiently impressed. She asked for questions, which was probably a mistake. Most of the soldiers had a few questions about compatibility with current mounting systems or battery life. I had a million technical questions. Surprisingly, Ms. Ogawa answered most of them off of the top of her head. Eventually, though, I either stumped her or annoyed her. She pulled a thick technical manual out of her bag and dropped it onto the table in front of me. "There is something for you to read tonight," she said.

With no more questions, the Professor dismissed us. Ms. Ogawa made certain that the lieutenant had her card before he left. "That is the easiest way to contact me if you have any questions about your units. I would also like to invite you to Japan to go through our training course so that you can be prepared to deal with any issues yourself, since my company will not let me deploy into the field with you."

"That's a damn shame, Ms. Ogawa," he replied with a hint of a smile on his face. "Something tells me you'd do very well out there." He bowed to her before leaving the tent. Halfway through the door, the Professor stopped and turned around. "You might want to give Pup your card, too. He might be a better choice for the training."

I turned to her and held out my hand for a card, but she was still looking at the door, smiling. See my problem with guys like the Professor? He's smart, charming, and looks like every woman's dream, even women from the other side of the planet. Compared to him, I'm just . . . well . . . me. I had to clear my throat to get the young lady's attention. She snapped out of her reverie and handed me a card. I was about to leave when I thought of something that I had wanted to ask her since I had realized who she was. "Ms. Ogawa, I was wondering why you never told me you spoke English."

"What do you mean?"

I helped her pack up her materials as I explained. "Well, when I . . . uh . . . ran into you at the airport, you never gave any indication that you spoke English."

She looked at me as if I had grown another head. "Seriously? Well, let me ask you this. Do you speak another language?"

"A little Klingon," I replied. It's a language! Really, it is!

"We will forget how sad that is for just a moment. Come around the table and stand here with me." I stepped around the table and stood a few feet away from her. She beckoned me closer, and closer, and closer still. Finally I was standing just a few inches from her. I could make out wisps of her hair that were escaping from underneath the cap. I could see that she wore contacts in her eyes, and I could once again smell her perfume. I could almost hear the romantic background music playing as she looked up into my eyes as well. I started wondering if I should kiss her.

I had just begun moving forward ever so slowly when she stomped on my foot. Hard. I mean really hard. My brain took note of the pain and tried to decide whether anything was broken. "Holy crap! What the hell?" I shouted out as I hobbled back a few steps.

She moved up close to me again. I actually cringed when she approached. "Now, why didn't you curse in Klingon?" she asked me quietly.

I stopped hobbling, forgot about the pain in my foot, and thought about the question. I'm strange like that (among a million other ways). A good intellectual exercise will make me forget all else. She obviously could tell that I was drawing the parallels because she nodded and returned to packing up her materials. "You could have just told me," I complained.

"But would you have truly understood?" she returned. Damn, she was good. I helped her pack up, and we talked a little in the process. It turned out that she had attended college in the United States, not far from my hometown. It explained why she was so fluent in English and how I recognized the accent. She was as intelligent as I had supposed she was, but she also had a quick wit and sense of humor. I found myself stumbling often over my words, which she seemed to find amusing. She laughed at the mistakes, but she didn't seem to be laughing at *me* quite as much. By the time we had packed up, I decided that I really didn't want her to leave.

She was almost to the door when she stopped. "I have a question for you, Pup."

"Yes, Ms. Ogawa?"

"It's Mayumi. Mayumi Ogawa. I was wondering if you think they will end up sending you to the training. I'm the one that teaches the classes, and I want to know if you will be there."

I'm no expert on these kinds of things. I've never really learned the art of flirting. To this day I know that if I were to try and flirt with a woman, the embarrassment resulting from the idiotic things that I would say would probably live on in movies for decades to come. However, even I heard what sounded like a flirtation in her question. "They just might," I replied as smoothly as I could. "I do plan to become an expert on your equipment." Now that I hear myself making that statement, I realize how incredibly stupid that sounded.

Mayumi seemed to mull that over in her head. I held out hope right until she got a look on her face that indicated disappointment. "No offense, but I hope they send your lieutenant instead. I mean . . . whoa!" She got a dreamy, faraway look in her eyes, then exited the tent, bumping into the doorframe on the way out, lost in her fantasies. Her stupid hormones.

Just call me The One . . .

*

Winter fell on Camp Wildcat and two things happened. First, the Professor traveled to Japan to take part in the training classes on the new night vision gear. I hoped that made Mayumi happy. I couldn't help but admit jealousy. Well, I guess that it was jealousy. Although jealousy would imply that I had any sort of chance with her to begin with, and I was pretty sure that wasn't in the cards. Maybe it was more disappointment than jealousy. I'm not sure. Still working on those inferiority issues. The Professor wasn't gone for very long. The training and travel only took a little over a week. Still, it was a long week. The Professor tended to be the only person in the whole platoon who was able to explain things to me in a way that I understood and had the patience to do it. I couldn't wait for him to return so that I knew I had someone in the camp who I could work with without pissing them off. Plus, the longer that jerk was in Japan, the more time he was spending with Mayumi Ogawa, which meant there was less chance that I would ever . . . sorry. I'm working on it. Really, I am!

Second, I discovered the true meaning of the word "cold." It wasn't like I was raised in the tropics or anything. I had experienced snow and ice and cold weather before. There were some important differences, though. My mother used to dress me up like the Michelin Man. I'd had enough layers on to stop high-powered rifle rounds. I hadn't been able to put my arms down, could barely move my legs, and turning my head had been physically impossible, but I'd always been warm. I couldn't depend on that kind of approach to stay warm in the Hiss. I had to be able to move, maneuver, and operate my weapon. The stuff the army gave me was pretty good, and it allowed me to move a lot more than my mother's preparation-for-spaceflight approach did, but it wasn't as warm. Also, if I got too cold back home, I would just go inside. At Camp Wildcat, "inside" was a tent. They kept heat going in all of the tents in various fashions. Some used electric heaters and others used old-fashioned stoves, but they all suffered from the same failure: if you were next to them, you were too hot. If you moved away, you were too cold. There was no middle ground. It was the worst of both worlds.

The cold was a living thing that invaded your body and sought out your weaknesses. My weaknesses were my extremities. I made that comment to some other soldiers once. The jokes continued for a month. Now do you see why I wanted the Professor to return? My hands and feet always seemed cold no matter what the weather was. When the cold crept in, my hands and feet stopped being cold. Instead, they started being absent. My brain forced my eyes to look down every once in a while to make certain that my feet hadn't gone off on a walk of their own. I was constantly fighting numbness in my feet and hands. It became a daily problem. Eventually, I wound up wearing gloves all day and night. The only time I took the gloves off was when I would take a shower. I even slept in them. It looked like I was trying to start a new fashion trend and failing miserably. It helped me out with the numbness in my fingers, but it didn't do wonders for my reputation. Of course, my reputation was already that of an oddball, so I reckoned it didn't hurt my reputation either.

My squad was sent to set up a security checkpoint on a road known to be used by enemy insurgents and saboteurs while the Professor was off on his training trip. (He better have been training. *Come on, LT, you can get any girl out there. You can at least leave this one . . .* sorry. Inferiority. You know the deal.) Naturally, this work required us to stand outside in the blistering cold for hours on end. Since we weren't on a patrol but instead manning a fixed point, it also meant that we weren't moving a whole lot. Within twenty minutes, I was starting to lose feeling in my hands, feet, ears, lips . . . I was wondering if I was going to go numb from the neck up. "I can't feel my hands," I announced.

Boom walked over to me and gave me a withering stare. "The only thing keeping you alive right now is the fact that I can't feel your hands either." Despite our earlier interactions, I was still scared to death of her. When she fixed me with a gaze like that, anything that she said to me sounded like a threat to my ears. The worst part was that she knew it. She held her fierce countenance for about three heartbeats before reaching out suddenly and grabbing my hand. I flinched. I always lost in the "two for flinching" game. She tore the glove off of my left hand. She took my index finger put it into her mouth, and sucked on it. Everyone's eyes went as wide as saucers, including mine. I had only heard stories like this being told in hushed tones in the mess hall. (I wasn't eavesdropping. I promise. I just have good hearing.) A few appreciative sounds were made by other members of the squad. She removed my finger from her mouth, but she didn't let go of my hand. She held it up a little above eye level. I found that I couldn't speak in actual words, but I think I made a few squeaking noises. She had a very mischievous grin on her face now. Everyone around still seemed in shock at what she had just done. Without looking away, she announced to all of them, "Wait for it . . ."

I wasn't exactly sure what she wanted them to wait for, because my mind was still locked up. That was when I started to notice some sensations. OK, some *other* sensations. With my hand held a little bit above my head, there was nothing blocking the blowing of the wind. I remembered hearing that the temperature was well below zero, and that was before the wind was factored in. My index finger had stayed warm for a moment, but then the saliva that encompassed it began to lose its heat. The blowing wind and the bitter cold combined with the saliva, which was beginning to freeze on my finger. Once my brain was able to unlock itself from its state of shock, it recognized the new sensation. It was known as remarkably excruciating pain!

Stifling a curse, I pulled my hand down and lowered it into a jacket pocket. Everyone was laughing, including Boom. She reached down and picked up the glove she had torn off and handed it to me. "Put this on before you get frostbite, Pup." I quickly donned the glove and felt the pain start to subside, though the throbbing in my finger continued for a little while longer. "I'm sorry, but sometimes you are just too much fun to pick on," she said, still laughing. She gave me a kiss on the cheek, then a punch in the arm, and then walked over to the other side of the road.

A few minutes later the temperature seemed to drop even lower. We all put on our winter face masks, which we all hated but they really did help protect our faces from frostbite-level temperatures. I hated the masks because I never felt like I could open my eyes all the way and I couldn't see anybody's lips moving when they were talking. It was scary. It turned our squad into the world's most creepy and well-armed ventriloquist act.

The day had been a pretty slow one. The trick Boom played on me was the most excitement that we'd seen all day. A grand total of seven vehicles had driven through our checkpoint, all filled with families. It gave me a chance to play around with the little kids. I love children. They find me goofy and funny. Adults find me annoying. This made the stop at our checkpoint much more acceptable to the parents until we had to put our cold-weather masks on. I discovered that trying to talk and be friendly to kids with a face-covering mask is both scary to the kids and concerning to the parents. The parents needn't have been concerned. Their children were very capable of defending themselves. I discovered this when I knelt down in front of one of the children to say "hello." He promptly kicked me in the face. The black eye remained for several days.

Night fell in earnest. We had spotlights shining down the road while Nickel scanned the distance with night vision gear. We all became restless and grumpy. This type of duty took a lot of time and energy, and it always felt to us like little was accomplished. I knew it was necessary. Saying that it wasn't effective was trying to prove a negative. Still, there were a lot of other things I would have rather done. Trimming my toenails, eating undercooked fish, and challenging Hannibal to a wrestling match to the death all topped the list. However, since no one had offered us any other option, we ran the security checkpoint.

I really had lost track of time. It was dark, cold, and boring, and checking my watch would have just reminded me of how long it had been. I looked over at Nickel and felt especially sorry for him. At least the rest of us were moving around or getting to shift our attention every few minutes. He was stuck with monitoring the distance with night vision goggles. I knew from experience that looking through them for that long could cause a nasty headache. He never said a word, though. I had asked him about it before. He told me that he was used to this type of thing. His old neighborhood was in gang territory. He'd never joined a gang, and neither had most of the people in his neighborhood. This hadn't set well with a local gang, and they'd started damaging properties and had even perpetrated a few drive-by shootings to try and convince the local high school boys that they needed the gang's protection. Nickel said that he'd had to spend many nights as the neighborhood lookout. It had become such a habit that he'd continued to do it even after the gang had been wiped out by rivals.

Even knowing this, I felt bad for him. The fact that he could do it didn't mean he should have to. No good deed goes unpunished. I would have offered to take a shift from him, but I'm pretty sure I would have lasted only about six minutes before I would have either gotten a headache, passed out from exhaustion, or gone insane from boredom. Still, I decided that I should risk it about the time I saw him move. It was apparent that he had seen something, and it had definitely grabbed his attention. Suddenly he grabbed his carbine. "Eyes up! Eight hundred yards and closing fast!"

We all raised our weapons. We started to hear the noise of a big engine running at high speed. At about five hundred yards we saw the outline of a four-wheel-drive truck with its headlights turned off. That was like a giant neon sign that yelled "imported insurgents!" Those trucks had been used by insurgents for decades in Afghanistan. That was when the first shot was fired from the truck, blowing out one of the spotlights. "Pup!" shouted Hannibal. "Light 'em up!"

Lifting the squad automatic, I didn't hesitate to pull the trigger. My first shots went through the windshield. I heard everyone around me fire as well. I didn't let off of the trigger but continued to pepper the truck with everything I had. At two hundred yards, we could tell that the driver and passenger were dead, but the truck kept coming. There were several men in the back, but our fire was keeping them down. It occurred to me that the truck was going to smash right through us and the Humvees we were using to block the road. It was going to be nasty.

That's when Jethro stepped up. He was our marksman and his rifle carried armor-piercing bullets. He took half a heartbeat to aim, which was about three heartbeats longer than we were comfortable with. When he fired three rounds, they were all perfectly placed. His rounds pierced the engine block, causing it to seize up. The wheels of the truck locked, and the riders in the back flew out of it. The truck started skidding sideways, but it had enough inertia to keep it moving. A quick calculation in my mind told me that the truck wasn't going to stop before it made it to us . . . and I was right in the path.

I've seen way too many movies. In the movies, this was when the hero would shoot out the wheels and make the vehicle flip over and go flying over the hero and his friends. Of course, this always happened in slow motion and with incredible camera angles. The problem was that I was no hero and this wasn't happening in slow motion. The truck ate up the distance with a complete lack of concern for our safety. Before I knew it, the vehicle was within what Jethro referred to as "spittin' distance." In my peripheral vision, I saw everyone else diving to one side or the other. I didn't quite do the same.

The Professor told me that he thought I had good instincts. I have a world of respect for the Professor, but I honestly think he was full of crap. My instincts lead me into doing some of the most ridiculous stuff. This entire incident is a great example. Every member of the squad had the good sense to dive out of the way. It was the right instinct. It made sense and had the greatest chance of success. My instinct was different. As the truck came so close that I could almost touch it, I didn't jump to the side. I jumped straight up.

I still remember everything that happened and how it felt. I jumped as high as I could and tried to draw my legs up. The next thing I knew, my feet felt like they were back on the ground, and I ran forward a few steps to try and get away from the wreck. After two or three quick steps, it seemed like the ground fell out from underneath me. I could feel myself falling, and then I was back on the ground and running. I heard the haunting sound of metal grinding on metal as the truck plowed into one of the Humvees, and then the night descended into an awkward silence, punctuated by the moans of some of the truck's passengers lying injured on the road.

The squad sounded off and reported no injuries. We quickly gathered the survivors from the truck, assessed their injuries, and had them bound and placed under guard as we awaited a Dustoff bird to carry out the wounded insurgents and for MPs to come and collect the prisoners. It had turned out to be a successful night after all.

Once the scene had been cleared, the squad gathered up its equipment and got ready to return to Camp Wildcat. Not more than ten seconds went by before Nickel, Jethro, Rabbit, Boom, and even Hannibal started to express their shock at my accomplishment. The problem with this was that I didn't have the first clue as to what they were talking about. "You're gonna tell me that you didn't plan that?" Rabbit asked in disbelief.

"I don't even know what 'that' is that you're referring to." Honesty. It always seems to lead me to the truth . . . that I can do some strange stuff.

"What did I miss?" chimed in Nickel. "I didn't get the NVGs off, so I missed it."

Hannibal didn't seem to want to encourage the discussion any further, but he reluctantly told Rabbit, "Go get the tape."

Starting in about the third year of the Second Korean War, security checkpoints began keeping a digital video record of the checkpoint. It was for the security of the soldiers as well as for civilians passing through the checkpoints. It was also transmitted in real time to a computer server in Japan where it could be monitored or stored. Rabbit grabbed the camera that had recorded the entire incident and set it to play back the attack. We all gathered around the tiny screen. Everything happened about like I expected. Nickel gave his warning, and I opened fire a split second before everyone else did. Jethro fired his rounds, and the truck began to skid.

What happened next was so fast that Rabbit had to rewind it and play it again in slow motion. The truck was coming dangerously close when everyone else dove to the side except for the skinny little idiot in the middle that seemed frozen in place. That was me, if you haven't figured that out. Just as it seemed certain that the truck's front fender was going to have an intimate meeting with my abdomen, I jumped up off of the ground. Appearing to break all laws of common sense and physics, I leapt high enough to land on the hood of the truck. With the truck still moving, I ran along the hood of the truck before dropping off of the other side and running away down the road.

I just sat there in silent shock as they watched the video. I couldn't have planned to do something like that if I had tried. I discovered later that one of the technicians checking the videos in Japan witnessed the stunt and sent the video to some friends in America. I made ESPN's Play of the Week. This from a guy who got cut from his high school's table tennis team for not being athletic enough.

The drive back to Camp Wildcat was a long ordeal of nonstop replays of the video and pats on the back. Everyone thought it was the most amazing thing they had ever seen. Freerunners do neater stuff than that all the time. Why did they think so much of me doing it? I was quiet the entire ride. Normally, I would have loved the idea of receiving this kind of attention. I knew I would never be the quarterback that throws the winning touchdown pass in the championship game. This was as close as I would ever get to that kind of adoration. Unfortunately, I couldn't enjoy it. Maybe it was because I hadn't planned to do it. Maybe it was because I was too embarrassed by it. Maybe it was because I was shocked by what I had seen and amazed that I had lived through it. It must have been that last one, because as soon as we got back to camp I went straight to my bunk and started to write a letter home. It started with *Dear Mom and Dad, I'm OK. There have been a lot of exciting times over here, but someone must be watching over me because I've managed to get through them all unscathed (that means I haven't been hurt, Dad). For example, tonight . . .*

And not a single kangaroo in sight . . .

*

The Professor returned not long after my world-renowned foray into parkour. As I was certain he would, he congratulated me on my "instincts." I told him that if these were my instincts and I was left to my own devices, Darwin would have used me as an example of natural selection causing a species to go extinct. "Did you live?" he asked me.

"I know that I'm pale, but I thought it was pretty obvious that I survived." I'm so glad that the Professor understands me and my sarcasm. I'm pretty sure that snarky comment would have caused me significant problems with a lot of other officers. They would have thrown me in the stockade, where you don't go on patrol and don't have armed men in trucks trying to run you over. Dammit! Oh, well. I don't look good in orange anyways.

"Your survival is proof that your instincts were good." Satisfied with his own answer, he turned to walk away.

Curiosity and, um, envy forced me to ask, "How was your training in Japan, sir?"

The smile on his face when he turned around was one of contentment and joy. "Very productive. Good information. Good food. Good company. I'm hoping to go back real soon." I hated that smug, good-looking, smooth-talking bastard! OK, I got that off my chest. I didn't mean it, Professor! Really!

Dejected, I turned to walk away. "Maybe you should go there for your R&R!" he shouted after me. I halted my retreat. "You should have some R&R coming up real soon. It's cold as hell here in the Hiss. I suggest you take that time when it's offered and go somewhere warm . . . even if the warmth is in the companionship you find there."

Not bothering to try and understand what that last comment meant, I started researching what options were available to me for R&R. I considered Tokyo in the hopes that it might allow me to bump into Mayumi Ogawa. The intellectual part of my brain sometimes takes a little while to get into gear. Once it did, it reminded me that Tokyo was one of the largest cities in the world. The odds of running into one particular person who didn't even know you were there consisted of numbers that cause theoretical physicists to wake up in the middle of the night sweating and short of breath. Plus, I had already been to Japan once. Sure it was just the airport, but I'm pretty sure that I made enough of an impression there that they wouldn't be falling all over themselves to get me back. I looked at several other destinations that were interesting and exotic. In the end I settled on taking my R&R in Australia.

This was going to be an all new experience for me. I had never really taken a trip without my family. Yes, I had flown all the way to Korea and spent months there, but given the circumstances, I don't think that counts. I was excited and nervous at the same time. When I get that way, I often tend to chatter somewhat mindlessly for long periods of time. By the time that leave had arrived, even the Professor was ready for me to get out so that he could have some peace and quiet.

I knew a little bit better about what to expect while traveling this time. I still had the iPod that the flight attendant had given me when I had flown over from the states, and I'd put together a collection of magazines and books that I had not read before. It was hopefully enough to keep me awake during the flight and not cause anyone to suffer the horror of my snoring. The plane was going to have a lot of soldiers trying to get away from the war for a little while to decompress, and I doubt that putting them into a murderous rage would do a lot to help them with that decompression. I try to be thoughtful. I don't always succeed, but I do try.

The flight was blissfully uneventful. No snoring from me, no death threats from others, and no turbulence from the plane. I certainly couldn't complain, except for the movie that was shown during the flight. I don't care if a film was a huge blockbuster in the theater, it probably isn't a good idea to show a movie about an airplane hijacking on an airliner. I don't have the sense that God gave the common dog ,and even I know that. Despite that relatively minor snafu, I walked into the Sydney airport terminal in very high spirits. I even caught the shuttle to the hotel I was being put up in and checked in with virtually no problem. After unpacking what little I had brought with me and making sure I knew where everything was in the room, I sat down on the bed and realized that I had run into my first problem: I had no idea what I was going to do in this city.

The problem with always taking a vacation with your family, besides the fact that you were on vacation with your family (I had fun, Mom! Still, how many goofy family photos can one person take?), was that someone else had always planned out the itinerary. As a kid, I never had to think of what I wanted to do when we took a vacation. I was told what we were going to do when we took a vacation. Now I was on a "vacation" on my own and had no clue what I wanted to do. It was already sundown, which limited some of my possibilities. I racked my brain for a few minutes, trying to think of what the members of my squad would do. I had heard them tell stories about some of their R&R trips. I had to dismiss some of them because of the physical impossibility of the acts that they described. However, there was often another unifying theme in their stories. So, I put on my boots, checked my hair, stepped out of the hotel, and looked around for the closest bar.

I guess I should point out that I didn't drink anything besides water and sodas at the time. I had only experienced alcohol once, and that was a sip of communion wine. It had taken me a day to get rid of the taste. Still, since virtually every soldier I spoke to seemed to drink, I figured I would see what all of the buzz was about. I entered the closest bar and found a seat. It turned out to be a sports bar, and there was a soccer match on. I'm sorry. A *football* match. I almost got thrown out of the bar in the first five minutes because of that mistake. Just about everyone around me was yelling and screaming and acting like they had already consumed a large amount of alcohol. At least that meant that if I had too much I would probably fit in. All of the bartenders and waitresses were incredibly attractive women. That was actually a problem for me. If this was the first time that I was going to drink, I would hate to ask stupid questions and look like a moron in front of a bunch of beautiful women. Of course, since that is the short description of my high school career, I guess it doesn't make much difference in the end.

The very eye-catching bartender came over and asked what I would like. I figured that I should try the drink that seemed to be a permanent part of the blood of so many of the people that I knew. "I'll have a beer, please."

"What kind, love?"

My brain seized up for two reasons. The first was that I didn't know anything about the different kinds of beer. The second was because I could have sworn that she called me "love." Was she flirting with me? Then I remembered that I was in Australia and that I was me. No flirtation involved. As for the beer, I decided to play it safe. "Give me whatever you think is the best beer that you serve." She returned a moment later with a mug full of foamy beer. With steely resolve, I lifted the mug and took a swig of my first beer.

To all of you beer drinkers out there, please do not think that I am trying to insult you, but why? Even now, many years later, I have tried several types of beer and I haven't found one yet that didn't give me nightmares and visions of men in a beer bottling plant dumping random things into a vat while laughing maniacally. I'm sure that there is probably something in me that doesn't quite understand it the way that other people do since beer is such a popular drink. However, that first swig convinced me that, at least for me, I would probably have to be drunk already before I found pleasure in beer.

I was fortunate that my gagging and choking noises were drowned out by the cheers of the *football* (see, I learned) fans after a goal had been scored. I wasn't completely hidden from notice, though. I looked over and the bartender was looking at me with a huge, beautiful, and very amused smile on her face. "You don't drink, do you, love?"

I had to cough a few more times and wipe tears from my eyes before I could answer. "No, ma'am, I don't. Is it that obvious?"

"Only to a person that has their eyes open." She chuckled and leaned over the bar to speak to me. I made a concerted effort to look directly at her face and avoid other . . . distractions. Yes, hormones again. Some guys take a while to work through them. "Why are you trying now? I mean, it's business for me, which is great, but I don't want you to wind up in any trouble."

That wasn't something that I expected. I never expected a bartender to question my drinking. That was when I realized that I had no idea why I was drinking. "I guess . . . well . . . it seems that every time I hear anyone in my squad talk about going out and having a good time, they're usually drinking a beer or something like that. I just got here, I have no idea what to do here, and I figured that maybe I should try drinking to have a good time."

The bartender kept looking at me like she was appraising me. I know, because I was still making sure to look directly back into her eyes. After what seemed like an agonizingly long time (at least five seconds!), she spoke again. "You aren't very comfortable relaxing around people, are you?" With a little shyness, I nodded. "I bet that makes things tough so far from home. I'll tell you what. Beer obviously isn't your thing. Let me make you a mixed drink that I guarantee will taste just fine to you and should loosen you up quite a bit." She went to the other end of the bar and appeared to be very busy with mixing and pouring what must have been a complicated drink. Finally, she walked over to me and set a cup with ice cubes and a dark liquid in front of me. "You will love this. I bet my pub on it."

With a little trepidation, I lifted the drink to my lips and took a little sip. My eyebrows went up, and a smile crossed my face. It tasted a lot like a coke, but there was just a little more of a twinge to it. I could tell in that instant that I had found a drink I could drink all night long and appreciate the taste, as it reminded me of home. "What do you call this?" I asked.

"It's a house specialty, love. I'm the only one that knows how to mix it, so make sure that you order it from me if you want another. Drink on it a while and enjoy the match." With a satisfied smile and what appeared to be a little extra sway to her walk, the bartender walked back to the other side of the bar.

I was about halfway through the glass when I started to notice some changes. I was feeling a tiny bit dizzy. I also felt the urge to move or talk or do anything so long as I was active. I started watching the football match to give myself something to focus on, but I decided that I wasn't at a good enough angle to see the screen very well. Before I knew it, I was sitting next to a complete stranger that had been vocally complaining about the officiating, but I didn't care. Pretty soon, I joined him in the jeering. After a few minutes, I realized that my glass was empty and that I had moved myself to a table to join a crowd of cheering and jeering fans. I looked up and found the bartender looking at me with that same satisfied smile on her face. I lifted a hand. She nodded and went to work on preparing me another drink.

A minute or so later I saw the bartender hand the drink to a waitress and point to me while saying something to her. The leggy blonde waitress walked over with an even more pronounced sway than the bartender and sat the drink on the table in front of me. "Thank you so much, beautiful," I said. Did I say that? "I mean . . . uh . . . sorry! I didn't mean to . . ."

The waitress let out the most wonderful and musical laugh. "I don't know what you're apologizing for, cutie, but I promise that whatever it is, you're forgiven." She playfully tapped my nose with her index finger and walked away with that same sway and even a little more laughter. It was one of the few things that could tear the attention of every man there away from the game for a few moments. The sound of a whistle from the television broke our trance, and we all went back to shouting once again.

I was at the bar for most of the night. I watched two soccer matches, learned most of the rules, drank six of the mixed drinks, made friends with a dozen locals, and gave and received hugs from three of the waitresses. I was amazed that I remembered anything given how many of the drinks I had consumed. When I stood up, I was a little shaky but not much more uncoordinated than usual. It surprised me. Most of the bar's patrons had left for the night, so I was able to walk straight up to the bartender. "Hey, I never heard you give your name." I also noticed that my speech wasn't slurred.

Wiping down the bar and some glasses, she didn't even look up. "Ginger. My name is Ginger."

I reached out my hand. She set down the glass she had just dried and shook it, finally looking up. "Pup. They call me Pup. I have to know, what was in those drinks? I might want to order it when I get back to the states."

I should have guessed when she went back to drying glasses and not looking at me. "Coke, lemon, a local lemon-lime soda mixed in, and a little bit of sour."

I ran all of that through my head, trying to work out the discrepancy. "Which part of that has the alcohol in it?"

"None of it does." She dried another glass and then looked back up at me. "I could tell it from the moment that I met you, Pup. You don't need to drink to have a good time. You just need to relax. If I could convince you that you were relaxed, you could enjoy yourself. Sorry for tricking you, love, but something tells me that a boy like you is better off remembering the good times. You'll get more out of them."

Everything made a lot more sense now. The only side effect I seemed to have from a night full of drinking was a little bit of shakiness. I wasn't drunk. I was on a sugar buzz. And Ginger was absolutely correct. I had had one of the most enjoyable nights of my life simply because I hadn't been afraid to talk to some people or show a little bit of excitement. My confused expression turned into a giant smile. "Ginger, you are an absolute sweetheart." This time I reached out for her hand, but rather than shake it, I kissed it. She blushed a little and then thanked me. I turned to the blonde waitress who was wiping down the tables. "Dory, I am sorry if I said or did anything to offend you. I hope you realize that your deadbeat boyfriend doesn't deserve you."

Dory came over and kissed me on the cheek. "Even when you thought you were drunk, you were more of a gentleman toward me than most of the blokes that come in here. Thanks for listening to me earlier. I think you're right. I'm going to take your advice and dump that loser and go back to school." Even when I think I'm drunk, I'm always trying to solve people's problems. It's like an illness or something with me.

Ginger and Dory told me to be careful in the Hiss ,and I walked out of the bar feeling even better than when I had walked in. I looked up at the sign and found out that it was called the Ego Boost Pub. I love truth in advertising. And I didn't even have a hangover the next morning.

One thing that I did have the next morning was a better idea of what I wanted to do while I was in Sydney. Ginger had provided me with a tourism book to help me stay occupied since even I couldn't be fooled by the fake drink bit twice. I decided that I wanted to go to the beach. I just had to decide which one. Because of my location, I wound up going to Manly Beach. Ironic, huh? I walked along the beach just to enjoy the sights. I had rarely seen the ocean, and one of those times was from an airliner, so I don't think it counts. I didn't plan to swim. There were a few reasons for that. First of all, I'm not much of a swimmer. I never have been. Secondly, I was already walking around in shorts. That's scary enough. Walking around with my shirt off might have constituted a crime against humanity. I didn't need to be in the ocean to enjoy it. The smell and sounds were a novelty for me. So were the voices. I was being treated to an amazing cross section of humanity. Not only were there the unmistakable accents of the Australians, but there were British, Indian, Chinese, Japanese, Vietnamese, and even some American voices floating through the air. I began to challenge myself by closing my eyes and seeing if I could guess the nationality of the speaker through their accent. Of course, I had no way to prove that I was right without asking, and something told me that walking around and asking a whole bunch of people where they were from might get the attention of the local constabulary. That's the cops, for any of you that haven't been overseas.

The walk along Manly Beach was relaxing and interesting. I allowed my mind to wander to wherever it wanted to go and didn't concern myself with any kind of danger or worries. After all, that's what R&R is for. Of course, it also prevented me from noticing a worry. The voices were becoming fewer and farther between, but I figured that maybe it was just getting hot and people were leaving the beach. February is a summer month there after all. I never bothered to look up at the sky. I might have noticed the massive rain shower forming if I had. I was too busy getting lost in my head. Boy, it's a labyrinth in there!

The first drop made me think that I was getting hit by ocean spray. The second made me think that maybe some kids were playing with water guns. There wasn't exactly a third drop. Instead, as my mother would have put it, the bottom dropped out! I don't think that the cloud decided to pour rain on me as much as I think that the entire cloud decided to descend and pummel me mercilessly. I began running without real direction. There was so much rain coming down and getting into my eyes that I couldn't make out a lot of what was around me. After about thirty seconds of pointless wandering, I was able to make out some window lights. What looked like a shopping center or mall was in the distance and across the street.

I ran for all that I was worth. Sometimes I wonder why I bothered. After all, I was already soaked through to my skin.

What was more rain going to do to me? Maybe some instinctually driven part of my mind didn't want to hang around and find out. Or maybe I was being driven by the hand of fate . . . or an impressive tail wind. Either way, I collided with someone that was running toward the same place for the same reason. The collision was a jarring one, but I kept my balance. The person that ran into me reacted differently, holding onto me in order to stay upright. There was something familiar about the situation, but I didn't slow down to think about it. Instead, I continued running with the victim of my non-vehicular accident being carried by me all the way to the mall entrance. Once I entered the breezeway, I stopped. The sudden deceleration loosened my passenger's grip, and they fell to the floor before sliding to a stop. I heard a remarkably familiar curse in a foreign language and looked down to see Mayumi Ogawa, soaked to the bone, looking up at me with equal parts confusion and surprise.

"This has got to be the coolest episode of *The Twilight Zone* ever," I thought. At least, I thought that I thought it. Turns out that I vocalize my thoughts more often than I realize.

"I don't think that I would list it as the coolest," she countered. "Maybe the creepiest."

"You've watched *The Twilight Zone?*" I know that my voice was flooded with amazement, both because she had watched the show and because I realized I had spoken aloud.

"Yes. I used to watch it all the time while soaking wet on a shopping mall floor." Sarcasm. It's like its own language, you know. Realizing how impolite I was being, I offered Mayumi my hand and helped her up. She took a moment to try and straighten her clothes before giving it up as hopeless. "I can't believe this has happened twice. I just . . . I . . . you . . ." In a fit of frustration and at a loss for words, Mayumi turned to walk away into the mall.

Maybe I had a little bit of that magical cola flowing through me because I reached for her arm and stopped her. "Ms. Ogawa, I'm not sure what you're doing here, but I'm here on R&R and I don't know a soul. I enjoy solitude as much as the next man, but I wouldn't mind having someone familiar to talk to for a few minutes." She looked like she was about to turn back away, so I added, "I also have no fashion sense. Obviously, I could use some different clothes to change into, and I would appreciate the opinion of a lady to help me look a little less like a sci-fi convention reject." After another moment's thought, she nodded. Self-deprecation. What a turn-on, huh?

I followed her into the mall and had her choose the shop where we would buy some clothes. It seemed the smart thing to do. I wouldn't know fashion if it hit me on the head. I actually had that happen once. I knocked over a display mannequin that landed on my head and gave me a concussion. I could have sued the store for damages, but since the mannequin was wearing some very expensive clothing that I thoughtlessly ruined with my bleeding head, the manager and I called it square. I have been known to suffer from psychosomatic headaches in clothing stores ever since.

Forty-five minutes later, Mayumi and I emerged with new and blissfully dry clothing. She looked amazing in her outfit. It was just the right combination of relaxed with accentuated class. I looked down at my new outfit and shook my head a little. "I have to admit, Ms. Ogawa, that your sense of fashion kind of surprises me."

She tugged a little at the pre-faded *Star Wars* T-shirt that she had chosen for me and then straightened the Darth Vader baseball cap. "Well, you said that you didn't want to look like a sci-fi convention reject. Now you look like a sci-fi convention attendee." Logic, you are a harsh mistress. She tugged again at my t-shirt playfully. "Besides, lots of Japanese girls find sci-fi geeks sexy."

I have no doubt that the extreme surprise that I felt showed on my blushing face. "Really?"

"Absolutely," she replied slyly. She began to walk away toward the food court but turned to continue. "I don't, but lots of Japanese girls do." I would like to take this moment to apologize to everyone that I've ever been sarcastic to. I understand how it feels now.

I joined Mayumi for a simple and completely non-nutritious meal in the food court. It seemed like forever since I'd had food that was incredibly tasty and had no redeeming health value whatsoever. I don't know if Mayumi considered this a first date or not, but I'm pretty sure that I broke first date rules by moaning with delight when I took my first bite of my hamburger. I didn't even realize I was doing it at first. Then I saw her take a bite of her chicken sandwich, and then I *heard* her eating her chicken sandwich. She was sounding just like me. It was like the scene from some old romantic comedy my mother used to watch. Half of the people in the food court were looking over at us to see what we were doing. Shortly afterward, there was a rush on chicken sandwiches and hamburgers. "I'd almost forgotten how good one of these can be," I finally said halfway through the burger.

"Same here," Mayumi mumbled around a mouthful of chicken sandwich. After she swallowed her bite, she continued her explanation. "There was a fast food restaurant near the college I went to in America that specialized in chicken sandwiches. I had never tasted anything so wonderful before. I ate there constantly. I haven't had a good chicken sandwich since I went back home. This isn't as good as what was in America, but it is close enough to make me happy."

I finished up my burger before continuing the conversation. "I never did ask: Why are you here?"

"The company gave me some vacation time after the last training classes were completed. I had heard a lot of great things about Australia, so I booked a flight to Sydney. I didn't know I would get picked up, literally, on my first day."

I smiled and started eating my fries. In mid-bite I started to feel a little queasy thinking about something she had mentioned. "Classes. That's right. You had a week of training with the Professor."

"Who?" she asked absentmindedly. "Oh, you mean Aaron! Yes I did. That was a really good time."

I tried to be nonchalant about it. "I'm glad you had fun. So you and the Professor . . . I mean Aaron," I had never heard his name before, "the two of you had some fun outside of the training?"

"Sure," she replied around her final bite of chicken sandwich. "He had some questions about the gear, so we decided to meet for dinner. I'll be honest, though. I don't think he understood most of what I was telling him. In fact, I know he didn't." She grabbed a handful of my fries. "He ended up asking me for all of the manuals to take back to you. He said that you would understand and then you could explain it in a way that he would understand. He's more of a history genius." She dipped the fries in my ketchup. Apparently nothing is sacred. "Honestly, I was disappointed. I expected more out of him."

I can say in complete candor that I wasn't disappointed. In fact, I was feeling hope again. I tried to play it coolly. "I thought you said it was a really good time."

"It was," she responded with a ring of ketchup around her mouth. "I introduced him to some of my friends. They all really liked him, so we hung out as a group and had a lot of fun. It was kind of like being back in school." I reached across the table with a napkin and wiped the ketchup off of her mouth. She thanked me with a little giggle. "We were all together when the news aired the video of your athletic skill at the road block. We were amazed. Aaron spent half the night talking about your potential. It got a little old."

"I apologize on his behalf."

"I didn't say that I wasn't impressed. Truthfully, I was just glad that you were all right." I nodded in appreciation. Then, as often happens around me, an awkward silence fell. I managed to break the silence by taking a sip of my drink, having it go down the wrong pipe, and then snorting it out my nose. If you've never done that with a soda before, it stings. Badly. Almost as badly as it feels doing it in front of a pretty lady. Trying to stifle laughter, Mayumi gabbed some napkins and began cleaning the table. "Well, you're a fun date, aren't you?" I choked again and snorted more soda. A date? The closest I had come in years was telling a lady what date it was. Like I needed more reasons to be nervous.

As suddenly as it arrived, the rain ended and the sun came out. Mayumi and I walked back toward Manly Beach. Not exactly the best choice for me. Walking along the beach were a bunch of men wearing skimpy swimsuits. Some of them had chiseled bodies that sculptors have been trying to duplicate for centuries. Though she never said anything, I knew Mayumi noticed them. How could she not? I swear that the sun actually shined special rays on them like spotlights! It was like being in some weird B movie. Still, I managed to keep the conversation going for a while by discussing technical information about her company's projects. It might not have been perfect date talk (not that I really know what that sounds like either), but at least it kept her from staring the whole time at their abs and pecs.

We were about halfway down the beach when she suddenly checked her watch. "Oh no! I don't want to be late!" she exclaimed in urgency.

Realizing that our surprise date was coming to an abrupt end, I figured I would bow out gracefully. "I've had a good time. Hope you enjoy the rest of your vacation."

She didn't run off immediately. "Do you have swimming clothes in your hotel room?" Befuddled, I just nodded. "Well, I have my swimsuit on under these clothes, so we don't have to go back to my room. Let's run to your room, you can change, and then you can come with me! My treat!" I didn't know what she was treating me to, but I had no intention of arguing.

I was interested to discover that when Mayumi said that we could run to my room, she actually meant run. She was four steps ahead of me before I thought to try and catch her. Once I got going, I lengthened my strides and came up alongside. It was about a mile run to my hotel, and I will admit that I enjoyed it. I know how to run. I know how to run while carrying a duffle bag. I know how to run while carrying a duffle bag with a Japanese woman hanging onto me for dear life. Usually I don't choose to do it on purpose, though. This time, I wished my hotel was farther away once the run was over. It was hot and humid, and we were both sweating and out of breath, but I could have run the rest of the day.

I changed into my swimming trunks and met Mayumi back in the lobby. Without a word, she began running again. This time, I was quicker to follow her. We wound up back out on the beach and running toward one end until we reached a building near a lagoon. Apparently we had reached our destination because she stopped running and walked the rest of the way toward the building. We went into a small office where there was a desk staffed by a pretty secretary. I looked around the room. I figured that looking at a pretty secretary while on a date wasn't very good etiquette. I have to say that I was proud of myself for figuring that out without making the mistake first. You know what they say about blind squirrels.

Mayumi spoke with the secretary while I looked around the room. It was plain, with white drywall sparsely decorated with pictures of sea life, boats, and the ocean. It was almost a stereotype of what you would expect to see at any business located by the beach. After about two minutes, Mayumi called me over and told me to sign a waiver. I hate those things. There are pages and pages of legal language that I know I could understand if I could take the time to read it all, but seeing as how most people get frustrated whenever you take an hour and a half to read a waiver, I usually just sign them. One of these days someone is going to show up wanting my firstborn child because of what was in one of those waivers, like in *Rumpelstiltskin*. Kids, now do you see why I tell you not to open the door for strangers? It's because Daddy doesn't always read the waivers!

We were sent into a small room filled with chairs and about six other people. I just smiled amicably and kept playing along. After a few minutes a guy who was way too buff and with one of those voices that ladies go to movies just to hear went to the front of the room. "Good afternoon, and welcome to your SNUBA instruction."

I glanced over at Mayumi, who was staring intently at the man and hanging on his every word. I waited for a long enough pause in the presentation so as not to interrupt, but when none was forthcoming I finally whispered to her, "Does he mean SCUBA? Are we SCUBA diving?"

"No," she responded quickly so that she wouldn't miss too much. "It is SNUBA. You don't have to get certified for this. The tanks stay on a float on the surface, and a hose runs down to your breathing mask. I've been wanting to try this for a while."

Hoping that the interest she held was in the underwater life she might encounter and not the instructor, I listened to the presentation with a certain level of trepidation. As I have mentioned, I am not much of a swimmer. Usually if I wind up underwater, it's an accident followed by me coughing up water while some lifeguard keeps asking if I'm OK. Going underwater on purpose wasn't exactly on my bucket list. It was more like one of the causes of kicking that bucket. I became more convinced that I would be kicking that bucket when the instructor mentioned we would be visiting a grey shark nesting ground near some place called Magic Point. Great. I got attacked by a largemouth bass once. Imagine how much fun a shark would have with me.

I looked over at Mayumi, prepared to ask if I could sit this one out, but I could see how much she was looking forward to it. Oh, well. I'll try anything once. Twice if it's incredibly stupid. After about thirty minutes of explanation of the equipment and how to use it, we stepped outside and were issued masks, mouthpieces, and flippers. With all of our gear, we were led to a small boat for the journey to Magic Point. I'm not the biggest fan of boats, but I could have stayed on there all day. One reason was because the longer I was on the boat, the less time I was in the water. The other reason was because of the sheer excitement that Mayumi was showing in anticipation of the dive. She wasn't like a kid in a candy store. That's too low-key. She was like a kid who had just been told they could pick any one hundred things they wanted from a toy store. She was like a sci-fi nerd who had just gotten to meet the entire cast of every *Star Trek* ever made. She was like me making it through an entire day without saying or doing anything stupid. I can honestly say that it was a lot of fun to watch.

Unfortunately, we did reach our destination. Now was our first time to try out our SNUBA gear. Our mouthpieces were hooked up to a set of tanks that were floating in their own little boat. Then we climbed out of our boat and hung onto a railing that had been built on the side. We all had on our masks and flippers and were breathing through our mouthpieces. The instructor then told us to keep holding onto the rail but to lower our heads under the surface of the water and get used to breathing there. I watched everyone go under, including Mayumi, and then took a deep, steadying breath before lowering myself down.

I have had bullets fly past my head. I have almost been run over by a speeding truck full of terrorists. I have had a man twice my size threaten to rip my nose off and eat it. I would rather have all of those things happen a hundred more times than to try SNUBA again. I had always believed, incorrectly it turns out, that SCUBA breathers used pressurized air. Wrong. When breathing in, not only is there not air being blown into your mouth, but it actually takes a little more effort to breathe in than normal. Here is what my brain thought as I dunked my head under: *You can do this. Going under . . . now. Interesting noise. Hey! I can see under here! There's Mayumi. She looks great in her bathing suit. Stupid hormones! Can't stay like this forever. Have to breathe. OK, inhale. That isn't happening as easily as planned. That's tough. Wait a minute. Underwater . . . hard to breath . . . oh, yeah! That's called drowning. Wait . . . did I say drowning? Holy crap! I'm drowning!*

I came up out of the water in a cold sweat. No one else could tell because, well, we were in the ocean. I was shaking. That was terrifying! I looked around and saw that everyone else was still under. I chose to try it again. Maybe that was an initial surge of panic that I would be able to get past. After another twenty seconds of submersion, I reemerged to the surface with absolute certainty that it wasn't an initial surge of panic. It was, in fact, life-altering, mind-numbing, inescapable terror.

Mayumi broached the surface with glee in her eyes. It dimmed quite a bit when she looked over at me. She removed her mouthpiece and asked, "Pup, what's wrong?"

I know that I often look like an idiot to people. That I have come to expect. But looking like a wimp on what, to my surprise, was a first date is another thing entirely. So, being the properly raised individual that I am, I did what seemed proper: I lied through my teeth. "Miss Ogawa, I never told you that I got captured once. They spent days dunking my head into saltwater. I only survived by . . . uhh . . . building a generator that kept me alive until I was able to escape . . ." Why did that sound so familiar? "I just keep having flashbacks whenever I'm under the surface."

I never did quite figure out the expressions that passed over her face as she listened. However, when I was done, she reached over and hugged me. *Sweet!* "I'm so sorry, Pup. Maybe you should stay with the boat while we go diving." With feigned reluctance, I nodded. I ascended the ladder into the boat and then looked back down at her before she began her dive. The smile she gave me now was more full of mischief than compassion. "After all, we wouldn't want your iron suit to rust or anything." Have I ever mentioned that I suck at lying?

I stayed in the boat and spent the time making small talk with the assistant. He said that there was usually at least one person who stayed on the boat when they couldn't deal with the dive. I felt a little better about things until he mentioned that it was usually a child. Thanks. After about forty-five minutes, Mayumi and the other divers returned to the boat. If Mayumi was disappointed in me for not diving, she didn't show it. She was busy describing everything that they had seen and the sensation of walking along on the ocean floor. Her excitement and wonder made me wish that I could have gone with her. Not enough to actually try again, mind you, but enough to wish.

The remaining two days went by in a flash of fun. Mayumi and I met for each meal. We discovered that we both had an appreciation for science fiction, although she liked Captain Janeway more than Captain Picard. That was a nasty argument. Janeway? Really? We visited a place called the Urban Jungle, where we went through a series of rope courses. This was probably the highlight of my R&R. I had gone through the Victory Tower obstacle course during training a lot. Probably because I kept screwing it up a lot. Compared to the tower, the Urban Jungle was a breeze. It was a lot of fun, and I managed to not screw it up. I actually looked like I knew what I was doing. You can see why it was the highlight for me. I took her to the Ego Boost Pub one night. It turned out that Mayumi could shoot whiskey with the best of them (while I sat there drinking my special soda). Ginger declared her "a keeper!"

I agreed. I could never have hoped for a more enjoyable trip. I should have known better than to think it could stay that way. It was the morning that I was going to fly back to the Hiss. Mayumi and I were taking a walk down the street. I was carrying my duffle bag and figured I would catch a taxi farther down the road just to eke out a few more minutes on the longest (and virtually only) date of my life. Mayumi had reached over and taken my hand, an action that stopped my heart for a few minutes. Hey, holding hands meant something, baby. Boy, I wish my mom hadn't played so much eighties music when I was a kid. We finally made it to a corner, and a cab was sitting there. Out of excuses, I had the driver open the trunk and put in my duffle bag. Standing next to the open cab door, we started to say our goodbyes. "Thank you for putting up with me, Miss Ogawa."

"It's the least I can do for a superhero," she said giggling.

"You aren't ever going to let me forget that lie, are you?"

"That's my current plan." She took both of my hands in hers. "If you have any questions about the night vision gear, please contact me. Or if you are going to be near me again. Or if you would like me to be near you."

Have you ever had one of those moments that you look back on and realize it was too perfect and was bound to get screwed up in some way? I have a lot of those. It is sometimes the most succinct way to describe my life. I should have known to leave right then. I know it would have spoiled the moment and would have not been the movie ending that everyone would want, but it would have been the safe thing to do. Naturally, that isn't what I did. Feeling as bold as I ever had, I decided to try and kiss her. Mayumi obviously felt the same and decided to kiss me as well. She was significantly shorter than I was, so I leaned low to compensate. Mayumi rose up on her tiptoes for the same reason. I overcompensated. In a rush of nerves, fast movements, closed eyes, and stupidity, I missed her lips and instead hit her nose with my forehead. That's right, kids, your father's first real date ended with him head-butting the woman he was trying to kiss. Now, if your schoolmates start making fun of your father, you can join in with all-new material.

I managed to catch my flight, but just barely. I was late because we had to take Mayumi to a clinic. They confirmed that her nose was broken. I could never tell if she was mad at me or forgave me, because she couldn't stop her eyes from watering and she wasn't in a very talkative mood. I'm sure I apologized a million times before she gestured for me to leave so that I wouldn't miss my flight. As soon as I could, I looked for a card to send her to apologize for what had happened again. It turns out that I was actually able to find a situation that no one had ever made a greeting card for. I didn't take any more R&R for the rest of my time in the army. It seemed safest for everyone involved.

And the war drums beat on . . .

*

Despite what could generously be called a disastrous ending, I was still feeling pretty good when I returned from Australia. I took a nap on the ride to Camp Wildcat. The countryside was familiar to me now, and even the questionable driving skills of the soldier at the wheel couldn't surprise or frighten me anymore. I knew that I snored. I knew that it was much louder than the engine and road noise. I didn't care. I had been in-country for longer than him, so he would just have to live with it.

I knew as soon as we got near Camp Wildcat that something had happened. Everything looked exactly like it should. There was just something in the air. It was like a dark cloud on a completely sunny day. As soon as I got into camp, I went to find the Professor to let him know that I had returned. I found him in his tent. The dark cloud wasn't just hanging over the camp. It seemed to be hanging over him as well. "Welcome back, Pup," he said with little enthusiasm. "I hope you had a good time. You might want to go say hello to your squad. I think they'll want to see you."

That very cryptic suggestion made me concerned about the squad. I ran as fast as I could to the tent, threw open the wood-framed door, and tripped over the frame on my way through. I looked up from the floor and noticed everyone watching me. Upon closer inspection, I realized that *almost* everyone was watching me. One familiar face was missing. "Where's Nickel?" I asked from the floor.

There was silence for a moment. Finally, Rabbit spoke up. "Nickel was hurt. He is in an evac hospital in Japan."

I had just barely managed to get into a sitting position when Jethro got up from his bunk and walked out, stepping on my hand as he passed. He did it on purpose, too. He'd had to change his stride in order to step on my hand. I was too surprised to register any pain. Leaving my duffle bag where it was, I got up and went after Jethro. I found him behind the mess tent. He wasn't crying, but his face was certainly haunted with pain. "Jethro, what happened?"

"Nickel hit a booby trap." Jethro's voice was strong but almost a monotone. "He saw a trip wire and stepped over it, but a second, chest-high wire was spaced so that he hit it after stepping over the first wire." He stopped and pulled out a hip flask. He took a long pull from it before continuing. "Right after the explosion, there were a dozen tangos waiting to ambush us. We beat the hell out of them, capturing three as prisoners, hurting four, and the rest were killed. Had to wait until we beat those shit-kickers before we could get an angel in to take care of Nickel." I finally heard some emotion enter his voice, and I realized that I liked it better when he was speaking in monotone. "I put a call in to the evac hospital. They say he'll probably lose his left leg and maybe his arm, too." I reached out to put a hand on his shoulder, but he slapped my hand away. "Get away from me, city slicker!"

I was really confused. I'd just gotten back. I hadn't had time to screw anything up yet. "Jethro, what did I do wrong?"

"You weren't there!" he shouted at me. "We were out on patrol and you were off in Australia being as useless to us as tits on a bull!"

In earnest, I was already feeling guilty about that fact. I knew I shouldn't. Everyone took R&R, and everyone needed to. I had been on patrols when some of the others had been away. I knew that logically I shouldn't feel guilty, but life isn't logical. "I wish I had been there, Jethro. I don't know what I could have done though. With as clumsy as I am I probably would have tripped every booby trap in the region."

Almost snarling, Jethro replied, "That would have been fine by me! At least Nickel wouldn't be the one in the hospital!" Ouch! That hurt. "Instead, you go traipsing off to the Outback to find some Aussie hussy."

"Actually, I ran into Mayumi Ogawa there." Now why did I tell him that? Did some part of me think he would really care? Maybe I'd been yelled at so much I wanted to remember what had made me feel good previously. Maybe I don't have a filter installed between my brain and mouth. Regardless of the reason, it was a useless piece of information for the moment.

Jethro let out a humorless laugh. "Oh, that's so much better. Instead of an Aussie hussy you went out and found yourself a Japanese slut. I hope her ass was worth Nickel's arm and leg!"

I'm not prone to extreme anger. I tend to help people through problems, and I insist on keeping all of my actions well-thought-out. Granted, my thought process makes very little sense to anyone else or even to myself, but there are thoughts involved. This time, my thoughts appeared to be somewhere along the lines of *Screw that! He just pissed me off!* Before I had given it a second thought, or even a first thought, I punched Jethro in the face. If I had done that prior to joining the army, he would have laughed. I mean, he would have honestly, audibly laughed. Even after I had joined the army, a punch from me would have probably just earned a chuckle. Months of being the FNG had changed that. I had been lugging around that squad automatic and all of that extra ammunition for so long that I had finally started to put on some muscle mass, and my punch showed it. Jethro's hip flask went flying, and he hit the ground. It was probably more from shock than from impact, but he hit the ground nonetheless, and my anger-addled brain wasn't going to let him recover. I got one knee on his chest, grabbed his collar with one hand, and began punching him with the other. "I didn't hurt Nickel! I miss him, too! I would've taken his place if I could! I never saw her booty!" Don't ask me why, even when blinded with anger, I couldn't make myself use the word "ass" when talking about Mayumi. Damn, those manners are like the world's most pervasive psychological conditioning.

I had hit Jethro three or four times. His lip was split and bleeding, and it looked like he was going to have a black eye, but it was obvious that he still had plenty in him to fight if he wanted to. He didn't. He just sat there looking up at me. The red haze that had clouded my vision cleared, and I lowered my fist. Jethro just lay there as I took my knee off of his chest and went to retrieve his hip flask. When I returned, he was sitting up and looking at me, but there wasn't any anger in his face. He was just looking off into the distance, like he was watching a bird flying all the way to the horizon. I stayed quiet and didn't interrupt his thoughts. "Nickel had the worst taste in music," he finally said. "He would play that rap shit so loud in his headphones that it was all I could hear in my bunk. He hadn't ever been fishing. He hadn't ever been hunting. Hell, he hadn't even been to a county fair. Only plant he'd ever seen was grass." Jethro was shaking his head, like he couldn't believe everything that he was saying. "How the hell did he wind up becoming my best friend?"

I chanced putting a hand on Jethro's shoulder again. This time, he didn't slap it away. "Nickel's alive. He's going to get to go home. He survived. That's what's important."

"He's going back to that pit he grew up in. The only thing that kept his family alive out there was the fact that nobody ever taught those gangbangers how to shoot. How is he supposed to survive out there with one arm and one leg?" Jethro finally looked at me, and the tears in his eyes were obvious now. "I was gonna take him huntin' for mule deer when we got back home."

I decided to take a risk with my response. "You still can. And I bet with one arm and one leg, he'll still be a better shot than you with a hunting rifle."

I saw Jethro's hand go back, and I prepared to receive a beating. Instead, I got a playful punch in the arm. "Why is it that I just took a whoopin' but you're the one talking like you've lost your senses?" I saw the corners of his mouth creep up, just a little. "You're right. He did survive. When I saw that explosion, I thought we were all gone. Damn miracle he made it out at all. I think I'm just worried. He's gonna make it home. I'm just hoping that I'll make it home to take him on that huntin' trip."

I reached out a hand, and we pulled each other up. He reached for the hip flask, but I didn't hand it to him. "I think that you've probably had enough of this for now." I opened the flask to pour it out, but the scent that escaped caught my attention. Casting an inquiring glance at Jethro, I took a sip from the flask. "Wait . . . isn't that . . . grape Kool-Aid?"

Slightly embarrassed, Jethro snatched the flask from my hand. "It reminds me of home," he muttered. He started walking off but stopped after a couple of steps. He didn't turn around but instead looked up at the stars for a moment before saying, "I'm glad you're back, Pup." Then he did turn around and looked at me. "Never saw her *booty*?"

Blushing brightly, I walked past him. "No, I didn't try to see her *booty* either, jackhole." Even though it was at my expense, it was great to hear his laughter as I returned to the tent.

Passing the torch . . .

*

It was only a couple of days after I returned that a replacement for Nickel showed up in the camp. He was about my age and . . . honestly, I didn't care a whole lot about who he was at the time. The important thing was that he was new. That meant that he was the FNG. Yes! A *padawan*! That was all that mattered to me. The Professor walked him into the tent early one morning. "Good morning, folks. This is your new grunt. He is brand new to the Hiss. Meet Shaggy. Shaggy, your squad." With that, the Professor left so that the low-intensity hazing could begin.

I took a look at Shaggy. He was tall and skinny to the point of being scrawny. When I can say that, it is a pretty bad thing. Still, I could have thought of better nicknames than Shaggy. "So where are you from back in the world?"

"I'm from central California," he responded, and I understood the nickname. His voice screeched like an owl. I suddenly realized that I didn't want him anywhere near me when it was time to eat just in case he had an appetite that was anything like the character he was named for. I also couldn't wait to go on patrol again so that I could relinquish the squad auto to the new FNG. My shoulders raised back up an inch or two with the thought of less weight.

I didn't have to wait long before I was able to pass the torch. The next morning, we received word that a heavy bomber had been shot down. The crew had bailed out and rescue operations were underway, but there was enemy activity reported in the area and we were the closest unit. I handed Shaggy the squad automatic weapon and all of the accompanying gear without comment or explanation. I smiled inwardly. I don't usually find joy in other people's suffering, but I was willing to make an exception in this case. I grabbed a carbine, reveled in the joy of its lighter weight, and then ran to the bird that was waiting for us. It was a short flight. I still didn't understand why the doors had to remain open, and I still didn't like it, but I had learned to live with it. Shaggy looked as white as a ghost. I gave him what I hoped was an encouraging thumbs-up. I still remembered that feeling on the way to my first combat mission. I still felt that way. I had just gotten better at hiding it.

The helicopter hovered a few feet off of the ground, and we all jumped out. It never ceased to amaze me that we were able to do that without a lot more ankle injuries. We made it to the closest tree line and established a perimeter. Hannibal got out his map and compass and started checking our position. He didn't trust using a GPS. He was convinced that if he ever decided to use one, it would be at the same time that the North Koreans figured out how to hack the satellites and send him off course. After taking a couple of readings, he called me over. I approached him with trepidation. He pointed to a spot on the map. "This is our LZ." He pointed to another spot on the map. "This is where the bomber crew is thought to have landed." He gestured over another area of the map. "This is where some enemy units are expected to be operating. We need to get between them and the crew."

I always appreciated having a clue about what we were doing, but Hannibal had never informed me before. "Thanks for the briefing, but why are you telling me this?"

That's when the other shoe dropped. "Because with Nickel gone, you are our new point man." There is an old saying that if you aren't the lead sled dog, then the scenery never changes. When you are a grunt on patrol, no new scenery is a comfortable thing. Being the point man didn't just mean that I was at the head of the line. It also meant that I was supposed to be the one looking out for enemy soldiers, booby traps, land mines, and any or all other dangers or impediments that would keep us from getting from Point A to Point B. Also, being at the head of the line meant that I was supposed to get us to Point B. I got lost in my own house once! And I was eleven years old when I did it! I now regret all of those times that I rushed to be the line leader in elementary school. It's nowhere near as cool when you're an adult.

I was going to bring up all of these objections, but I could see by the look on his face that Hannibal wasn't in a talkative mood, and I knew that time was of the essence. I nodded and started moving in the direction of travel. Hannibal called for Jethro to follow me, or "take up my slack." Jethro was supposed to watch out for me while I watched out for everything else. Although I was pretty sure that we were OK, I couldn't help but remember how he had wished I had set off the booby trap instead of Nickel. I knew that he'd been speaking out of anger and guilt, and I knew that Nickel was his best friend and I was just another member of the squad, but it still kept a little worry tickling the back of my brain.

After about two hours we had covered the same number of miles. That was a pretty slow pace, but we happened to be walking through an area that was more densely forested than most of the rest of Korea, and there was also snow on the ground. The forest provided plenty of hiding places for North Korean troops or their allies, and the snow would help muffle any noises they would make. The same snow would also make certain that my squad left a trail behind us, so the tail-end Charlie and I were the two most nervous people in the entire Hiss. OK, Shaggy was more nervous. I know because even though he was in the middle of the squad, I could hear him shaking. It was cold outside, sure, but not cold enough to sound like your own personal earthquake. I wanted to try and help him through with some advice and comfort, but I had issues of my own at the time. The snow made it so that I couldn't see what I might be putting my foot down on. Every time I snapped a twig I had a little heart attack.

We were getting into our third hour when I thought I saw something. Just ahead and off to the right was a little bit of green that seemed a slightly different shade from the other plants in the area. I signaled for the squad to halt and continued to stare at the slightly different shade of green. The longer I stared, the more sense that it made. The green slowly began taking a human shape. After about thirty seconds, I was able to make out the shape of an American airman. He hadn't seen us yet. I guess I was a little quieter than I thought I was. That was when I made a mistake. Instead of trying to raise the airman on the radio, I stepped toward him. My foot rested upon one of those heart-attack causing twigs, and it snapped.

It is amazing how loud a small sound can be in the silence. I remember trying to sneak downstairs to get a snack one time when I was a kid. Things were going well until I decided that I wanted a soda to drink along with whatever I'd decided I wanted for a snack. Bad choice. When I opened the two liter bottle of soda, the sound of the CO_2 escaping was like fireworks going off in the house. It echoed off of the walls. Everything short of flashing lights and sirens seemed to occur in my house as my mother and father came running downstairs to see what the "ruckus" was. I wasn't allowed to have sodas after sundown ever again.

The snapping of the twig alerted the airman to our presence, but it didn't tell him who we were. After hours of being wound tight with fear and adrenaline, he wasn't in the mood to take risks. With the reflexes of an Old West gunfighter, the airman snapped up his pistol and fired toward the sound of the snapped twig. Luckily for me, Jethro thought that Old West gunfighters were a bunch of slow-moving grandfathers ready to be put out to pasture. He flew through the air and tackled me to the ground, out of the way of the incoming bullet. The bullet impacted with a tree near Shaggy, who froze in fear and wet himself. "Americans!" Jethro called out to the airman.

Lowering his pistol, the airman stood and walked toward us. "Damn! I didn't know you guys were here yet."

Hannibal had run up to the front as soon as the shot was fired. He went straight to the airman and asked, "What are you doing here? You should be a klick or so east of here."

"Couldn't stay," the airman replied as he holstered his weapon. "We heard some Koreans moving in on our location, so we bugged out. The others are about fifty yards north of here. Where's your bird?"

"We aren't the rescue team. We were sent to keep the Korean forces just west of here away from you and the rescue team."

"Oh . . ." the airman replied. I struggled to figure out why his response had an air of fatality in its tone. That's when I realized that if we were supposed to keep the North Koreans off of the bomber crew, we had just failed miserably. That pistol shot made my snapping twig sound like . . . well, a snapping twig. If the enemy hadn't known where we were before, they certainly did now.

Speaking of the devil, he arrived with a vengeance. Before Hannibal could order us to pull back, an enemy rifle opened up on our position. We all took cover, including the airman, who must have trained as an acrobat with the distance he achieved in his leap to safety. Two other rifles began firing on us as well, and we returned fire with practiced teamwork that we had honed in the months of patrols we had done together. Everyone except for the bomber crew and Shaggy. The bomber crew, not exactly accustomed to warfare on the ground, all drew their pistols and emptied them without bothering to realize that their targets weren't within range. Shaggy had hit the ground where he was, but he was not doing anything except holding his hands on top of his helmet.

Every soldier wonders what they will do the first time that they are in combat. Some wonder if they will freeze. Some wonder if they will run. Some wonder if they will remember their training. All wonder if they will be brave. I still wonder what I did when I first saw combat. Honestly, I know that I followed my training, but in what way and if I looked like I had a clue, I still don't remember. What I did know was that I at least contributed to what the squad had been doing. Shaggy wasn't. I didn't think less of him for it. There is absolutely no way to know what you will do when things get real, and in a draft army the chance of negative reaction goes up. Even so, we needed him, and we needed him now.

When I am freaked out about something, I don't need a lot of instructions or explanations or details thrown at me. My mind is just concerned with living. I'd always operated under the assumption that everyone else was the same. That probably wasn't the smartest assumption to make since

I tended to not be the same as anyone else, but what else could I do. I decided to keep it as simple as I could. "Shaggy!" I called out over the sound of the rifles and carbines. I called out twice more before he looked over at me. I pointed in the direction that the enemy fire was coming from. "Weapon! Point! Shoot!" With a frightened nod, he began to position his weapon. He made several mistakes at first, but finally he had his weapon set up and pointed toward the enemy. Once he pulled the trigger and started sending rounds downrange, his entire demeanor changed. Not only did he get himself into the fight, I actually heard him begin shouting and growling at the enemy. No longer feeling helpless, Shaggy became a soldier.

The North Koreans that had fired on us were only a half squad of light infantry, and when Shaggy put the squad automatic into play, they realized that they were outgunned. They pulled back and we hightailed it out of there before the enemy could bring reinforcements. During the much faster return trip to our LZ, Hannibal radioed ahead that we had rescued the aircrew and needed gunship support. In a very short time we heard helicopter gunships fly overhead and begin strafing the trees to our right with gunfire and launching rockets farther away. It gave us good reason to keep up a fast pace.

We all boarded the waiting helicopters and took off with no further incident. Once we were high enough and speeding back toward our base, we all let out a celebratory whoop, even Shaggy. I got Jethro's attention. "Thanks for saving my sorry booty!"

Jethro smiled at the mention. "Couldn't let anything happen to ya, Pup. It would get too boring around here."

As we all exchanged fist bumps and high fives (some of us hadn't figured out how to fist-bump without injury yet)

Shaggy got my attention. "Thanks, Pup! Thanks for straightening me out!"

I felt like it was my responsibility now to pass on some of the knowledge that I had learned from the Hiss to the FNG, but I could only think of one thing to say. "When you get your Combat Infantry Badge, if a girl from home sends you a picture, don't try to burn it!" Shaggy looked at me strangely for the rest of the flight home.

Those are some serious raindrops . . .

*

The next couple of months passed without major incident. We went on a few more patrols and provided security for some other shot-down pilots and aircrews, but none of them resulted in enemy contact. Shaggy continued to learn his way around the camp and settled in a lot more quickly than I had. I even helped pull the shower trick on him, stealing his towel and watching him streak across the camp to the tent. Yes, it was fun. I get it now. We thought for a while that we were going to lose Boom and Jethro, but they both volunteered for another tour rather than be stationed stateside. I couldn't imagine anyone doing that on purpose. When I asked them about it, they both laughed. "Look at yourself, Pup," Boom told me.

I looked down at myself and checked my reflection in a shaving mirror hanging in our tent. I still looked like a cartoon character. "I've always needed a fashion consultant. What's your point?"

"You look like ten pounds of crap in a five pound sack," Jethro clarified. "When was the last time your uniform and appearance were good enough to pass inspection?"

I had to think back on that. I'd never really been good at passing inspection to begin with, but I did what I could to scrape by during all of my training because I was really bad at push-ups and got sick of peeling potatoes. What did they do with all of those potatoes, anyway? I know we didn't eat that many in the mess hall. "I think the last time I could've passed inspection was the day I showed up here."

"Exactly," responded Boom. "I mean, I know that I look good every day," she didn't receive any argument from me or Jethro, "but making my uniform look good every day isn't something that I'm worried about anymore. Me and some fresh lieutenant would probably wind up in a fight, and I'd be in the stockade after kicking his ass." I understood what they were saying. It was certainly a lot safer to be stationed stateside, but it was also a very different mindset. We kept everything in proper working order at Camp Wildcat because our lives depended on it. Keeping our uniforms straight and proper didn't do anything to keep us alive in the field, so we didn't expend too much energy worrying about that. The Professor kept us functioning like a well-oiled machine, even if it wasn't a shiny one.

There was something else that I suspected the two of them left unsaid. I thought that they were both worried about whether they would be able to settle in back home. I understood their concern. I'd never fit in anywhere, so I figured that I would have trouble whether I was stateside or in the Hiss. I didn't let it bother me but just accepted it as another chapter in my infamous existence. However, I understood how hard it would be for them to wind up back somewhere that was full of people who hadn't seen what they'd seen, experienced what they'd experienced, or felt what they'd felt. Playing video games or watching movies and the news simply wasn't the same. I knew that neither of them would ever admit to being afraid of anything, but I thought that going home scared them as much as anything in the Hiss, and at least they had some means of defense here.

I have so many fears that I don't think I can list them all. I have an unnatural fear of the game Jenga. There is something about all of those blocks missing out of a structure and it still not falling that seems so unnatural. I immediately knock the tower over before any blocks have been removed. Many family game nights have been ruined by that fear. However, one fear that I didn't even know existed came to life as the rainy season began in Korea. The Professor walked up to me as I was going to lunch in the mess hall with a smile on his face. "Hey, Pup! I thought you would want to know that Mayumi Ogawa is going to be coming on some patrols with us!"

A flash of lightning and clap of thunder followed his announcement. No Hollywood director could have timed it more perfectly. "Mayumi . . . she . . . uh . . . patrol . . . why?" I can be so eloquent when I'm frightened.

Leading toward the mess tent so that we wouldn't be caught in the storm, the Professor explained. "I have informed her company about some concerns I've noted about their equipment. They want her to help field-test it, especially during the rainy season, which is where some of my concerns are."

I was mindlessly walking through the line at this point. I grabbed myself a heaping spoonful of . . . something. Honestly, I don't think that I could have identified it even if I had been paying attention. "Well, OK, but she's a civilian. She can't go on a patrol with us."

"The Japanese Self-Defense Force has granted her a temporary commission. They are very interested to see how well this equipment works and are pulling out all the stops to get it fielded."

I was running out of options. "But . . . you're too happy about it!" Now how could he possibly argue against such flawless logic?

We sat down at a table with my squad. There must have been something about my expression because they all decided that they were going to listen in, not even worrying about an officer sitting at the table with them. "Of course I'm happy about it. I had a great time with her and her friends in Japan. I would've thought you'd be thrilled to see her after your time in Sydney."

Everyone leaned in to hear my response. I swear, it was like some bad television show following high schoolers. "Well . . . I . . . she hasn't spoken to me since then." Everyone leaned back into their seats again with their eyes wide in disbelief. What was this? Some weirdly scripted play? "I don't think things ended the way that she expected, so I never heard from her." I guess I should mention that I'd never told anyone at Camp Wildcat exactly how my R&R had ended. After all, how do you keep any of your dignity after telling people that you broke your date's nose? Sure, that might be the talk of cocktail parties for years on end, but only cocktail parties that I don't get invited to . . . which is all of them.

I spent the rest of the week dreading Mayumi's arrival. I really wanted to see her. I missed her. I'd had such a fun time with her in Sydney before I put her in a situation in which she required medical attention. Still, without having spoken to her, I could only imagine how much anger and frustration she might have built up and wanted to unload on me as soon as she could. You know what they say about hell's fury and all. That's for a woman scorned. I wonder what it is like for a woman injured. Plus, she was going to outrank me. She would also be armed! There was no way that this could end well!

After all of my fear and concern, I wasn't even aware of when Mayumi made it into camp. I was just outside of my tent and heard a familiar laugh. I looked up and saw the

Professor and Mayumi walking toward officer's country. She looked amazing. Her nose had healed, and I think I've already mentioned my appreciation for women in uniform. Her smile was as bright as ever, and it was all that I could do to not run up and hug her. Of course, with my luck I might have broken her arm in the process and made things that much worse instead of better. She never noticed me, but I watched her all the way to the tent she was being assigned.

It was another hour or so when the situation changed in a way that I had not foreseen. The Professor called my squad to his tent, where Mayumi was waiting. It was crowded, but we all fit in and awaited an explanation. I avoided looking directly at Mayumi. I was scared I might shout something out without thinking about it, like some sort of emotional Tourette's syndrome. The Professor began the introductions. "This is Lieutenant Mayumi Ogawa of the Japanese Self-Defense Force. She will be with us for the next couple of weeks to help us work out some issues with the new night vision gear. She will be accompanying your squad."

From out of nowhere, Boom raised her hand. "Permission to be excused, sir." Without waiting for permission, Boom left the tent. Rabbit followed right behind her. Even the Professor seemed surprised by their sudden departure.

"I . . . uh . . . just wanted to introduce you all. I guess you're dismissed." Everyone filed out except for me, the Professor, and Mayumi. I don't know why I didn't leave. I think that part of me wanted to go ahead and get it over with. If I was going to die at the hands of a beautiful woman, better sooner than later. When Mayumi looked up at me, she didn't have fire in her eyes. She was actually trying to keep her expression neutral and professional. She failed. Her eyes took on a look of sorrow, then she averted her gaze and ran out of the tent. The Professor sat there looking at the empty tent for a moment. "Pup, I don't know what you did, but I don't think you ever want to do it again."

The next two days found me in a daze. I was trying to figure out what was going on, but I had no clue. Mayumi didn't try to exact some kind of revenge on me. In fact, she wouldn't speak to me. She purposely avoided me. While that was going on, Boom and Rabbit seemed to go out of their way to make her life miserable. They kept bumping into her in the chow line. They got up and walked away whenever she would come near. They would begin whispering in a menacing tone whenever she walked past. It was starting to scare me.

Finally, after two days I decided to ask Boom and Rabbit what was going on. After the joke they had pulled after I first arrived, we had begun a very unusual habit of discussing anything we were concerned about in the showers. I still turned away whenever they entered, and I still wore boxer shorts, and they still thought that all of that was funny. Despite this, I had become a bit of a confidant for the two because they knew that I would approach all of their problems from a neutral point of view and not try to get something out of it for myself. I did that because it was right, it was appropriate, and I knew that I would never get anything out of it anyway! Setting low expectations for yourself sometimes prevents you from being let down.

I had only been in the shower for a few seconds when Boom and Rabbit entered. They greeted the back of my head (I told you I still turned around) and stepped into their own showers. Once I was certain they were behind their dividers, I turned around and questioned their behavior from the past few days. "Why is it that you've been giving Lieutenant Ogawa such a hard time? Did she do something to either of you that I don't know about?"

They looked at each other in confusion over their shower dividers. "No," answered Rabbit. "We never met her before she got here."

"So why are you giving her the cold shoulder?" I pressed.

Boom responded, "You." I appreciate the fact that she left the word "duh" off of the end of that sentence. "She hurt you, Pup. That's reason enough."

I was so surprised that I stood there in shock until the cold water hit me. Even after that, I stood there silent for a minute. "I didn't know you guys would do something like that for me."

Rabbit sounded about as close to caring as she ever did. "Pup, you may be a dumb shit, but you're *our* dumb shit." That was one of the nicest things anyone had ever said to me.

"Thanks to both of you, but I guess you can lay off. There's no reason to make her life more miserable than I already have." Then I described to them what had happened just before I left Sydney.

When I was done, both of them had already turned off their water and were standing there in silence. You could have heard a pin drop (which is actually kind of loud if you've ever tried that). Then they broke out into simultaneous laughter. I mean uncontrollable, side-splitting, out-look-on-life-changing laughter. I couldn't help it. After the first few seconds, I started laughing, too. I had never really looked back on what I had been through without seeing it through a prism of regret. Now that I saw it from someone else's point of view, I could see the comedy in it.

It took us a couple of minutes to settle down enough that we could speak again. "Damn, Pup!" Boom managed between laughs. "I've had some guys do some crazy stuff to me before, but none of them ever broke my nose!"

"I gotta say," Rabbit added, "I think I would have dumped you, too!" She managed to sober up a bit. "When you told us that she hadn't spoken to you since your R&R, we figured that she must have dumped you and didn't have the guts to tell you. We'll lay off of her for a day or two. That should give you enough time to talk to her and get your shit straight." I couldn't argue with that. I did need to speak to Mayumi and at least get her to end things with me officially. I started to walk over to thank them, but Rabbit stopped me. "Don't come near us, Pup! We're both in the shower, and I don't want to find out what you might manage to break on either of us!" I had to agree with that logic, so I gave them a goodbye wave over the dividers and left the showers.

As soon as I got an opportunity, I went to Mayumi's tent. I knocked on her door and was told to enter. I walked in and was greeted with the words, "Oh. It's you."

Amazingly, that isn't the most unpleasant greeting I've ever received. "Do you think we can talk?" I asked.

"Oh, so *now* you want to talk?" That response brought me up short. She seemed to be the one that was avoiding speaking to me. When I pointed that out, she decided to set the record straight. "I have been sitting around in Japan for months waiting to hear from you! No e-mail, no phone call, and no letter? You didn't even have the decency to dump me with a message!"

I stammered for a minute. "I... but... you... it's just... broken nose!" If that didn't make my point, I didn't know what would!

"What about it?" Was it possible that I might have met someone a little more naive than me?

"Miss Ogawa, I don't know what things are like in Japan, but where I come from, breaking someone else's nose doesn't raise one's future dating potential."

"Well it doesn't in Japan either!" she shouted back. I figured that pretty much made the end of our very brief relationship official, so I turned to leave. I stopped when I heard a much softer tone of voice call after me. "But neither does picking someone up and running with them, or knocking over tables, or saying you're going to become an expert on someone's equipment." I had forgotten about that one. Why couldn't she? "None of those things kept me away from you."

"So I didn't write to you because you hadn't written to me, and you didn't write to me because I hadn't written to you?"

"How messed up are we?"

"Well, I can't speak for you, but I plan on having a psychological disorder named after me." She giggled. Wow, had I missed that giggle!

Have you ever noticed how there are some movies where the main characters always find themselves in a romantic situation and start to move in for a kiss and then always get interrupted by someone or something? I used to laugh at those movies. I don't anymore. Whoever wrote those movies was also cruel enough to write the narrative of my life. Just as Mayumi and I started to move closer together, the camp PA system shouted out, "All squads form up for emergency briefing! All squads form up for emergency briefing!"

I ran to the door and then made myself stop and hold it open. See what I mean about that conditioning of manners? "After you, Mayumi."

In a voice that would have done my drill sergeant proud, she replied, "That's Lieutenant Ogawa to you, Private!" With an instinct borne out of basic training, I immediately straightened to attention. She began to walk out with military-crisp steps but stopped beside me and ran a finger along my cheek. "You are so much fun!" She broke into a run, and I found myself chasing after her to formation.

As soon as we were all in formation, I knew something serious was going on. We were standing in the pouring rain at sunset, and the Professor was already geared up and looking more serious than I had ever seen him. He ordered us at parade rest and then spoke loudly over the rainfall. "The North Koreans and their allies are trying something new this year! They've decided to take advantage of the rainy season and the obstacles it creates. They have begun a large-scale infantry offensive, exploiting the difficulties that heavy armor and wheeled vehicles can have on the soggy ground." As if to emphasize the point, the Professor's boot sunk several inches into the mud. He had to stop his briefing for a moment to extricate himself. (Extricate! Another multipoint word!) "There is a small village about forty klicks northeast of here that is going to be overrun soon. That village is now our responsibility. Do not mistake this for a defensive mission. We cannot hold this village. There are not enough of us and the advancing North Koreans are supported by heavy artillery that we cannot counter at the moment. Our job is to evacuate the village and get the civilians to safety while division command prepares for a counterattack." Thunder and lightning interrupted him, and it made me think of what flying to the village in a storm like this was going to be like. I started feeling a little sick to my stomach. "The main road to the village is not paved, and our trucks cannot reach them. We will be brought in by helicopter, and we will organize an evacuation to two klicks south of the village, which is the closest paved road. Trucks will meet us there to carry the civilians to safety."

The Professor stopped talking for a moment and looked at each squad as if evaluating whether we were ready to hear what he had to say. After checking on our demeanor, he came to the conclusion that we could handle it. "As soon as the evacuation is over, we will return to Camp Wildcat and make preparations to bug out. The enemy will have a large force less than an hour's drive from this camp. If division can't stop them, then we have to leave. Most of you have already seen combat, and many of you are on your second or even third tour, but let me make this very clear: this war just got real. Even if division stops the advance, we can plan on being part of any counter-maneuvers that are implemented. We are going to be doing large-scale infantry versus infantry contacts, and it is likely to be bigger than any of us have ever faced. I know you all. I trust you all. I know that if we are faced with the enemy's greatest soldiers, or even their most fearsome dogs, the Wildcats will prevail!" A cheer rose up from the platoon, and several nearby soldiers clapped me on the back. Would I ever live down the dog incident? At least they hadn't heard about what happened the first time that I went fishing.

As soon as the Professor dismissed us, we all ran around in what can be politely referred to as a chaotic ballet to get our gear, weapons, and anything else we might need for a rapid deployment. I had taken a few steps and realized that not everyone might know what to do. I glanced back and saw Mayumi looking confused. Before I could turn around to try and help her, I saw Boom and Rabbit grab her by the arms and lead her away. They were either going to help her get equipped rapidly or take her behind a tent and beat the snot out of her. I was really hoping it was to help her get equipped. Unfortunately, I didn't have time to concern myself with it since I had to get myself prepared, and the clock was ticking.

The helicopters arrived a few short minutes later. This was about as nasty a situation as we could have been put into. The rain was pouring down in buckets, it was getting dark, we didn't have time to study maps of the area, we were uncertain of the enemy's strength, and flying in helicopters still scared me and this time it was going to be in a storm! Somebody throw in a *Godzilla* monster rampaging through the center of the camp and my worries would be complete. My squad plus Mayumi rapidly boarded the helicopter and strapped ourselves in. The helicopter took off with a lurch, and the winds caused it to shake in a way I had not experienced. Just as I thought that panic would overtake me for the first time since diving, someone did what they had refused to do before: they closed the helicopter doors. It was a little stuffy inside because of the enclosed space, but at least we weren't getting pelted with rain and the wind noise decreased significantly.

Not everyone on the bird thought that the closed doors was such a good thing. Mayumi shuddered when the doors closed as though someone had just closed her into her coffin. I noticed that she nervously flipped the safety switch of her carbine on and off underneath her dripping poncho. She wasn't looking at the windows or the doors but instead at her feet, as if she were preventing them from running somewhere by sheer force of will. Now I truly understood how I looked when I was a cherry. I wanted to reach across and take her hand to comfort her, but she was supposed to be an officer from an allied nation. It would have looked bad for both of us. I floundered about for some way to surreptitiously (man! I am cranking out the cool words!) comfort her and get her settled before we reached our landing zone. Looking about the cabin of the helicopter, my eyes settled on the front of Jethro's helmet. There, attached to a bracket, were the night vision goggles that Mayumi was there to evaluate. "Lieutenant Ogawa!" I called out over the drone of the helicopter's motor. "Are we going to have any problems with our goggles in the rain?"

Mayumi's eyes shot up from her feet at the mention of her name, but it seemed to take her a moment to realize what I was asking her. "Goggles?"

"Yes, ma'am," I pointed to the goggles mounted to my own helmet. "Are there going to be any issues with them in the rain? If so, how do we correct?"

Mayumi stammered for a moment, but she soon fell into the familiar and comfortable technical aspects of her work. All of the soldiers in the bird were quiet and listening as she began her impromptu briefing on the gear. "The full-color NVGs have been tested in simulated typhoon conditions and suffered a malfunction rate of less than five percent. In the unlikely event that your goggles should cease function . . ." I listened carefully to what she was saying and was happy that she was saying it with a calm and even voice. I guess that techno-babble is her happy place. Mine is the bridge of the starship *Enterprise*. That's a whole different story. I saw Rabbit looking over at me. She gave me a thumbs-up. Another thing done right. If I wasn't careful I was going to make this a habit.

It didn't take long for the helicopters to eat up the distance between Camp Wildcat and the village we were charged with evacuating. Mayumi had just finished explaining how to reset the goggles when I heard a noise that I had never heard before. It sounded like the world's biggest zipper being torn open, and it was coming from just a few feet from where I was sitting. With a start I turned around and saw that the side gunners in the cabin were firing their miniguns. If you've never seen one before, there is nothing "mini" about a minigun. It's a .30-caliber multi-barrel machine gun that spins at a remarkable speed and spits out bullets faster than Hollywood makes bad movies. The guy who named it a minigun probably also had a five-hundred-pound brother that he called Tiny. The tracers create the appearance of a laser shooting from the side of the helicopter to the ground. When aimed well, it is devastating to its targets. This was the first time that the gunners had ever had to use it on a helicopter I was riding in. It was terrifying. I could only imagine what it was like for the guys on the ground that they were shooting at.

"Heads up!" Hannibal shouted to the cabin. "The gunners just opened up on an enemy advanced recon patrol. They say they saw no more movement after they sprayed the area, but it means that the enemy is getting closer. Consider this a hot insertion, and be ready to fight the moment your boots hit the ground!"

"Can I keep my boots in here and not have to fight?" I thought.

"No, Pup! I'll drag you out of here by your family jewels if I have to!" Wow . . . I guess I must have said that out loud. I really have to watch that sort of thing.

The helicopter flared and the doors opened. The gunners didn't fire out of concern for civilians in the area, but their fingers were resting on the triggers. As soon as we were low enough, we stood in a crouch and moved to the doorway, jumping out onto the muddy ground. I saw Mayumi start to stand up and then wince in pain before reaching down and unfastening her harness. Has there ever been a study by the army about how often that happens? I know it's happened at least twice. Isn't that enough to peak anyone else's curiosity?

As soon as we hit the ground I could hear the Professor shouting out orders. "We've got enemy interference on the radios, so listen up! Camper, you and your squad advance to the road and make certain that we have a clear path! Psycho and Gameshow, your squads need to organize the villagers and escort them to the road! Hannibal, deploy your squad north of here about half a klick and delay any advanced enemy elements! Move out!"

I lowered my night vision goggles and got a much better picture of what was going on. Villagers were being gathered in several locations already. The village only had a couple hundred occupants, and although they we getting soaked in the storm, none of them showed any illusions of taking shelter in their homes. Although none of the buildings had any damage to them indicating enemy action, everyone knew that wouldn't last long. I turned toward the north when I heard Hannibal order us to spread out and find observation positions. The view to the north was terrifying, and despite the number of times that I had already met with the enemy, I felt like I was seeing war for the first time.

All of the fighting wasn't taking place directly in front of us, but the unobstructed view we enjoyed for the moment gave us a front-row seat for enough of it. We could make out the afterburners of jets flying overhead. That gave me a moment of calm until I realized that some of the planes were shooting at the others. That was a really bad sign. The North Korean Air Force had taken a serious pounding about two years before. If they were sending up some of their few remaining planes, then they were serious about this whole offensive. Missiles and tracer rounds streaked across the sky, occasionally punctuated by small explosions indicating that they had found their target. Helicopters of various styles and nationalities flew overhead in massive swarms like a biblical plague. Many of them began trailing streams of flares to decoy heat-seeking missiles, bringing a new light source to the busy night.

Then there were the flashes. We were in the middle of a thunderstorm, so I expected there to be lightning. There was plenty. The lightning danced across the sky in a show that I normally would have found beautiful and exciting. Instead, when happening as a backdrop to the aerial warfare, it was terrifying. Still, those weren't the flashes that concerned me. The flashes on the horizon were accompanied by their own thunder. There was nothing natural about their creation and source. It was the visual indication of heavy artillery being used, and since it was in the north, that meant that it belonged to our enemy. I hadn't faced artillery yet. It wasn't on my immediate to-do list either.

The squad fanned out and moved half a kilometer north of the village. Movement was rapid but messy. The mud was beginning to coat our boots, pants, ponchos, and even our helmets. I was loving the night vision gear, as it gave us an almost daytime view that I knew prevented me from a large number of accidents. We took positions behind boulders and small copses of trees and watched the light show as we kept an eye out for movement.

The gunners on our helicopter had been spot-on with their fire against the first enemy advanced patrol. None of them had survived the onslaught by the miniguns. Of course, they weren't the only advanced patrol, and it only took a few minutes before another stumbled into our position. They moved remarkably quietly. There was a talent to their steps that managed to avoid snapping twigs or even squishing in the mud. They knew their jobs well and performed them flawlessly, but they were at a distinct disadvantage. It didn't matter how quiet they were. We were able to see them the entire time. They moved within about three hundred yards of our position and were still not aware of our presence.

I looked to my left and saw Mayumi lying prone behind a shrub with her carbine trained on the approaching patrol. She looked over toward me. Since she was wearing her goggles I couldn't make out her expression, but I'm sure that if I could, there would have been steel staring back at me. She held up three fingers, then lowered one, then another, then as she lowered the third she lined up her sights and shouted "Contact front!" as she squeezed her trigger. The entire squad followed her example and added a rain of lead to the water falling from the sky. Most of the advanced patrol was decimated within the first few seconds. A couple of them managed to take cover themselves and return fire. We could hear them speaking loudly, but none of us spoke Korean, so we assumed they were trying to inform each other of our positions. Shaggy provided cover fire as Jethro maneuvered to their right flank. Within three minutes of the initial shot, it was over.

Hannibal kept us all in defensive positions but called Mayumi over. I had to remind myself that she was, officially, the ranking officer in the squad. Although Hannibal was giving the orders, it was at least proper for him to consult with his superior. That's why I thought he was speaking to her. What a shock; I was wrong. A minute or two later, Mayumi came over and whispered into my ear. I really enjoyed the sensation of her breath in ear. Damn it! I'm in combat! Go away hormones! "I speak Korean. I heard them reporting our position. We think they were calling in support. Prepare to fall back to the village." She got up and ran to the next man in line. She could speak Korean? I didn't know that.

Mayumi had just informed the last person in the squad when her suspicions were confirmed. I saw the flashes on the horizon and awaited for the distant thunder that had accompanied them up to that point. It didn't happen. Instead, a dreadful whistling began to pierce the air. It was remarkably similar to the noise that you often heard in old movies, especially those about the World Wars. I found myself having flashbacks of watching *Sergeant York* with my parents. Then, about a hundred yards away, I saw the earth turn into a fountain of mud, followed by an earthquake and a sound that rivaled thunder from inside the cloud. *Hello, Artillery. I hope you don't mind if I make a snap judgment, but I really hate you. Feel free to leave ,and don't let the door hit you on the way out.* Ever notice how no one you ever tell that to leaves right away? Neither did the artillery. The second salvo was on the way, and it landed ten yards closer. "Fall back to the village!" I heard Hannibal yell. None of us needed further motivation.

During the run back to the village we intercepted a runner from another squad who was coming to tell us that the villagers had been evacuated and that we could pull back. Gee, thanks for the permission. We wound up running more or less in a line as fast as we could to get back to the village. I was the fastest, but I wanted to make certain that everyone made it, so I held back a bit. Mayumi was the last in line, and I tucked in front of her and made certain that she was able to keep up and stayed sufficiently far ahead of the artillery. I even saw her shoot me a smile under the goggles. I actually felt happy at that moment.

I should have known better than that. Now please understand that I am not the biggest fan of low-brow humor. I like a good mindless movie now and again, but mostly I appreciate humor that requires at least some level of thought to enjoy. I point this out because I don't want you to think that I am trying to entertain you by appealing to the lowest denominator of humor. In fact, kids, if you are reading this, skip the next paragraph or so. I don't want you discussing this at dinner tonight. I'm just trying to divulge the facts as they occurred.

We were just getting to the edge of the village and were still running at a pretty good clip. When we had eaten in the mess hall earlier that day, none of us had known we would be going into action that night. If I had, I probably would have eaten less and made different choices. Naturally, I hadn't, and it came back to haunt me as we entered the village. We had just passed the first building, and it happened. I farted. Loudly. When I say loudly, let me clarify. There were still artillery shells falling a couple hundred yards behind us. I heard myself over those explosions. So did Mayumi. So did the soldiers running in front of me. Everyone slowed down a little and looked back at me. I could feel my face burning with embarrassment. I felt my foot step on something unusual, and I picked it up. It was a teddy bear. "Look what I found," I said with false cheeriness to try and distract them. It didn't work. I was mortified.

Though the teddy bear didn't distract them, the artillery shells did. The next volley was getting closer to the village. We resumed our run and made it to the other side of the village when the shelling seemed to stop for a moment. We were about three or four hundred yards past the village when we heard the next volley heading toward us. The sound was different this time. The whistling seemed to have a different pitch. The shells passed over the village and then seemed to explode a hundred or so feet in the air with much smaller *booms* than I would have expected. What looked to be pieces of the artillery shells began to splat down into the mud between us and the village. They must have had their fusing wrong. Their shells were exploding prematurely. I've heard that can sometimes happen with age.

Not wanting to see if they could get their fuses set correctly, we began running again. We didn't make it three strides before I heard a scream behind me followed by a *splat*. I looked back and saw Mayumi on the ground cradling her ankle. She had stepped into an overly deep puddle of mud and twisted it. I was about to pick her up and carry her when I saw movement in the village. A little girl stepped out from one of the buildings searching the ground desperately.

She found the teddy bear that I had stepped on and picked it up, hugged it, and ran back into the building. "Hannibal!" I called. The big man showed up with amazing speed for someone his size. "Mayumi . . . I mean Lieutenant Ogawa's hurt, and there's a little girl back in the village." He looked toward the village about the same time as another volley of shells exploded prematurely and shell fragment fell to the ground between us and the village again. "You take the lieutenant. I'll go get the girl."

I was already a few steps away when Hannibal yelled out to me, "Get back here, Pup! It's too late!"

I ran backward as I replied, "Running while carrying some poor scared person that doesn't know who I am? This is what I do!" With a smile I started running toward the village again. I ran through the area where the shells were dropping their fragments. In fact, some shells dropped their fragments while I was running through there. They fell with surprisingly solid *thuds*, and it made me feel like I was running through a hail storm. Rather than frighten me, it just spurred me on.

I made it to the village in what had to be Olympic record time. I ran straight to the building that I had seen the little girl run into. She was in the corner of the first room, huddled with her teddy bear. "Hi!" I said in my friendliest voice. "Do you speak English?" Did you know that a three-year-old girl can still manage to look at you in a way that makes you feel incredibly stupid? "Of course you don't. Then I won't bother introducing myself and telling you why we have to run for our lives." Instead, I knelt down and opened up my arms and beckoned her over to me. Slowly and reluctantly, she walked up to me. She got near me, looked at me closely, and then punched me in the nose. Is there some kind of newsletter passed around by children in foreign countries that tells them to treat me this way? I tried to keep a smile on my face as my eyes watered and I picked her up, teddy bear and all.

I stepped out of the home and back into the pouring rain. That was when my goggles became one of the five percent that failed in monsoon conditions. I went from having a nice color picture of the world to pitch black. I pushed the goggles up from my eyes on their swivel and didn't bother trying to fix them. I was too concerned with getting out of the village before any more advanced patrols arrived. Flares from helicopters and flashes of lightning allowed me to orient myself enough to find the way out of the village. I began to run with the little girl under my arm still clutching her teddy bear. I started to pick up speed and saw that Hannibal and Mayumi were still waiting for me in the distance. They were gesturing and shouting, and I could have sworn that they were telling me to stop, but I figured I would ask them what they were really saying once I got to them. With all of the rain and noise and confusion, there was no telling what they might be going on about.

I lost a lot of respect for the North Koreans as a fighting force when I saw that they had not corrected their fusing issues. I saw another volley of shells explode in the air and rain chunks down onto the ground. Some of their smaller shells must have been fused properly because there were small explosions at random places throughout the field of debris, and if any of that debris were to hit me it could certainly be deadly, but it seemed like nothing compared to the massive artillery explosions I had seen earlier. The girl I was carrying seemed to think otherwise. The closer to the field we got, the more agitated she became. By the time I entered the debris field, she was kicking and screaming and wailing. It was all that I could do keep a grip on her. Another volley of shells caused debris to rain down around us, and I heard more random small explosions. Sure, it was scary, but that little girl was acting like it was the end of the world. Of course, for a girl that young, it probably did seem like it.

I made it through the debris field, and the girl stopped kicking and screaming. I guess the most immediate fear was gone. Both Mayumi and Hannibal were wearing astonished looks as I approached. I would have loved to have asked them why, but I didn't want to meet up with advancing enemy forces because I was curious about someone's mood. "Come on, guys! Let's go!" I jogged past them at a slower pace to give them time to catch up. They gave each other a look of surprise, then decided to pursue the matter later. Against her objections, Hannibal picked Mayumi up in a fireman's carry and began running with her. We kept up a fast pace all the way to the road.

When we arrived at the road, we found most of the platoon providing security as the trucks were loading. A fairly young couple were trying their best to speak to the Professor, but his Korean was limited and they were in such a distressed state that I doubt that he could have understood them anyway. When they saw me carrying the little girl, they stopped talking and ran toward me. The little girl tried to squirm loose, and this time I let her. I couldn't help but smile as she ran to her parents, both of whom hugged her tightly with tears visible even in the pouring rain. After a few minutes, the little girl moved away from her parents and walked to me. I was still grinning like an idiot and squatted down so that I would be at her level. She walked up to me, and then kicked me in the shin. I howled in pain as she ran back to her parents and then boarded a truck.

I was still grasping my shin when Hannibal walked over to me and Mayumi hobbled up behind him. "You deserved that, you know?" Hannibal said.

"Why?" I asked. "Because I passed gas?"

"That was you? I thought someone had tripped a booby trap!" He shook his head. "You still don't know what you did, do you?"

"I ran back to the village and got a girl that stayed behind to find her teddy bear. The North Koreans couldn't seem to get the fusing right on their artillery. As long as their shells were blowing up prematurely, it was possible to get to the village and back. I know it was a little dangerous, but since they couldn't get the range right, I figured I was OK."

Mayumi sat down next to me in the mud. She was already covered in it, so I guess it didn't bother her any. "Pup, those shells weren't exploding prematurely. They were dropping submunitions."

The Professor had been listening in on the conversation and stepped forward, addressing Hannibal. "You mean to tell me that Pup ran into the village and back again *after* the NoKos started dropping submunitions?" Hannibal nodded. "That's decoration-worthy."

"What's the big deal?" I found myself asking in an almost whining voice. "Parts of the shells were dropping, and I'm sure that wasn't safe, but I'm sure anyone else would have done it."

Mayumi put her hand on my shoulder. "Those weren't parts of the shells dropping, Pup. They were submunitions. They were *mines*. The North Koreans were cutting us off from the village."

I sat there for a minute trying to comprehend what I was being told. Some of my questions wound up vocalizing themselves. "So . . . I ran through a minefield?" Everyone nodded. "I picked up the girl and carried her back through a minefield?" More nodding. "The girl knew it was a minefield, and that's why she acted like she did?" Smiles and nods. "And that is why you guys tried to stop me?" They didn't bother nodding now. Their eyes said it all. "I ran through a minefield twice in the middle of a rainstorm. Wow." I don't know if anyone else was as impressed with that realization as I was because it was at that moment that I decided to pass out. It seemed like the smart thing to do.

Intelligent choices . . . wonder what those are like?

*

I regained consciousness just a few seconds later and stumbled through the rest of the evening in a haze. We marched along the road for a couple of miles before some trucks were dispatched to pick us up. I climbed in the back and ended up falling asleep almost as soon as I sat down. I don't think that I snored. I honestly didn't care. The rising sun brought an end to the rain for a time. We drove into Camp Wildcat, and I got to see my world actually coming apart.

While we were gone, the non-combat soldiers had begun the process of dismantling the camp. Wood frames stood where most of the tents had been. A steady stream of trucks and helicopters were ferrying equipment, furniture, food, and everything else that we had needed for our daily life away from the camp. "Are they that close?" I asked to no one in particular.

"We passed a convoy of our soldiers hell-bent for leather heading north to try and stop the advance," Jethro responded. "Even if they stop it, we are awfully close for some of their long-range tubes. It seems like a good time to skedaddle." And that was that. I found myself holding back a few tears. I had been living at Camp Wildcat for about ten months, and somewhere along the way I had started seeing it as a home. I can't imagine why. I had to shower in my boxers there. If my mother had cooked like the mess hall did, I would have run away when I was five years old. I still couldn't look at the latrine without feeling phantom burning on my buttocks. Still, I had settled there. I didn't want to see it go.

There wasn't any time for a tearful farewell to our old digs. As soon as we got off the trucks we were instructed to collect any personal belongings that remained and get back to the trucks within fifteen minutes. I ran to where my bunk had once been and grabbed my duffle bag. I began stuffing everything that I could into the bag and was startled when my hands got tangled up in someone else's. I looked up and saw Mayumi. She was still hobbling a little, but she was smiling at me. "I never really settled in," she explained. "I figured that I would lend you a hand. My ankle is still a little tender, but my arms still work fine." I was too tired and on too much of an emotional roller coaster to feel either thankful or concerned. I just nodded and continued packing. She grabbed my pack of snore strips and asked, "What are these?"

I glanced at the package and responded, "Personal safety equipment."

Mayumi shrugged and continued helping me pick up my personal things. She grabbed a stack of letters and stuffed them into my duffel, but an empty envelope fell out of the stack. She picked it up, glancing at the return address. "I don't recognize this name. Who is Korika?"

I guess that I never got around to throwing away the envelope that the latrine-destroying picture was sent in. I grabbed the envelope and stuffed it into the duffle bag. "Wrong number," was my lame explanation. My imagination disappears when I'm stressed.

The rest of the packing went on in silence. I guess that Mayumi realized that I was far too preoccupied to be chatty. Looking back on the situation, I realize that she, too, was under a lot of stress. She had just returned from her baptism by fire. Maybe she was like me and had a habit of becoming very talkative when she got nervous. Part of me feels like a jerk for not being there for her when she needed someone to talk to. Another part of me says that I'd needed to take care of my own issues at that moment. I'm really not sure which side is right.

Fifteen minutes later I was back in the truck and watching the skeletal remains of Camp Wildcat disappear behind us. I was still very taken aback by how attached I had become to the place. The Professor had been right. We were really starting to see what war is. It isn't just fighting the enemy and protecting your brothers- and sisters-in-arms. Sometimes it means letting go of things that you didn't even know you cared about. The movies and video games never seemed to point that out to me.

We were relocated to a small town several miles farther south. Our platoon was temporarily assigned an elementary school building as our new camp. After spending the better part of a year being surrounded by olive drab everywhere I looked, the riot of bright primary colors that dominated the school hurt my eyes. I found cots set up in the gymnasium and library and grabbed an empty one near the rest of my squad. I had seen cots lining the hallways as well and really didn't want to try to sleep as people walked past me. After claiming the cot and putting a few things from my duffle bag on there in order to make certain that everyone knew it was mine, I went to find the Professor. For some reason I felt lost ,and I really needed him to provide some clarity. It didn't surprise me to find out that he had claimed the principal's office. I informed his clerk that I wanted to speak to him and then had a seat in the outer office. I felt a little shiver of familiarity to the situation. I had rarely gotten in trouble at school, but the one time I did, it was principal-worthy. I had just wanted to make certain that my chemistry teacher wasn't exaggerating about how some different chemicals reacted with each other. It turned out that he was actually understating the reactions. It took a month for my eyebrows to grow back. The chemistry teacher's toupee didn't make it.

I was fortunate that I didn't have to relive that memory for long. It only took about three minutes before the clerk informed me that the Professor could see me. I walked into the office and was impressed with how quickly the lieutenant had managed to transform the principal's office into his own command center. Multiple radios filled the desks ,and a detailed map of the area with suspected enemy locations covered one wall. The one thing that he did leave on the desk from the office's previous occupant was a name plate. It was written in Korean, but someone had decided to put a translation under it. It read "The Boss." It was obvious that the Professor had been receiving overwhelming amounts of information, orders, stress, and underwhelming amounts of sleep. Put simply, he was looking haggard for the first time since I'd met him. Despite this, he smiled when he looked up at me. "Pup! Come in. Have a seat."

My feelings of being lost paled in comparison to what the Professor was obviously going through. I suddenly felt very silly. "Never mind, sir. It's not important. Sorry to have disturbed you."

"Stay, Pup, and shut the door." His voice was still friendly, but it also had another tone mixed in. It sounded like desperation. Maybe he needed to talk as much as I did. I closed the door and sat down. "I thought that you would like to know that based on the reports given to me by your squad leader and Lieutenant Ogawa concerning your actions during the evacuation of the village, I am submitting your name to receive the Bronze Star. I don't know how long it will take before we hear back about it, but I have no doubt that you will receive it." He offered to shake my hand.

"I don't deserve it," I replied immediately, not taking his hand. My quack therapist says that I have issues with inferiority. He's right (for once). However, that had nothing to do with my response. "I had no idea that I was running through a minefield to get that little girl."

"No, you thought that you were running through a downpour of shrapnel. That isn't exactly safe either, is it?" I shook my head and was about to protest, but the Professor raised his hand to silence me. "It comes right down to the simple truth that you would have done it even if you knew that it was a minefield. You might have walked a little more softly, but you saw that little girl in danger, and you chose to put your own life at risk to save her. It was damned brave. If you doubt that, you can always consult this." He handed me a piece of paper with a crayon drawing on it. There were what looked like explosions on the left side of the paper. On the right was a little stick person kicking the leg of a taller stick person with a funny hat that I assumed was supposed to be a helmet. "We received that a few minutes ago. The little girl you saved drew it."

I looked at the picture for several moments. "She doesn't look very happy with what I did."

The Professor laughed. That was good. I knew that he needed it. "In that picture she surely does not. However, I know that she is. She drew the picture and gave it to her parents with a big smile on her face and told them to give it to 'the idiot.' They spent two hours finding out your name. You did well, Pup. You deserve the recognition. And God knows that I need something to look forward to."

His last statement brought me up short. It worried me to hear him sound fatalistic. "Are things that bad?" I finally managed to ask.

The Professor stood up and looked at his map. "The brass says that it's not. As a matter of fact, they are certain that this is the beginning of the end for our enemy's forces. I agree with them. They appear to have committed almost everything that they have for one last desperate assault. The North Koreans, the jihadists, the communist guerrillas, and everyone else who is here fighting us seem to have found their second wind and run out into the rain to fight. They are losing. We stopped them dead in their tracks about ten miles short of Camp Wildcat a couple of hours ago. The powers that be are preparing plans for a counterattack, and we are sure to be part of it." He turned to me, looking like the weight of the world was on his shoulders. "I know that we can do this, and I will never shy away from a fight. This is the last battle. I am sure of it. That is a good thing. I just don't see us being able to finish it without taking more casualties than I am comfortable with."

"How many are you comfortable with?" I still don't know why I asked that. Was I going to take a survey later and see who would volunteer to be a casualty so that we could meet our quota?

"With this platoon, any casualty is too many. I've lost my objectivity as an officer and become too close to those I command. I don't want to see a single thing happen to any of you. I'll follow my orders. I will send us all into danger if I am told to, but I will regret it for the rest of my life."

I stood up, convinced myself I was doing the right thing, and placed my hand on his shoulder. "I think that all of the great officers regret the risks they are forced to have their soldiers take. That's what makes them great officers." I then looked around to make sure that Hannibal wasn't nearby, came to attention, and saluted. The Professor returned the salute with textbook precision (he really did belong in movies). "Just don't give me that Bronze Star. I don't deserve it." I turned to leave.

"Screw you, Pup. I outrank you and will do whatever I want!" I could hear the humor in his voice and left the office happy in the knowledge that I was leaving it better than how I found it. That was more than I could say the last time I had been to the principal's office.

As I walked down the hallway, I found myself thinking about some of the things that the Professor had said. There was no way that this platoon was going to be sitting this battle out. We were located close to the front lines, we had knowledge of the region, and we were an infantry platoon in what was clearly going to be an infantry battle. That meant that we would fight, and in a fight this large, some of our people would get hurt. My squad had been remarkably lucky in only having one casualty since I had arrived. I knew that in any war, that was unusual for a frontline combat unit. I think that I might have started taking it for granted. I always expected that every time I went into battle I would have Jethro and Rabbit and Boom and Hannibal and even Shaggy at my side. We had fought in our fair share of firefights together and come out on the other side as a unit. This time was different. This time was a great deal bigger. We weren't going to have to go out and find the enemy. The enemy wasn't bothering to hide this time. He was standing out in the open and daring us to come and get him, and we had to accept the dare. I couldn't see a way that we could get through this fight without someone going home before they should. I found that this thought frightened me even more than my first taste of combat had. I couldn't seem to think straight. I couldn't catch my breath. I had no idea what I was doing. My subconscious had taken over my actions.

Before I knew what I was doing, I was knocking on the door to the school nurse's office, which was the room assigned to Mayumi as quarters.

She opened the door quickly after I knocked on it. She had gotten a little bit of sleep and managed to clean herself up. I know that I looked like death eating a cracker, but it didn't stop her from looking thrilled to see me. I really wished that she hadn't done that. "You need to go back home," I found myself saying.

The look on her face fell. "What do you mean you want me to go home?"

I really didn't know what I meant. My mind seemed to be on autopilot. The autopilot seemed to have an answer. "You need to go home. As long as you're here, people's lives are at risk."

She stepped back out of her doorway and sat down on her cot. I took her place, filling up the open frame. "Why am I a risk?" she asked in a weak voice.

"Because you aren't as well trained, and you haven't been fighting with us." My responses were instant and strong and logical . . . and I hated them all. I just couldn't seem to stop them.

"But I fought with you at the village. I can handle combat. Plus . . ." She looked up at me with tears in her eyes. "I want to be with you."

"Well I don't want to be with you." My voice was even and strong. My heart was screaming and cursing. Of course, Mayumi could only hear my words, not my heart. "We had a good time in Australia, but here you are holding me back. Getting a smile or kiss from you isn't worth having to look over my shoulder all of the time to check and see if you are OK. We are from two different worlds for goodness sake! Call it what it is: two goofballs having a few laughs."

Mayumi seemed to deflate. She wouldn't even look at me. When she spoke, it was barely above a whisper. "Go to hell, Pup."

I nodded and turned away without another word. I thought that I heard her whimper a little as I walked out, but I didn't turn around to see if I was right. My heart was racing and I felt sick to my stomach, but my mind was perfectly focused and certain that it had made the right choice. I wasn't five or six steps down the hallway when I ran into Rabbit. She was also showing the same fatigue as I was, but she suffered the same annoying habit that everyone else seemed to have that day: she seemed happy to see me. "Pup! Glad I found you. I just wanted you to know that I heard about what you did. I'm impressed. You're really growing as a soldier." She leaned forward and kissed me on the cheek. Then she turned and walked away. I looked over just in time to see Mayumi slam the door to her room. I still wasn't entirely sure what I was trying to accomplish, but I was pretty sure that I had accomplished it. Yay for me.

Melvin seemed to deflate. [illegible] even [illegible]
me. What she [illegible] above a whisper. [illegible]
said.

He nodded and turned away without another word. [illegible]
thought that [illegible] I walked out
[illegible] head was
[illegible] my mind was
[illegible] focused and certain that I had made the right choice.

I was [illegible] five or six steps down the hall [illegible]
Kubota. She was also [illegible] the [illegible] but
she [illegible] everyone
[illegible] seemed to [illegible]
[illegible] I [illegible] and you [illegible] wanted [illegible] to know that I [illegible]
[illegible] what you did [illegible] really [illegible]
said. She [illegible] kissed me on the cheek.
Then she turned and walked away. I looked at her [illegible]
[illegible] the door to her room. [illegible]
[illegible] what I was trying to accomplish [illegible] I was
[illegible] for me.

Welcome to the war. We hope you enjoy your stay . . .

*

I managed to get about four hours of sleep. I assumed that it was restful. I was so completely exhausted and physically and emotionally drained that when I woke up I realized I was in the exact same position that I had fallen asleep in. I had been too tired to move even in my sleep. I hadn't even snored. I didn't know that it was possible to be too tired to snore. Even though I don't think that I consciously said all of the things that I'd said to Mayumi, I remembered them all with perfect clarity as soon as I woke up. That wasn't really something that I wanted to remember. Part of my brain wanted to try and figure out why I'd said those things, but it had no time to investigate. (I know that it's obvious now, but that's now. You know what they say about hindsight. Then again, who can see out of their hind?) The reason that I had woken up was because the school's PA system was calling all members of the platoon to the auditorium for a briefing. It seemed that the Professor was right. There was no way that we were going to be sitting this battle out.

I filed into the auditorium and sat in the first seat I could find. I wasn't near the other members of my squad, but I wasn't all that concerned about that. I didn't feel much like socializing anyway. Just before the lights went down in the auditorium so that the projector could be seen, I managed to look around. I didn't see Mayumi anywhere. It surprised me. It was the first time in my existence that someone had actually chosen to do what I'd asked them to. Why did that have to start now?

The Professor was standing at a podium on the stage of the auditorium. There was a map of the surrounding area projected next to him with the location of allied and enemy forces marked on it. There was more red on that map than I had seen so far in my time in the Hiss. Maybe the Professor was right. Maybe this was the big one. "Ladies and gentlemen, this is the big one." See? I told you. "The North Koreans and their allies are trying to take advantage of the weather situation by attacking during this monsoon in the hopes that it will negate some of the advantages that we enjoy. They have been partially successful in that respect." He flipped through a few slides that showed a tank stuck in mud, a drone that had crashed into a tree during a storm, and a spy satellite photo that only showed clouds. "I don't show you these pictures to worry you. I show them to you because they prove that the enemy was wrong. The advantage that we have isn't because of technology. Here is the greatest weapon that the United States has ever fielded." The next slide was predictable but still welcome. It was a picture of a soldier. The auditorium erupted into cheers and screaming. The Professor couldn't suppress a little smile. I think he might have been a male cheerleader in college. What do they call them? Yell leaders? Whatever. I think he might have been one of those.

It took a good minute or two before the shouting finally died down enough for the briefing to continue. I had no doubt that the Professor could have ended the cheers anytime he wanted to, but I think he knew how much the troops needed it. He was a natural leader that way. "The

North Koreans have miscalculated because their choice of tactics has allowed us to exploit our most capable weapon to its fullest potential. We have halted the enemy advance and the brass have decided that it is time to bring this war to a close. Our counterattack begins in two hours." He brought the map of the region back up, but this one showed arrows indicating the directions that the blue forces would be traveling. "As you can see on this map, we are going to start rolling up the enemy forces, but we can see an obvious opening for the enemy to swing around and hit our left flank. That is where we come in. This platoon will be part of a brigade-sized force that will protect the left flank and advance with the main force to help roll up and eventually surround this main enemy formation. NCOs, you will receive detailed information about your area of operation. The rest of you, just go out there and do what you know how to do best. It's raining, it's muddy, it'll be a tough fight, and you'll be telling your grandchildren with pride that you were a part of it. Dismissed!"

I got up and went straight to my preparations. I'm pretty sure that I was nervous as hell. I'm pretty sure that I was scared to death. My therapist would no doubt love to delve into how I was feeling at that moment. I don't bother to now because I didn't bother to then. I kept my mind on what I needed to do and what was expected of me. It was probably the only thing that kept me sane. I know that people asked me questions and gave me orders. I know that I responded to all of the questions and orders. I can only assume that I responded automatically because I'll be damned if I can remember what I said. What I do know is that two hours flies by a lot more quickly than you think it would when you are getting ready for something major.

I found my squad and waited with them for the helicopter that was going to carry us to our area of operations.

Everyone was remarkably subdued. I guess that we all really did understand how big of a thing we were about to take part in. We double-checked each other's gear, helped tighten straps, and exchanged rations with each other, but there was very little conversation. Jethro wasn't humming a country song. Boom wasn't shouting at some guy for looking at her wrong. Hannibal wasn't threatening me with bodily harm. Shaggy . . . well, Shaggy was eating a protein bar. It turned out that he did tend to eat as much as the cartoon character he was named for. Once our bird landed, we boarded quickly and quietly and lifted off with barely a word.

The rain had started again, and lightning and thunder was accompanying it. It was not the kind of flight you would ever want to take in a helicopter, but I don't think that any of us really noticed. The silence became an almost physical presence, pressing down on us with an imminent feeling of doom. Was that dramatic enough? I'm trying to work on my wording a bit in case I ever decide to write a movie. Regardless, the silence got to be too much. I couldn't stand it. It had to end before it swallowed us whole. Without notice or context, I shouted out the first word that came to my mind. "Vacuum!" That was the first word that came to my mind? I don't get me. I really don't.

Everyone in the cabin of the helicopter turned to me in confusion. I just kept a neutral expression, like this was a perfectly natural thing to have shouted out in the middle of a helicopter full of soldiers on their way into battle. Finally, in his typical, threatening, angry voice, Hannibal asked, "Pup, what the hell are you talking about?"

Still with my neutral expression, I replied, "I have no idea, Sergeant."

Rabbit smiled. "That doesn't make it any different than any other time that he opens his mouth."

"At least he ain't talking about someone's booty," Jethro added.

"Or his mommy," said Boom.

"Or getting himself blown off of the latrine," Shaggy said in his high-pitched screech. How did he know about that?

Most of the soldiers in the cabin of the helicopter were showing signs of a smile, except for Hannibal. He still looked like his normal, surly self. "You know what, Pup?" he growled. "I should have ripped your nose off and eaten it when I had the chance." He reached forward, and I have to admit that I was awfully scared as he did. His hand went straight for my nose, and I found myself briefly wondering if this was going to hurt as badly as I thought it would. Instead of ripping my nose off, he honked it. I still tried to jump out of my seat. Half of Hannibal's face went up with a grin. Aw, look. I think I made a friend.

The lightened mood only lasted a few seconds because word came back that we were thirty seconds from our landing zone. Everyone checked their weapons, and the miniguns on the helicopter began their world-ending buzz that shook the entire bird and sent untold amounts of lead hurtling to the ground. Whether the enemy was there or not, we were treating this as a hot insertion. It was only my second. I could've done without it.

We each had to make a conscious effort to not move in front of the gunner's position. Although he had stopped firing for the moment, which meant that we might not be facing enemy fire as soon as we deployed, he could restart at any time, and it wouldn't be good to be standing in front of him if he did. We all flipped the safety off of our weapons and leapt out of the hovering helicopter. I was less than thrilled to discover that we were deploying into a rice paddy. I splashed down into waist-deep water and barely managed to keep my weapon from being submerged. Without even having time to complain about it, I dragged myself up onto one of the levees and lay in a prone position searching a nearby tree line for movement. Once the rest of the squad had joined me on the ground, the helicopter flew away with a deafening whine of power, and a spray of water kicked up into our faces. Three people were sent to check out the tree line while the rest of us helped pull everyone out of the water.

Once everyone was on what passed for dry land and we were certain that we were not surrounded by enemy troops, Hannibal made an appraisal of our surroundings, checked his map, and then radioed our position to the Professor. Hannibal apparently got a response because he put his hand up to one side of his helmet over his ear and listened intently. I've never understood why people do that. If a bunch of people are talking to you, I understand wanting to block them out by covering your ear so that you can hear the radio, but no one was talking to him, and putting your hand on your helmet accomplishes nothing. I have come to the conclusion that it is a method of displaying status. It is like looking at everyone and saying *I'm important enough to have someone speak to me on the radio and you aren't. Nanananaboo-boo!* Of course, I don't think I could ever picture Hannibal saying that last part. I'm pretty sure his version of taunting when he was a tiny child included a threatening growl.

Hannibal called out to all of us once he had completed receiving his own instructions. We gathered around to make certain that we could hear him over the rain while a few flankers made sure that no one could sneak up on us. "Here is the situation. The main attack is proceeding as planned and with the expected level of success. Command attempted to secure the left flank with some armor, but it was as ineffective as they feared it would be. That means that we will be flank security against any North Korean maneuvers. We are to proceed about two miles north of here and set up defensive positions along a railroad track and service road there. If we are unable to hold that position, we will make our way westward toward a SoKo company positioned there. We may have artillery support and some light vehicles to assist, but don't plan on air support. Any questions?" I always wanted to chime in at moments like that with a question like *why is the sky blue?* I doubt Hannibal would have found that amusing. "Very well. Intelligence doesn't think that we will begin seeing any advanced enemy patrols for another few hours, so let's get to our position, dig in, and get ready to kick some ass."

The march to our defensive position was a messy one. Days of pouring rain had created a morass of mud and standing water. I was already wet from the waist down after being dropped off in a rice paddy. The rain made certain that I was wet from the waist up, too. Most of us were wearing ponchos when we started out, but after the first mile of the march we ditched them. We were soaked even with the ponchos, they restricted our movement, and air didn't flow through them. It was like being on a long march in your own personal sauna. I don't recommend it. After we entered another field after passing through a copse of trees, I had a thought: *Shouldn't the treads on the tanks spread out their weight so that they can operate in these conditions?*

I hadn't asked the question to anyone in particular, but since Rabbit was closest to me, she obviously felt the need to respond. "Pup, am I in a tank?" I gave her the obvious negative response. "Then how the hell should I know?"

"Well, I . . . uh . . . just . . . kinda . . ." I have such a great way with words. I should write song lyrics.

I found an answer to my question a few minutes later. Two burnt-out tank hulls were sitting in the middle of a field, blackened. I discovered later that they had been crossing the field and were forced to go much slower than usual because of their weight and the mud. As they lumbered across the field, a couple of jihadist insurgents were able to hit them with rockets. Unable to maneuver, the tanks had little chance. A nearby infantry squad captured the insurgents later, but it showed that the weather was going to be a detriment to the heavy armor that the United States enjoyed fielding so much.

It took a little longer to cover the distance than I was happy with. That's because every step that you took involved your foot going ankle-deep in mud and then having to pull it out again. Still, we made it to the railroad tracks with plenty of time to prepare for a defensive action. The tracks ran east to west, as did the service road beside it. This worked in our favor since the North Koreans or their allies were likely to approach us from the north. The train track, which was elevated to prevent flooding, would help provide a barrier to small arms fire. We all got out our entrenchment tools and dug some shallow foxholes. We couldn't dig anything very deep because the mud kept collapsing into the holes. We positioned our squad automatic weapons to provide the maximum field of fire, and then we took our positions and waited.

Waiting is a terrible thing to be subjected to when you are in a life-or-death situation. It's like fate is teasing you. You have to find ways to fill the time but not make yourself vulnerable in the process. Most of us ate. It's usually a really bad idea for me to eat whenever I'm nervous or might be in a stressful situation. The food doesn't tend to like me in those instances. However, I had learned through my previous encounters to get food and sleep whenever I could because I never knew when the next opportunity would arrive. Food I could eat with one hand and still keep an eye on my zone. Sleep would have been an entirely different story. Since I couldn't do one, I figured that I had better take care of the other. The food was getting soggy from the rain and hadn't been good to begin with, but it provided me with sustenance. It was almost like eating in the cafeteria in my elementary school.

I was beginning to think that the North Koreans were going to be no-shows to their own party. The sun went down, which did nothing to stop the rain but did force us all to put on our night vision gear. We were fortunate that this time none of our goggles suffered due to the weather conditions, and we were able to watch the field ahead of us almost like it was daytime. That probably saved some of our lives.

Jethro was the first to see them. He always claimed it was because of his time spent hunting. He would spend hours in a blind or a tree stand just waiting for the sound or movement that would indicate he would be going home with a feeling of triumph. I guess it's a good thing that I never went hunting with him. I would have been flipping my safety on and off or playing games on some electronic device to give myself something to do, scaring all of the animals off in the process. Patience is not one of my virtues. Thankfully, it was one of his. He noticed movement at a pretty good distance and used his goggle's magnification feature to zoom in on that movement. He reported to Hannibal that he had spotted enemy infantry about a half mile away.

Hannibal wasted no time. He radioed in the sighting and called for artillery support. Less than a minute later I heard the telltale whistling of artillery rounds flying overhead. They sounded much different when they were flying away from you than when they were flying toward you. I liked the sound a lot more when it was outgoing. Then I saw the explosions of earth and fire in the distance moments before I could hear them. I had been on the receiving end of artillery fire and found it terrifying. It was much more satisfying when it was going the other way.

The artillery fire made it obvious to the North Koreans that they had been located, so they decided not to bother hiding anymore. They announced their presence by jamming our radios. Everyone in the squad heard a faint but definitive *click* and then nothing. Whatever they were using was effective because we couldn't even communicate by radio with people in our own squad. The artillery support ended almost immediately. Without information coming in from the front lines, they couldn't risk dropping shells on their own men. Not since the time I had gotten lost in the mall had I ever felt so alone. At least at the mall I didn't have people trying to kill me. Not that I knew of.

The North Koreans began moving across the field carefully and with impressive skill. They obviously knew that we were there and that we were going to fight against them, but they weren't going to make it easy for us. They moved in leapfrog patterns, and I could have sworn that I saw mortars being set up in the distance. The only thing that gave me comfort was that I had seen our own mortars being set up behind us a ways. Hannibal, thinking of the same subject as I was, low-crawled to another member of the squad and ordered them to fall back to the mortar squad and inform them of the situation. The soldier scurried off as best as he could, but he had to move slowly and low to the ground or he would give away our position. I was certain that by the time he made it to the mortar squads we would be under fire.

Before I go any further, I think it is only fair to warn you that I have never described what happened over the next several hours all at once before. My therapist thinks that I need to do it so often that it becomes second nature and doesn't affect me anymore. My therapist is an idiot. I don't try to pretend that all of this didn't happen. I know that it did. I just don't want to relive it so often that it defines everything that I do, no matter what kind of impact it has on my life. It's kind of like having a bad teacher. Everyone has had a teacher that they didn't like or didn't get along with. That is nothing new. What amazes me is the number of people who let that control their point of view for the rest of their lives. They tell their kids to never trust teachers and that they are all out to get them. They become cynical and think school is a waste of time. I've had a teacher or two say some nasty things to me. I dealt with the problem and didn't let it define me. I don't want this event to define me either. I'll describe it all in one sitting, but don't expect me to do it again. You can just reread it if you have questions.

The NoKos were about eight hundred yards away when they started firing their mortars at us. They didn't know exactly where we were, but it didn't take a genius to see the raised railroad tracks and realize that they made for good cover. The shells rained down in a haphazard manner, but that made it no less frightening. Knowing that there is nothing you can do prevent a shell from landing on your head will definitely give you the shakes. Our own mortars began to answer back and walked shells toward the enemy positions. High-detail radar told our crews exactly where to send their shells. Thank you to the light artillery. Within a few minutes the NoKo's mortars had been chased off. There was one less nightmare I had to deal with. To help with things, our tubes continued to drop rounds on the advancing infantry. It's always nice for the trouble to be on someone else's side of the fight.

Having shells falling on you is never an enjoyable thing, but it can be a great motivator. Where the North Korean troops had been advancing carefully before the bombardment, they were now trying to close the distance quickly so that the shelling would stop. That was an even more dangerous situation for them. The mortar fire was blind. Our fire was aimed. Once the advancing soldiers were within range, we opened fire with everything that we had. Several of them took hits, and the rest of them hit the ground. It made targeting them more difficult, and it gave them an opportunity to return fire. We were in excellent defensive positions and it never gave them a clear shot at us, but that didn't mean that there weren't some close calls. Seeing a bullet impact the dirt a foot in front of your face will certainly get the heart pumping. We stood our ground and gave a lot more than we got. I know that I hit several soldiers. I tried not to think about it, only about doing what I had to do. The North Koreans were determined, though. They continued to close in no matter how many they were losing, and there were a lot more of them than there were of us.

Things were beginning to get loud and confusing. Since our radios were jammed we were yelling back and forth at each other over the gunfire. Warnings, sightings, requests for cover fire were a constant barrage in the height of battle. It got to where I wasn't certain who was yelling, even if it was me. The situation was becoming very tense. The enemy soldiers continued to close even as their ranks were thinned out. They were getting close enough that I could make out the details of their faces. They ceased to be just silhouette targets anymore and became humans, as grim and determined to survive as I was. Seeing that frightened me, not because of what might happen to me but out of fear of what I might become. It didn't force me to pause in my fight, though. I think my therapist told me that what it forced me to become was a soldier and a survivor. He might have gotten that right. He's still a quack, though.

I was truly becoming worried that we were going to be overrun. The soldiers were getting close enough that I started to wonder if one of them had a good enough arm to throw a grenade at us. That's when two Humvees came flying up on the service road. Both had .50-caliber machine guns mounted on top, and they began pounding away before we could even hear the motors of the oncoming vehicles. The cavalry had arrived. Some jerk even shouted out "Hi ho, Silver!" It could have been me. I don't remember. Heat of battle and all.

The heavy machine guns were the straw that broke the camel's back. The North Koreans that had made it so close to our lines were talked out of any further advance by half-inch bullets digging new trenches all around them. They tossed several smoke grenades to cover their withdrawal. We kept the pressure on them until we were certain that they had left the area. The two Humvees pulled up, and the soldiers in the cupolas dismounted. Once they were out of the vehicles and walking toward us, I recognized them. It was the Professor and Mayumi. "The NoKos are pulling back all along the line!" he announced proudly. "We'll proceed westward in a few minutes to assist the SoKos. Things are pretty tense there. Medics are on their way to look at the wounded here." He clapped several of his soldiers on the shoulder. "It looks like we did it, folks!" A cheer rang out.

I wasn't cheering. Mayumi was standing ten feet from me and looking at me with a look of betrayal. I couldn't blame her. Even combat can't overcome heartbreak. I really needed to talk to her. "Lieutenant Ogawa, may we speak please?" She barely nodded and followed me a few dozen yards away, where we could not be overheard. "Why are you here?" I know it was a stupid way to start off the conversation, but I had asked her to go away. The absolutely microscopic, minuscule ego that I had was angry that she had ignored me.

With a very superior air, she replied, "Apparently I'm looking over my shoulder and taking care of you!"

There was nothing about that I could argue with. My ego shut up. "You know that I didn't really want you to leave."

"Do I?" She wasn't going to make this easy. Once again, I couldn't blame her. I once heard a comedian say that there were two ways to argue with a woman, and neither one works. I should have learned that lesson sooner. "Why should it matter to you? We were just having some laughs."

Fatigue hit me like a rock. Despite the mud, I flopped to the ground. She remained standing in a dignified manner. "It was a lot more than that. I was scared for you, Mayumi. I knew that this was going to be rough, and I didn't want you to be at risk. I know that you can fight, but you never know when you might get stuck in an artillery barrage or an air strike or . . ." Something started tickling the edge of my brain.

Whatever it was, Mayumi didn't notice. "Pup, it's dangerous everywhere. I could get mugged walking around Kyoto. I could get stuck in a house fire. I could . . ."

"Shut up," I commanded.

"*What?*" There are some things that you should never tell a woman, but it was a definite necessity.

"*Shut up!*" I commanded again with greater urgency. I stood up and looked toward what had been the battlefield. Some of the smoke released by the retreating North Koreans was beginning to dissipate, and my full-color goggles were seeing something unusual. "Mayumi, can these goggles make out the color of smoke?" She didn't answer at first. I think that she was still shocked at my brazenness. Let's face it, I'm not usually a very confrontational person. She might have thought it was another sign of the apocalypse. "*Can they?*" I repeated.

"Ye-ye-yes they can," she stammered.

I looked at the dissipating smoke again. I could see a little more clearly through the dark grey haze that they had created. Somewhere in there was another smoke. It would have been awfully hard to see at night, but maybe you could if you knew where to look for it. There was a yellow smoke billowing out of a can nearby. Almost as if it were marking the position for someone. Several latches unlocked in my brain, and I realized what was about to happen. "*Incoming!*" I shouted, but was too late.

As I mentioned before, the North Korean Air Force was a corpse of its former self, but apparently they had one or two attack aircraft still in their inventory. One of them came swooping down on our position, firing rockets. It was obvious that the pilot was inexperienced because most of the rockets landed in the field, but they kept getting closer. Unable to reach the rest of the squad, I tackled Mayumi to the ground and covered her with my body. There were multiple explosions, and I felt something burning along my back. The jet roared overhead before blowing up in midair. An American fighter flew past at breakneck speed, performing a barrel roll to celebrate its victory.

I'm glad that the fighter pilot had something to celebrate, because things on the ground were terrible. Once the ringing in my ears subsided a little, I checked on Mayumi to make certain that she was OK. Once she signaled that she was, I got up and turned to run toward the members of my squad. I didn't make it a single step. The rocket hadn't scored a direct hit, but it was close enough. The vehicles looked to still be intact, but there were people laying all around them, some moaning in pain, some not moving at all. I found myself frozen at the carnage for a few seconds, then my concern for my brothers and sisters kicked in.

Rabbit was the first person that I came to. She had burns all across her back. She was conscious, but it was obvious that she wasn't happy about it. After checking her pulse and breathing, I went to the next soldier, which was Hannibal. His leg had been hit badly with shrapnel. I could tell it was bad, and blood loss was already causing him to lose consciousness. I tore part of his sleeve off and made it into a tourniquet. It might not have been pretty, but I didn't know what else to do. Jethro, Boom, and Shaggy all looked to be suffering from concussions or some kind of head trauma. Both of the Humvee drivers were already dead. Then I found the Professor. He had taken a chest full of shrapnel but was somehow alive and awake. It was obvious that he would be neither for much longer. "Professor, I'm here. You're going to be fine," I lied.

"Don't ever play poker," he replied weakly. "I have one question for you." I leaned in closer. "Why did you burn that picture?"

Despite the situation, I couldn't help but be shocked. "How did you . . ." I asked in an unnaturally high voice.

He just answered with a weak smile. With his last bit of strength, he put his hand on the side of my face. "Good instincts, Pup." His hand dropped, and his eyes closed. He looked like a movie star, and his death looked like a scene he was playing. Damn, Professor. You were the best I ever knew. Aaron, my son, now you know where your name came from. Maybe making your middle name Professor was taking the honor a bit far, but I don't think so. Not one little bit.

Some people are born to greatness; others get lost and step in it . . .

*

I glanced over at Mayumi. She was giving Rabbit a shot of morphine and trying not to look up at me as I pulled a poncho over the Professor. I could tell that she was crying. I might have been, too. In the constant rain it was impossible to be sure. We performed what first aid we could on everyone there. She bandaged up my back where shrapnel had cut a long, shallow wound. After a few minutes we sat down together, leaning our backs against the bumper of one of the Humvees. "We're the only ones conscious here, you know?" I pointed out.

"I do," she replied. "Aaron . . . Aaron . . ." She couldn't seem to make herself get past his name. "He said that medics were on the way. We should wait."

I looked at the wounded all around us and was hit by a wave of uncertainty. "That smoke grenade gave away our location, and that jet seemed to be waiting. For all that we know, the medics could have been intercepted themselves. What about the mortar crew?"

Mayumi shook her head. "We had them pull out a while back. They should be a couple of miles west of here by now."

That got my mind to thinking. "The Professor," my voice cracked a bit when I said his name, "mentioned us heading west to meet up with the South Koreans. Maybe we should move the wounded in that direction."

Doing a quick count, Mayumi shook her head. "I know that you can run while you carry someone, whether they want you to or not, but there are ten of us here. That's more than you can carry. I don't see how we can pull it off."

I banged on the bumper we were leaning on with my fist. "These aren't just paperweights, you know." Realizing that we might have a solution, new energy flooded our systems. We jumped up and I ran to the driver's seat. We carefully removed the body of the driver and covered him in a poncho as well. Then I got in and tried to start the vehicle. The engine did not make a single sound. It didn't even try. "Well, maybe this one is a paperweight." With considerably less enthusiasm, we approached the second Humvee. Once again, we removed the driver and covered him. This time, when I tried to start it, the engine sputtered for a moment and then roared to life with the most glorious sound I had ever heard. I giggled with delight. I am not kidding. I giggled. I'm man enough to admit my giggling. Just don't mention it to my friends. "Help me get everyone loaded up!"

It didn't take long to see a flaw in our plan. We had a working vehicle, but it was not big enough to carry ten people. In a brain cloudburst (still not big enough to be called a brainstorm) I backed the working Humvee up to the useless one and connected them with tow cables kept in the toolkit. Mayumi seemed impressed. Apparently she held low expectations. It took another ten minutes, but we got everyone loaded into the two vehicles. Mayumi jumped into the seat next to mine, I put the Humvee into gear, and I gave it gas. I guess towing required a lot more power than I expected, because we didn't go anywhere. I continued to give more throttle until we started moving, but we were moving very slowly and the tires were spinning so much that they were smoking. I allowed this to continue for a few seconds before I stopped and took the vehicle out of gear. I pondered the situation for a moment and then gave myself a face-palm. Getting out of the lead Humvee, I walked to the towed vehicle, reached in, put it in neutral, turned off the hill break, and then walked back to my vehicle. I guess that I should mention that it took me a few tries to pass my driver's test in high school.

Once I had taken care of the initial problems, driving with the second vehicle in tow was easy. We stayed on the service road that followed the railroad tracks. We kept our headlights off so that we couldn't be easily spotted by aircraft or enemy soldiers. Besides, with our night vision gear we didn't need the lights. It wasn't exactly a pleasant drive through the countryside. All around us were signs of battles having been fought. There were fields that had managed to catch fire despite the rain. Wreckage of aircraft and helicopters littered the landscape. Large craters left by artillery or bombs were everywhere. Fortunately, none of them had hit the service road, and it allowed us to continue without detour. While all of these things showed that the land had been fought over, we still did not see any sign of allied forces anywhere.

The decision to follow the service road made sense for two reasons. The first was that although the paving was old and weather worn, it still allowed us to travel at relatively high speeds. The other reason that it made sense was because the road and railroad tracks traveled from east to west at our defensive point. I have no sense of direction, so this gave me an absolute means of making sure I headed west toward allied forces. What no one had told me, probably because I had no reason to know, was that the tracks and service road made a gradual turn to the northwest. A half hour of driving had sent me a few miles into North Korean-held territory.

I didn't know. I told you that I have no sense of direction. There wasn't a sign or anything. A map might color the area red, but the ground doesn't change color just because someone else controls it.

The detrimental thing about headlights is that they allow you to see a few dozen yards in front of you, but others can see those lights from miles away. The headlights on the big deuce-and-a-half truck had blackout covers on them, making them pinpricks of light instead of giant torches, but we could see them easily nonetheless. With almost giddy joy, Mayumi focused on the truck and zoomed in with her goggles to get a better look. "It's old, but it is definitely an American truck. It is traveling on a dirt road that will cross the train tracks in another mile or so." She stopped her description for a moment and studied what all she was seeing intently. "Pup, something isn't right. There are smaller vehicles all around it. There are four of them. They look like . . . what do you Americans call them? Dung buggies?"

I laughed. It sounded like something that I would say. "You mean dune buggies?"

"Yes, whatever," she responded impatiently. Fear had crept into her voice. "Each of them has a gun mounted on top. They . . . they're wearing North Korean uniforms! They must be trying to capture the truck!"

"Oh shit!" Sorry, Mom. Sometimes life calls for that kind of reaction. I took stock of our situation. There was no one else nearby. If we didn't do something, there was no way the driver of that truck would be able to get out of this mess. I made a quick decision. "Take the wheel!" I ordered. Mayumi looked like she was going to argue, but I didn't give her a choice. I began climbing out of the driver's seat and up into the gun turret. In the movies, such a change in drivers happens pretty smoothly. What a load of crap! If I didn't have my helmet on I would have cracked my skull open several times, there was so much swerving and jerking as Mayumi tried to get settled in to drive.

Once Mayumi did get settled in to drive, things didn't get much better. There was still an unbelievable amount of swerving and overcorrecting, and she couldn't seem to decide on a speed. The vehicle we were towing was going crazy, being thrown from one side to the other and hitting our rear bumper as we kept changing speed. The wounded in both of the vehicles should all be glad that they were unconscious. It was better for them that way. I steadied my vision enough to find the dune buggies. They were almost in range. I made sure that the electric traverse was still working on the gun, and as soon as they were in range, I unleashed hell.

The first gun that I had ever fired in the Hiss had been the machine gun when I was on sentry duty with Rabbit. Part of the reason I had fired so much was because I thought that I should protect the base. The other part was because I had found something about the raw power of firing it enjoyable. It turned out that I still did. I could hear myself whooping, hollering, and even growling as I pumped round after round of high-powered projectiles at my targets. The first dune buggy never had a chance. The rounds went straight through its engine, causing it to seize. The buggy flipped in a spectacular crash. The other buggies responded quickly. Although we had no headlights on, the muzzle flash from a heavy machine gun was like a giant beacon. There was no mistaking where we were. That was when Mayumi's very erratic driving became useful. There was no pattern, rhyme, or reason to her driving, which made us a nearly impossible target to hit. It also made it very difficult for me to aim, but I did my best. It surprised me that the dune buggies fought to the very last man, but in the end determination and a little touch of crazy won out. The truck was safe.

Throughout the entire fight, the truck had remained on its course. Then again, where else could it go? Mayumi brought the Humvee to a stop directly in front of it. For a moment, I thought that the truck was going to ram us. Finally, I heard the squeal of the truck's breaks and let out a breath I hadn't realized I was holding. I squirmed down out of the cupola. "Where did you learn to drive like that?" I asked. My neck was still trying to recover from her maneuvers.

"I didn't," she replied sheepishly. "You told me to take the wheel. You never asked if I had learned how to drive." I guess what they say about assuming is true.

"I'll check on the driver, Mayumi. You check on the passenger. Let's see if they can give us a ride to a medic station."

We dismounted from the Humvee and began to approach the truck. Something didn't quite seem right. The occupants seemed to be watching us with more concern than appreciation. You would think that if we just saved their lives that they would be all smiles. The passenger pulled out some small electronic device, punched a few buttons on it, and then put it away again. Their uniforms were correct, but something about the way that they wore them seemed wrong. It was like they weren't comfortable in them. And then there was the driver pulling out a pistol and shooting at me. That was the final giveaway that not everything was what it seemed. Just call me Sherlock.

I dove and rolled away. Mud covered my goggles and I ripped them off. The driver had opened his door and begun to step out so that he would have a clearer field of fire. I realized that I had committed a cardinal military sin by leaving my carbine in the Humvee. I grabbed a rock and hurled it with all of my might. It hit the driver in the shoulder. It elicited little more than an *ow* from him. He raised his pistol and aimed at me. I thought about closing my eyes but then wondered what that would accomplish. My eyelids wouldn't stop the bullet. Multiple shots were fired, and then the driver crumpled over, dead. I looked over at the Humvees and saw Rabbit in the turret, giving me a thumbs-up, a morphine induced giggle, and then passing out again.

The passenger must not have been carrying a sidearm because instead of shooting at Mayumi, he had leaped out of the truck and tackled her. He had managed to catch her by surprise and had her pinned to the ground. I saw him punch her, and my vision went red. I heard him draw a knife, but it didn't make me pause a single heartbeat. I ran up and tackled him with the ferocity of an NFL linebacker during a goal line defense in the Super Bowl. At least I assume that it was something like that. I don't really watch sports. It just sounded good. We hit the ground, and his knife went flying out of his hand. I put my knees in his chest, pinned him down, and snarled, "*Don't touch my girlfriend again!*" punctuating each word with a vicious punch to the face. I watched his eyes roll back in his head and realized that I had just knocked someone out. Boy if that bully from my high school gym class could just see me now. Steal my deodorant, huh? I heard a squish of footsteps and jumped up ready to fight again. It was Mayumi. She already had swelling around her cheekbone, but she looked to be all right. She looked at me, then looked down at the unconscious man at my feet. Almost as an afterthought, she gave him a vicious kick in the crotch. I cringed. I don't care if a man is friend or enemy, that just hurts! "Are you OK?"

She gave a slight nod. "So I'm your girlfriend? Shouldn't you check with me about that? After all, you still haven't seen my *booty*." Jethro! Can't you keep your mouth shut?

"Well, you weren't there to argue at the time." I knelt down and began removing the shoelaces from the passenger's boots. I didn't happen to carry handcuffs on me, so

I figured I could bind him with those until we could turn him in as a prisoner. As I was doing that, I took a good look at him. He seemed familiar. I ran through all of the movies that I had seen, but he didn't fit into any of them. I thought of all of the stupid commercials that got stuck in my head and forced me to sing jingles out loud whenever I thought no one could hear me, but I couldn't picture him singing any of those, either. For some reason I kept thinking about playing solitaire on a cell phone. That's almost a way of life, you know. That's when it hit me. Cards. "He's the King of Spades!" I realized that he was one of the men on the "capture cards" that the military used to familiarize troops with high-value targets. "He's one of the generals in the military junta that took over North Korea. That's a funny word, 'junta.'"

"Focus, Pup."

I guess that meant that I shouldn't point out that I would have thought he would be tougher than that. Oh, well. "I wonder what he was doing out here in a plain old truck?"

"Who cares?" Mayumi replied. "We can fit all of the wounded in here and get everyone back to the American lines." I couldn't argue with that logic, so I bound the still unconscious general with his own shoelaces and then accompanied Mayumi to the back of the truck. It was already partially occupied by a large wooden crate. "I wonder what this is." Mayumi said.

"As long as it's not beeping or ticking, I don't care." Sometimes you can't sweat the small stuff . . . or even the large, crated stuff.

Mayumi climbed into the back of the truck and approached the box carefully. She stood there studying it for a moment before she announced, "Well do you care that it *is* beeping?"

I thought about that one for a second. Then I returned to the general and searched his pockets. In one pocket I found a small electronic device with a few buttons covered in Korean symbols. I looked at it for a moment and decided not to overthink it. I pressed the red button near the top. Nothing happened. "Did it stop beeping?" I yelled.

Mayumi continued listening for a moment, then replied, "It stopped."

"Good. I can go back to not caring now. Let's get everyone loaded in." Ten minutes later I was driving a deuce-and-a-half southbound with a general tied up in the back being guarded by a Japanese woman whose specialty was electronics next to a giant crate that stops beeping when you push a red button on what looks like a really old cell phone. Perfectly normal night in the Hiss, right?

And I'm still trying to figure it all out . . .

*

Most of you should know the rest of the story. Of course, if you are anything like my children, that would mean that you would have had to study something, and they would rather get a paper cut and pour lemon juice on it than do that. Let me save you the Internet search. The Professor was right. That battle was the final death throes of the North Korean military junta. They'd put everything that they had into one final assault. Their allies weren't well trained in large-scale warfare, so they didn't fare well. The North Korean military had been fighting a long and drawn out war with very limited resources, so they didn't have much of a chance to begin with. The generals had decided that they would go down fighting, though. Naturally, with the exception of the general in the truck, the rest of the leaders had been far away while they'd expected their soldiers to go down fighting. There was a lot of celebrating when the junta members were captured three days later in a Special Forces assault. A lot of that celebrating was done by North Koreans.

My platoon had been involved in some of the lightest fighting. The biggest thrust had been several miles east of us. However, our end of the battlefield turned out to be the most significant. The North Korean generals weren't under the delusion that they had a good chance of winning the battle that they had started. What they had needed it for was a diversion. With a huge infantry battle taking place, surely no one would notice a plain old covered truck driving south. No one would have tried to intercept it as it drove toward the docks at Incheon. Then the only other nuclear bomb in North Korea's inventory would have ripped through that city. Even if the North had lost the battle, the threat of being able to deliver another nuclear bomb unnoticed to somewhere like Seoul may have helped them win the war. What they didn't plan on was one lost idiot who wasn't afraid to push buttons. Good thing I didn't try the green button.

The truck wasn't easy to drive. While Mayumi had never learned to drive, I had never learned to drive a manual transmission. I'm pretty sure that this truck had been captured during the First Korean War. Everything about it was old, rusty, and cantankerous. (I think I used that word correctly.) I ground the gears a lot, and I'm pretty sure that the clutch was never the same again, but I finally got us going. I'm pretty sure that I never broke fifteen miles per hour. Changing gears was difficult enough. Changing gears in a large truck that had tiny headlights in a nighttime downpour when I'd been spoiled by full-color night vision goggles was damn near impossible!

I managed to make contact with American forces without getting us shot. I'm not saying that it wasn't a close thing, mind you. Most soldiers tend to be a little more observant than I am. They noticed that the truck was of an older vintage, an older paint scheme, and the driver didn't seem to know what he was doing. However, after getting screamed at a lot, I was finally able to identify myself and inform them of the prisoner and casualties in the back of the truck. They worked quickly to secure the general properly and cart off the wounded and dead from the back. Someone asked me what was in the crate. I proclaimed ignorance, and they believed me. Some people just give off that air. When they opened it with a crowbar, many curses were uttered and a few pants were wetted. I spent days afterward being interviewed by every intelligence agent in the Hiss, and a few more that I believe were imported, about where I obtained a nuclear warhead.

I was able to attend the Professor's service at Arlington. It was the playing of "Taps" that finally did me in. I had managed to hold back the tears until that moment. It was the only time I've ever cried when no one told me that I needed to "man up." I still visit him whenever I can.

The Professor had been true to his word. His recommendation that I receive a decoration for what I did during the evacuation of the village was approved. Instead of the Bronze Star, I was given the Silver Star. I really wanted to refuse it, but it seemed disrespectful to his memory. The little girl I'd rescued was there at the ceremony. I think she gave me the finger. That's the last time I carry her unwillingly through a minefield!

The capture of the North Korean general and the prevention of the use of a nuclear weapon brought a lot more attention to me. Once again, I was recommended for a decoration. This one turned out to be an even bigger deal. I had to travel to Washington to receive it. With a lot more pomp and circumstance than I am comfortable with, I was awarded the Medal of Honor. Some people, when they are nervous, have their mouth go dry. I am the opposite. When I am nervous, my salivary glands go into overtime. Being in front of a whole bunch of cameras while the President of the United States talks about your bravery and merit can, to say the least, make you nervous. As a result, I had an overabundance of spit in my mouth. The President came up to me, put the medal around my neck, and then saluted me. I returned the salute and said, "Thank you, Mr. President." I really didn't need to say any word with the letter 'p' in it. The resulting spray hit the President right in the face. Despite the fact that most politicians can keep a straight face in unusual situations, a face full of spit will break the concentration of the most focused individual. The President recoiled suddenly and the Secret Service jumped in and covered him for protection. I didn't think they would ever stop showing that video clip on the news.

Even though these events were years ago, I'm still not comfortable with the medals that were given to me. There are, and always have been, true heroes among our soldiers, some of whom received the recognition that they deserved, and others that deserved more recognition than they got. I'm just some poor schmuck who didn't know when to stop running or which direction he was driving. I hope that the true heroes don't hate me. I don't want to take anything away from what you accomplished.

The Medal of Honor and Silver Star brought me a lot more attention than I had hoped for. My mother kept telling me to remember where I came from. She was almost like the guy who used to ride with Roman heroes and tell them, "Remember, thou art mortal." Don't worry, Mom. I never forgot where I came from. The dog is still trying to run away from there.

The high school that I graduated from decided that they wanted to rename it in honor of me. The faculty must have conveniently forgotten what an annoying, sarcastic little pain I had been. I finally relented and told them that they could, but I suggested that they just use my nickname. They refused and insisted on using my full name. I'm sure that they regret that now. The John Z. Pupulowinazowski High School. They had to reposition the lettering three times to fit it all on the building. The football jerseys have to be ordered with special lettering to try to put the school's name on there. They also decided to change their mascot to the "Pups." You know that strikes fear into the hearts of their opponents. What we need is to have another school become the "Kittens" and we can have a heck of a rivalry. I'd love to read that sports page article.

The squad had a reunion a few weeks ago. I'd say that things worked out well for most of us. When Rabbit woke up in the evac hospital in Japan, there was a doctor there watching her sleep. She didn't find it creepy at all. They were married two years later. She's a stay-at-home mom now and loves every minute of it. She's also turned into an animal lover. They have several dogs and cats in their household. I'm forbidden from visiting.

Jethro returned home and began feeling claustrophobic. Even his frequent hunting trips couldn't prevent him from feeling trapped in his tiny hometown. He moved out and is now the mayor of a city in Southern California. His family disowned him for becoming a "city slicker." They have their own reality show now. I'm still trying to figure out what reality they're in.

Hannibal lost his leg in the airstrike. It doesn't appear to have slowed him down any. He is a personal trainer. Rumor has it that he achieves remarkable results, largely because the people he trains are scared to death of him and put in extra effort to make certain that he stays happy. He still hikes mountains and says that having a prosthetic leg adds to the challenge, which makes it all worthwhile. He has become a vegetarian. My nose has never felt safer.

Boom went to college and became a teacher. While all of the boys at the school tend to drool over her, she has the most disciplined classes in the school. It only takes one boy getting out of line once a year for them to discover the explosive temper behind that pretty face. Her principal also commented on how the level of respect being shown among the students had risen dramatically since her arrival. Apparently, Boom liked to teach her female students what type of behavior they should never put up with from guys. I dare someone to tell her that she's a member of the weaker sex.

Shaggy wandered for a while after he was discharged. He had never really had much of a plan for life, and even facing death in the Hiss hadn't changed that. He might have wound up shuffling along the streets in a bathrobe if he hadn't accidentally bumped into a television producer and apologized. As soon as the producer heard his voice he grabbed him by the arm and took him to his studio. His is now the most well-known voice on children's television shows on the planet. He's also gained nearly three hundred pounds from his snacking. It all comes back to haunt us someday.

Nickel did lose an arm and a leg. During his recovery, he began taking some online college courses. By the time he was done, he was teaching American poetry classes at a college near his hometown. He has started a project in his old neighborhood, where he teaches some of the local boys how to turn some of the graffiti into something a little more artistic and poetic. Amazingly, he still hasn't thought of a word that rhymes with "last."

While it might not surprise some of you that I got married to Mayumi, it certainly surprised the hell out of me. Once the war was over, I figured that she would start to see me for the clumsy, socially awkward goof that I am. She did. For some reason it made her like me even more. We got married and had a couple of children. Despite the fact that I have the local high school named for me, I know that I'm still not a local celebrity. I still confuse or frighten people. I know that half of my neighbors swore that they would have nothing to do with me after Mayumi and I dressed up one Halloween and had a phaser battle in the front yard. Maybe it was shouting at each other in Klingon that frightened everyone off. The other half of my neighbors swore they'd have nothing to do with me when they saw me mow my lawn. I don't believe in clearing off the lawn or mowing around things. If it's there, it's fair game and will get mowed over. That Tonka truck never had a chance. They never should have started making them out of plastic.

I spent some time in college, got a couple of degrees, and I'm working on starting my own practice. I'm a psychologist. I've been practicing self-diagnosis. I told you my therapist was a quack! Yes, I do charge myself eighty dollars per hour. It's a tax thing. Oh yeah! I found my keys! They were still floating around the same transport plane that I took for part of my flight back to the states. They had gained an almost ghost-story status for attacking unsuspecting soldiers. Nice symmetry, huh? I once read a T-shirt that said "I'm in my own little world, but that's OK! Everyone there knows me!" I think that shirt sums me up quite well.

Welcome to my world. Everybody calls me Pup. Stay as long as you like. We're pretty friendly here, and we don't tell stories about heroes. We just tell stories. We let others decide what to call them.

Acknowledgements

*

Since this is my first published book, I feel the need to acknowledge a great many people. The first and most obvious appreciation must be extended to my family. Angela, you have taken so much pride in my accomplishments that I'm not sure I can ever repay you. I love you greatly. Joe, I am always proud to be your father, and your encouragement makes that pride grow even more. To my parents, you always let me explore my talents (or lack thereof) which helped lead me to so many things that I now enjoy.

My friends and colleagues, you keep me going through each day. DeAnn and Tommy, you provide me with a smile when I need it most. Mrs. Edwards, I can't promise you lots of money for your retirement, but drop by and I'll get that chicken sandwich I promised for you. Mrs. Golson-Saunders, thank you for helping me get *Pup* ready for competition. To the front office ladies, all of the faculty, administration, and students that put up with me throughout the year, I appreciate your enthusiasm and support.

I have to extend an enormous amount of thanks to Lou Aronica and the folks at Authors First and The Story Plant. You have given me a once-in-a-lifetime opportunity and you have guided me through it with understanding, patience, and insight. You helped me find a pride in my work that had remained hidden from me. I hope that your faith is well rewarded.

I know that there are a great many more people that I can and should thank. However, for once in my life, I'm going to try to avoid saying too much. You know who you are, and my love and thanks goes out to you. Thanks for visiting my world. You're always welcome here.

About the Author

*

Christopher Slater was born, raised, and continues to haunt Middle Tennessee. His love of history led him to teaching that subject, which gave him the opportunity to hone his storytelling skills with a captive audience. Once he thought he had sharpened his abilities enough, he decided to start writing for a more voluntary audience. When not writing, Slater enjoys historic reenacting, playing airsoft, and converting oxygen into carbon dioxide. He teaches middle school in Tennessee where he still lives with his entertaining son, very patient wife and a cat that won't get out of his seat.